The Mistress Chronicles

Gina Marie Martini

PAGE PUBLISHING, INC.
New York, NY

First originally published by Page Publishing, Inc. 2019

The characters and events in this book are fictitious and based on the author's imagination. Any similarities to real persons, living or dead, or business establishments are purely coincidental.

ISBN 978-1-64462-671-9 (Paperback)
ISBN 978-1-64462-672-6 (Digital)

Printed in the United States of America

For my brother, Bobby, who is always in my heart.

Surround yourself with people who motivate you and challenge you; then reciprocate.

—Anonymous

Acknowledgments

My greatest achievement in life is reflected through the kind, witty, smart men I have raised – my sons, Joe and Anthony, who make me proud every day. I am so fortunate to be your mom. I love you!

Special thanks to my mother, Carolyn, and my stepfather, Carl, for the love, encouragement, and generosity you have given me throughout my life, and for always cheering me on. Love you!

Aunts and Uncles enhance our existence with unconditional love. I have been blessed with many who love and support me. Thank you all for making my life extra special: Uncle Eddie and Auntie Ann; Aunt Pat; my Godmother, Auntie Pat; my Godfather, Uncle Joe, and Pat; and in loving memory of Aunt Phyllis and Aunt Joyce.

Many thanks to friends, Diana Barone, Cate Beaumont, Beth Foster, Denise Marenna, and Stephanie Sherman for your review of my initial manuscript or sample chapters, your feedback, as well as the immense support you have given me during this amazing endeavor.

Thank you, Joe Giordano, for sharing your knowledge and offering your vast expertise in real estate.

I would also like to thank Page Publishing for championing a novice in this business, allowing me the opportunity to share my stories with the world. More to come!

Chapter 1

June 22, 2010

WITH TREMBLING HANDS, I turned the small, silver key in the safe deposit box.

The bank manager removed the large container from a slot in the wall and placed it gently on the clunky table with a wobbly, metal leg.

Shivers flew up my spine in the cold room.

"I'll give you some time alone, ma'am," his voice echoed.

A nod in return signaled my desire for privacy. I sucked in a deep breath before peeking at the contents within the steel case. At the top sat a manila envelope. With tender care, I released the clasp. Numerous photographs slipped out; a mix of black and white, and color, depending upon the year. I smiled, despite the tears that jumped down my blushed cheeks. Pictures of a younger version of myself at a pivotal time in my young-adult life.

"Hawaii, 1971. No. '72." A brief chuckle escaped as I recalled that scandalous bikini I wore on Waikiki Beach. Scandalous for that period anyway. My fingers brushed across the handsome face of the man standing next to me in the photo. Tommy was so good-looking and charming. "We were so happy back then," I muttered.

Several notebooks with faded black and white covers lay beneath the photographs. Goosebumps sprang across my porcelain skin. I quickly rubbed my arms for warmth before opening my old journals. Doodles of hearts and flowers with Tommy's name written in block letters across the page brought me back. I chronicled the significant moments of our time together, beginning on that special night, New Year's Eve, 1970. Meeting Tommy changed my whole world.

I can't help reminiscing as I scroll through these journals. Recollections in my own words and handwriting, countered by my withered memories. So many wonderful memories stuck with me through the decades, blended with wounds that still linger long past their prime.

The seventies. A time before Google, social media, and cell phones. Laptops and personal computers weren't invented. If you didn't read the newspaper or watch the evening news, you were out of touch with the community and the world.

Richard Nixon was president. The Vietnam War persisted at a dreadful pace. Protests against the war and in support of equal rights for women were a part of a typical day. Society was quite different in that era, yet people somehow remain the same.

Chapter 2

December 31, 1970

THE LAS VEGAS Strip was lit up for New Year's Eve. When I was a little girl, I believed the lights and parties were in honor of my birthday. Daddy always told me I picked the best day to be born. New Year's Eve was the biggest party of the year. Today, I'm eighteen, legally an adult. Life's been dull thanks to my controlling father and uncle. My birthday wish was to have an exciting 1971 with blooming friendships and romance, but I can't share my wish with anyone. My diary holds all of my secrets.

Uncle Vince hosts a party for the holiday at his club, Spritz, off the electrifying Las Vegas Strip. I get to sing! I never sang in front of a large audience before. What if I forget the lyrics or feel faint? A part of me was grateful he allowed my cousin, Katie, and me to attend the affair at Spritz at all. After Daddy died, Uncle Vince never let me out of his sight. I loved living with my uncle and Katie at his beautiful estate in Rancho Circle. Now that I'm eighteen, my uncle was loosening his grip, ever so slightly.

He bought me a new outfit for the party. A gorgeous silver dress that hugged my curves and a pair of tall black boots. I can't believe he let me buy this dress. It's really short.

Katie straightened my long, black hair with a hot iron beneath a paper bag. I prayed she wouldn't singe my hair or scalp. She also found me a pretty, multi-colored scarf with a swirled pattern to wear as a headband. Katie wanted to enroll in beauty school someday to learn how to spruce up women's hair, making them feel beautiful. I don't mind her playing with mine. She seemed to have a knack for it.

The club was crowded as we entered through the back. The noise from the crowd and humming from the band's instruments stirred my anxiety to perform. I detested the smell of cigarettes, but I was too nervous to fret about it.

Diana Ross's "Ain't No Mountain High Enough" was blasting through the speakers. I wanted to sing early and get it over with in a way. Sing before the crowd was wasted and the air was thick with smoke.

I made Uncle Vince promise me he wouldn't tell anyone my last name was Russo and I was his niece. The last thing I needed was pity applause, or people praising my voice to get on his good side. My uncle was a popular man in Las Vegas with connections. He knew Frank Sinatra and met President Kennedy before his unfortunate demise back in '63. I wanted people to hear me sing and notice *me*, Angie Russo, not Vincenzo Russo's orphaned niece.

Katie ran into a boy from school. I envied her. I was homeschooled. Daddy wanted it that way, and my uncle did what Daddy wanted.

Sipping from a bottle of Pepsi at the bar, the coolest-looking guy I'd ever seen in my life strolled in. Sandy brown, shag hair, and large broad shoulders with a muscular build, easily noticeable through the dark blue shirt that clung to his body. He was at least five inches taller than my five feet, five inches. His eyes appeared dark, but with the dim lighting and distance between us, I was unsure of the color.

My heart skipped a beat, uncertain if it's from seeing this man or the fact that my name was announced over the microphone, calling me on stage for my number.

I remember standing on the stage, high above a large crowd. Patrons mostly in their twenties and thirties, out on the town, welcoming in 1971. They were distracted with their own conversations and drinks in hand.

The club manager introduced me simply as "Angie," no last name, thank goodness. No one seemed to pay any attention until the piano began to chime.

My eyes gazed around the room for Katie's familiar face to calm my nerves before I belted out the Carpenters "Close to You" with as much passion as Karen Carpenter herself. People stopped talking. They smiled at me, swaying and dancing to the beat while I sang.

As I glanced toward the bar to see if my uncle was listening, that beautiful man spun around the barstool and looked right at me. For a split second, I felt like we were the only two people in the room. I blinked my dark brown eyes away, but couldn't resist another gaze in his direction to see if he was still watching me. And he was.

As my song ended, the applause sounded like thunder. Katie and Uncle Vince were cheering. What a rush! So many people shook my hand and told me I had a great voice as I skipped off the stage. Even if they were drunk or high, I didn't care. I felt amazing!

I picked up my bottle of Pepsi from Sam, the bartender, taking a long slug. I nearly spit the soda out when that man at the bar tapped my shoulder. I swallowed the fizzy drink so hard, he surely heard the loud gulp.

"Hi. You have a beautiful voice. Are you a professional singer or something?"

"Who, me? No. I mean I'd love to be a professional singer someday."

Gray with a hint of green, his eyes.

"Well, you've got talent. What was your name again?"

"Angie."

"Hi, Angie. I'm Tommy. Tommy Cavallo." He shook my hand and held it firmly for several seconds before releasing me. "Can I buy you a drink?"

I held up my Pepsi bottle. That was stupid. "It was my first time," I said.

"Excuse me?" he chuckled.

My cheeks suddenly felt warm. "Singing in public, I mean. My first time."

"Wow, that's cool. I'm impressed."

Uncle Vince stepped directly between us. His long legs and commanding presence purposely disrupted my introduction to Tommy.

"Tommy, how's your father?" he asked, running a hand through his slicked back, dark hair.

I was surprised my uncle didn't stand between us the moment Tommy tapped my shoulder.

"Pop is the same, Vince. Thanks for asking," Tommy answered while shaking my uncle's hand.

"It's a shame what happened to him. Your father and I did a lot of business together. Stroke, right?"

"Yeah, stroke. I was just talking with Angie here. Where did you find such a talent?"

"She's my niece, Tommy. I'm her guardian." Uncle Vince turned toward me with a brilliant smile, expressing his pride. "You were fantastic, Angie! I'm so proud of you." His eyes softened.

Tommy's eyes stared into mine as he spoke to my uncle. "Frank's daughter?"

"You knew my father?" I asked, extremely curious how he knew Daddy.

"I knew of him. Through your uncle."

"Angie, I need to talk business with Tommy. Do me a favor and look for Katie. I lost sight of her."

Since I was a little girl, anytime business was discussed, I was dismissed. Being eighteen didn't seem to change that. Five minutes until midnight and the man of my dreams sat with my uncle.

At a corner table beneath an orange glow from the light fixture hanging above, Katie leaned against this tall, blonde boy from school she liked. Brett is his name. She'd ramble on and on about this star of the high school basketball team. I envied her, being able to go to a real school and make friends. Katie wouldn't want to be interrupted. Surely, she's hiding from my uncle's sight. She looked so happy, and I was happy for her.

I found a clear spot at the bar, hoping to get another Pepsi, but the bartenders were busy pouring champagne into glasses for the midnight extravaganza.

The club manager rushed to the stage and began the countdown. Ten... nine... eight...

Excitement filled the air. Seven... six... five...

Most people had a date to kiss at midnight. I glanced to the left and right of me. The options were not pleasing. I strolled away from the bar area toward the back. Four... three... two... one. Happy New Year cheers amidst "Auld Lang Syne." I suppose there was nothing magical about turning eighteen on New Year's Eve.

"Angie!"

I heard someone yell my name over the loud music and cheers.

Tommy suddenly stood before me with a bottle of Pepsi in his hand outstretched. I smiled, accepting the drink. He actually paid attention to what I was drinking.

"Happy New Year, Angie." He stared into my brown eyes then gently kissed my cheek.

I hoped for more. Dreamed of more. But he was a perfect gentleman. "Happy New Year," I responded with a huge smile, a breath away from the softest lips I ever felt.

"Would you like to have dinner with me, Angie?"

I gulped before nodding. I couldn't get the word *yes* out.

"You live with Vince? I can call you there?"

Again, I nodded. My brain and mouth were not in sync. What was wrong with me?

"How about tomorrow night?"

Another nod.

"I'll call you tomorrow, and maybe I can pick you up around seven?"

"Sure." Thank God my vocal chords worked again.

Chapter 3

January 1, 1971

KATIE WAS SURELY sick of me talking about last night. Between my stage performance and a date planned, I wouldn't shut up. Naturally, she helped me pick out an outfit and let me borrow some of her jewelry that matched perfectly. Katie was more like a sister to me than a cousin. We resembled each other a little too. She had a slim build like me, but a bit shorter. Her jet-black hair was tightly curled, thanks to a perm, while I preferred my hair very long and straight.

I've lived with Katie and Uncle Vince for the last three years, since my father died. I felt closer to her than I was to my older sister, Connie. The heroin destroyed her and my family. I couldn't be close to her. It killed me watching my sister slowly kill herself with that poison.

I didn't dare tell my uncle about my date with Tommy. He's so overprotective of Katie and me. He seemed to like Tommy though. Fortunately, Uncle Vince had dinner plans tonight, so he won't be home when Tommy picks me up.

As promised, Tommy called me to confirm dinner. We didn't talk for long. My tongue seemed to be tied whenever I heard his voice. I didn't want to be a total freak tonight.

At seven o'clock sharp, the doorbell rang. Katie insisted she answer it, so I wouldn't look overly anxious, which I clearly was. My hand traced along the dark walnut railing as I strolled down the staircase, wearing a short tangerine-colored dress with brown heels. I felt my cheeks heat up as Tommy's eyes moved up and down my body. The dress hugged my curves, and seemingly caught his attention.

"You look really nice, Angie," he said when his gray eyes met mine.

"Thank you, so do you." I could make out the definition of his strong, muscular arms through his buttoned down, brown shirt.

"Are you ready to go?"

I was surprised he didn't ask where my uncle was, but I grabbed my purse and followed him out to the red Camaro parked in the driveway. A beautiful car with some speed.

His car raced us to Palmieri's, an Italian restaurant off the Strip. It was a quiet place, but very elegant. Chandeliers in rows overhead. Dim lighting. A bottle of chilled champagne was waiting at our table for us. I noticed Tommy tipped the maître d' after escorting us to our table near the fireplace in the back of the restaurant. A very private spot.

Twisting my fingers was a nervous habit. I placed them on my lap beneath the table, hoping he wouldn't notice how jumpy I was.

"Would you like champagne, Angie?"

"Yes. I guess I'm legal now."

"Legal?" He grinned, displaying a confused expression.

"Well, I just turned eighteen."

"Eighteen? When did you turn eighteen?" His eyes exposed the shock he clearly felt.

Did he think of me as a child now? "Yesterday," I answered somewhat delicately.

"Really? New Year's Eve is your birthday? I wish I'd known that. I would've wished you a happy birthday last night too."

"And you're how old?" Assuming it's appropriate for a woman to ask a man his age.

"Well, I'm a little older than eighteen." He paused with a brief laugh. "I'm twenty-seven, but it's just a number, right?"

I nodded and took a swig of the champagne.

"Did you tell your uncle I was taking you out tonight?"

"Should I have?"

"Well, he's your uncle. It's up to you."

"I got the feeling you were friends."

"He did business with my father. I own the Montgomery."

"That tall, beautiful hotel on the Strip?" I was surprised someone as young as Tommy would own a luxurious hotel. "You mentioned your father had a stroke. Is he okay?"

"His mind doesn't work the way it once did. He was a shrewd businessman. Taught me everything about the family business. I have his power of attorney, and legally took over the hotel and casino. He groomed me for this role. I never thought I'd have to take the business over this soon though. Pop was the smartest man I knew. That's why it's so hard to see him in a nursing home, unable to take care of himself."

"That's terrible. Do you have any other family?"

"My mom died about seven years ago. I have an older brother, John. He's a great guy."

"If you don't mind my asking, why are you running the family business instead of your older brother?"

"John is deaf. He's also in a wheelchair, unable to walk without help. My father always made sure John was taken care of. Now he's my responsibility. He's able to live on his own. He likes to be as independent as possible and hates to be waited on. It's a shame that a lot of people can't look past the wheelchair and him being deaf. He's really a normal man otherwise."

"How do you communicate?" His family and his brother's disabilities fascinated me.

"I learned sign language from the time I was born. It's like learning French or Spanish. Just another language. I've been signing with John for as long as I can remember. He also reads lips. He's not just my brother. He's my best friend."

"I think that's amazing."

"What about your family, Angie?"

I couldn't answer. Instead, I clumsily gulped down another slug of champagne.

"I'm sorry. I meant no disrespect. I know your father was killed. That must be difficult to talk about."

"Yes. Sorry. I… I just have a hard time talking about my family. Thank God for my uncle and Katie."

"You can tell me when you're ready. That is if you ever want to talk about it."

Perhaps I didn't make a total fool out of myself tonight. The last real friend I had outside of family was back in the fifth grade before Daddy insisted I be homeschooled. Socially awkward, I was.

"There's something very special about you, Angie Russo." He raised his glass of champagne. "Happy belated birthday." Our glasses clinked. His eyes never left mine until the maître d' returned to take our dinner order.

Throughout dinner and the drive home, Tommy shared some funny stories about his family and amazing vacations around the world. His father was truly a good, family man. The effect seemed to rub off on Tommy.

I hated to tell him about my childhood. My parents were not happy. They tolerated each other. If I told him the truth, he would run in the opposite direction. It's too soon. I didn't want to end the evening on a sour note.

Then there's my uncle. Do I tell Uncle Vince I went out with Tommy? I'm eighteen now. He can't keep me locked up in his mansion for the rest of my life.

The Camaro pulled up in the driveway. I didn't see Uncle Vince's Mercedes. Maybe that's a good sign. The gentleman that he was, Tommy jumped out of the car and opened my door for me. He took hold of my hand tightly and walked me to the front door. The outside light shined in my eyes. As I turned to avoid the light, Tommy pulled me close to him, wrapping those strong arms around my waist.

"I had a nice time tonight, Angie. Did you?"

"Yes. Thank you again for dinner."

Tommy's head lowered as his arms continued to embrace me tightly. I hoped he would kiss me, but he pulled away.

"There's something I haven't told you, Angie. I'm not sure how to say this, but I don't want you to hear this from your uncle or anyone else." His weight shifted from side to side. His hand released my body and cupped my chin. He took in a deep breath before uttering the words, "I'm… married."

"What?" Did the rug just lift out from under me? "Married?"

"For now. I'm getting a divorce. There are a lot of issues that tie into my marriage."

It took a few moments for this information to sink in. "What kind of issues?"

"Legal issues because I didn't have a prenuptial agreement. My lawyer has concerns that she can be awarded a portion of my family's business, my father's legacy, the money. I can't let that happen. The marriage is over. It's been over for a while now. I just don't know when the divorce will be final."

"You should've told me last night."

"I'd like to get to know you, Angie. I was afraid you wouldn't want to see me, but I had to be honest with you about my situation. Your uncle is well aware of my marital status. You needed to hear this from *me*."

My head felt dizzy and slightly numb.

"I will be divorced, Angie. It will take time to make it official. I'd hate to lose out on the opportunity to spend more time with you. We can be friends and get to know each other, right?"

I lifted my head up to meet those unusual, gray eyes. Why do I want to kiss him after hearing this? I controlled my desires and stepped a couple of paces back. "How soon, Tommy? When will the divorce be final?"

"I can't really say. I hope this year. She knows it's over. We sleep in separate rooms. If I pack and leave the house, it looks like I abandoned the marriage, which gives her ammunition against me in court. My father is a sick man, Angie. Any part of his mind that still works will be destroyed if he thought I let Sadie take the hotel from us. My lawyer is on top of this. He knows I want this divorce finalized."

I struggled to look into his eyes. "Why are you divorcing her?"

"There's no love left between us, but I mean, I'll always care about her. My pop expected me to be married and have a family someday. Sadie fit the bill. All the pressure was put on me because of

John's physical impairments. Pop had a lot of expectations of me to fulfill, with a lot of demands. Marriage was one of them."

He inched near me and caressed my cheek. "I knew I had to meet you from the moment I heard your voice up on that stage. I turned away from the bar and saw your sweet face." His fingers brushed away a strand of hair from my brow. "I hope you'll give me a chance, Angie."

"I need some time to think."

He nodded his head then kissed my cheek without pulling away as he did last night. Our eyes met, noses touching. I wanted to run inside, but I stood frozen before him and let his lips meet mine. The sweetest taste my mouth ever experienced. Feeling a tad woozy, the champagne may have gone to my head. I tasted the sweet sparkling wine on his lips. But I had to pull away. His being married changed so much. Yes, he's getting divorced, but he had a wife right now. She was on my mind as I tasted his lips. What was wrong with me?

"Good night, Tommy." I withdrew from his grasp and stepped inside, closing the door behind me and catching my breath.

Chapter 4

January 2, 1971

MY FIRST KISS and it was bittersweet. The kiss itself exceeded my expectations. How can I get past the fact that he's married? Sleep wasn't an option last night. Maybe he won't call me today, but a part of me wanted to hear his smooth-sounding voice. Uncle Vince would never approve.

I sat near the phone all morning. The few times it rang, I jumped to answer it. Come two o'clock, the phone chimed again. I'm not sure if I was relieved or worried when I heard Tommy say my name.

It was difficult to talk to him with my uncle somewhere in the house. I didn't know if he would sneak up behind me and listen in on the conversation. I don't have a social life. He'd want to know who I was speaking with. There's really no privacy here, despite the enormity of the house.

In spite of my better judgment, I chose to follow my heart.

Never in my entire life had I met anyone half as interesting as Tommy Cavallo. His family, lifestyle, and business fascinated me. It doesn't hurt that he's sexy as hell and kissed me until my knees buckled beneath me.

I agreed to meet him at the deli down the street. I could easily walk there. I'm not ready to tell my uncle about him yet. I just needed Katie to cover for me.

Katie became my co-conspirator. She may have had extra freedom attending a real school and having friends, but Uncle Vince never allowed her to date anyone he hadn't met and approved of. I'm surprised he allowed us to learn to drive a car. Katie asked him, "Why did you let me learn to drive if I can't go anywhere?"

We told Uncle Vince we were having dinner together then seeing a movie downtown. However, Katie was meeting Brett, her unexpected New Year's Eve date, and I was meeting Tommy. There was something exhilarating about sneaking around, as long as we didn't get caught. The trick would be to make sure we met back at the same time to drive home together.

Katie took her car and dropped me off at the deli, where Tommy's red Camaro was parked, waiting for me. He must have been early, or maybe I was late. Katie promised she'd be back at midnight to meet me here. Then we went our separate ways.

I wasn't sure how I'd feel when I saw him, but when he flashed his big smile and stormy gray eyes my way, my knees weakened.

He brought me to Caesar's Palace. What a luxurious place! As soon as he helped me out of the car, he whisked me close to him and kissed me long and hard on the mouth. I could barely catch my breath! We had dinner first then spent time in the casino.

He won a little and lost a little. I played roulette! Tommy gave me some chips to place bets. I didn't know what I was doing, but I was winning! He showed me the slot machines and sat beside me, hoping to get all the sevens to line up. I started to lose. Tommy kissed me for luck with each spin. Although I loved the kisses, my winning streak was over. I didn't think I'd ever had this much fun before in my life.

Midnight was upon us. I promised Katie I'd be at the deli by then. We needed to go, but I didn't want the night to end. I could see the disappointment in Tommy's eyes when I told him it was time to leave. His arms lifted me up, pulling me in for a long kiss, devouring my lips and tongue.

"I don't want to let you go, Angie."

"I can't keep Katie waiting."

Reluctantly, we left the casino and he drove me to the deli.

It was twelve-fifteen the next morning and no Katie. I was getting worried. Tommy kept glancing at his watch.

"You can leave me here if you have to go."

"What? No, I won't leave you here alone late at night. I need to make sure you get home safely. I'll drive you home myself. Maybe your cousin is having fun and lost track of time?"

"You can't take me home. My uncle is there."

"We can't sneak around, Angie. He will find out. Besides, I don't want you lying to him. I'll talk to him. I'll explain everything. Maybe he won't kill me." He paused to see the surprised expression on my face. "I'm kidding."

"I will tell him when I'm ready."

"Why are you waiting?"

"Because he won't let me see you. He'll forbid it."

"You are eighteen. You have to respect him, but he has to respect you too as an adult. The problem he'll have with me is understandable. I am still married and a little older than you. Of course, he doesn't want his niece seeing a married man. I will explain to him, man to man, that I am working on a divorce and that my intentions with you are honorable."

"Honorable?"

"That means I am crazy about you, Angie Russo."

I laid my head upon his broad shoulder, feeling his bicep squeeze me in closer. Honestly, I was so concerned Katie was late.

Suddenly, headlights blinded us in the parking lot. It was Katie's car, thank goodness. She waved to me.

I kissed Tommy good night, although I didn't want to let him go.

"When can I see you again?"

"Call me tomorrow after four o'clock. My uncle is going out around four."

"I want to take you somewhere special tomorrow night."

Katie beeped her horn, expecting me to hurry.

"Okay. I have to go!"

Chapter 5

January 3, 1971

UNCLE VINCE LIKED a traditional Sunday dinner with family. Family did not necessarily mean blood relatives. There are very few blood relatives alive in the Russo family.

He had a lady friend, Nancy, who I knew was more than a friend to him. She was very nice. My uncle smiled brightly whenever she was around. She's a beautiful strawberry blonde with the brightest blue eyes I'd ever seen. Her long legs equaled my uncle's height.

He'd been single since he and Aunt Dolly divorced many years ago. Katie talked to her mother on the telephone regularly and visited her several times a year. Aunt Dolly moved to California. I never understood why she chose to leave Nevada and her daughter after their marriage ended.

Other guests at family dinner included my uncle's three business associates, Sal Maroni, Benny DeLeone, and Angelo Francisco, along with their wives. A couple of times these "family" members brought their grown sons to dinner in hopes of pairing one of them up with Katie. She hated when that happened. She would be graduating from high school this year, and she wanted to go to beauty school. Not that marriage was off the table for her, but she really liked Brett, the basketball player.

Sure enough, Sal and Alice Maroni arrived with their son, Louis. He looked about twenty-two years old and was home from college for the holidays. He was handsome in an Anthony Perkins kind of way. Tall, thin, and youthful-looking. Didn't look like he had any facial hair whatsoever. And he wore a suit to a casual family dinner. What is this, 1950?

Katie rolled her eyes at me. I couldn't help but chuckle as she pretended to hang herself at the table. Next, I expected them to play musical chairs to ensure Louis sat right beside her.

Much to my surprise, as the Maroni family greeted everyone, they introduced their son to *me* and encouraged we sit and talk about things like the weather or, God help me, politics! He bragged about being a political science major and graduating from college this year.

Uncle Vince took time away from Nancy and his guests to sit with Louis and me for a few minutes. I understood how Katie felt. I caught her pointing and laughing at me from a distance as my uncle tried to sell Louis to me like he was a lovely home on a piece of swamp land in Florida.

"You kids keep talking. Get to know each other," he said after springing up from the plush, striped sofa and strolling into the dining room.

Louis appeared very sweet and kind. I pretended to be interested, but really, I was being polite. Maybe if I never met Tommy, I'd have more of an interest in what he said. Frankly, he was boring. Safe was a good word to describe him. That's probably why Uncle Vince liked him for me. Always the protector, my dear uncle.

When dinner was served, Louis and I were finally called to join the rest of the "family" in the dining room. What a surprise, two seats next to each other in between Sal and Uncle Vince. I'd never met more proud parents than the Maronis, who boasted about their son's achievements in between bites of homemade manicotti.

"Louis, did you tell Angie you're on the dean's list? Louis, did you tell Angie about your trip to Washington, DC, where you met President Nixon?"

I got it. Louis was a genius! Louis would give a girl a stable, financial future someday. Louis would probably be a perfect husband. Louis might be a mayor, congressman, or senator someday. But Louis was as dull as a butter knife, awkward, with zero self-confidence. I couldn't wait until four o'clock when Uncle Vince took

Nancy away somewhere for the night. Then I could see Tommy. I just couldn't get him out of my mind or my heart.

Uncle Vince and Nancy left at four o'clock as they usually did on Sunday afternoons. Shortly thereafter, I heard from Tommy. The noisy traffic racing by in the background told me he's calling from a payphone. He was actually nearby, not far from the Strip. He sounded anxious to see me and was in route. I quickly scrambled through my closet for something to wear.

He arrived at my door with an exquisite bouquet of large, red roses with baby's breath bursting from the bunch. The sweet fragrance filled my senses. Butterflies tickled my stomach walls. I brought him into the kitchen and fumbled through the cabinets for a vase.

Katie kindly offered to arrange the roses for me so we could leave. I knew she was a little disappointed because Brett had plans and couldn't see her tonight. I hugged her tightly before Tommy took my hand and led me out to his car.

"Where are we going?" I asked Tommy. He was driving so quickly with a smile plastered on his face.

"It's a surprise. I hope you're hungry."

I wasn't very hungry after family dinner. Not to mention my nerves were rattling. We arrived outside a green, ranch-style house with black shutters in what seemed to be a very quiet neighborhood further away from the Strip in North Las Vegas. No vehicle in the driveway. We walked up a ramp to the side entrance of the quaint home. Tommy didn't knock. He just stepped inside, and I trailed behind. The air was filled with a delicious aroma of a roast of some sort.

Approaching us in a wheelchair across the kitchen, I could only assume was his older brother, John. He was handsome like Tommy, but with a crewcut as if he just enlisted in the army. His hair was as black as mine, and his eyes were more of a green color than Tommy's gray shade. I could definitely tell the family resemblance in their cheekbones and especially that similar, flirtatious smile, despite their physical differences.

Tommy used his fingers and hands in specific motions to talk to John. It was difficult for me, not knowing what they were saying.

"Angie, this is my brother, John." His hands continued to move while he spoke.

"Hi, John," I said with great fervor. I didn't mean to speak so loudly, but I wanted to be sure he read my lips.

Tommy laughed. "He can't hear you, sweetheart, no matter how loud you talk."

My cheeks warmed from blushing.

John used sign language and Tommy translated to tell me how nice it was to meet me. He was very flirty like Tommy, with his eyes and the way he looked at me. Tommy put his hands around my waist, moving my body in front of him. He spoke while he signed with John, teasing that I was his girl, so John shouldn't waste his time trying to win me over with his boyish charm and playful eyes.

Despite the wheelchair that contained his body and moved him around the house, John was quite a chef. He fixed up a lovely meal. Pot roast, seasoned potatoes, diced carrots, and a Caesar's salad. I told him if I had known he was cooking, I would have baked dessert.

John and I had a funny conversation, with Tommy as our translator, about how he destroyed a lemon meringue pie once, so he doesn't bake. I told him the meringue is tricky. You can't get any yolk in the egg mixture. He asked me to visit and show him how to properly make one.

Tommy stopped translating the rest of the sentence, cutting off his brother, telling him he's not going to leave me alone with him because he's such a *smooth talker*. We all laughed. I enjoyed the brotherly banter.

Before we left, I asked Tommy if he'd teach me sign language, so I could communicate directly with John. I don't know why he looked surprised. John smiled and winked at me. They exchanged some signs before I kissed John on the cheek and thanked him for dinner. Tommy and I trekked out the door with his arm draped around my shoulder.

The smile couldn't leave my face. I had such a nice time meeting John. I looked over at Tommy who seemed quiet. "What's wrong?" I asked.

"Did you mean what you said about learning sign language?"

"Yes. I'd love to be able to talk to John directly. It was so much fun meeting him. I really liked seeing you both together. Why do you seem upset?"

"Oh, no, I'm not upset. Surprised maybe. I never met anyone who would take the time to learn a language to speak with someone they just met. You amaze me, Angie Russo."

Chapter 6

January 15, 1971

SOMEHOW I MANAGED to convince my uncle to let me sing at Spritz for a small paycheck. I didn't make much money, but it was a job that got me out of the house. I loved to sing, and people seemed to like my mezzo-soprano voice. It was also a way for me to see Tommy. He popped in every night when I performed.

Tommy was the real reason I asked for this gig. It was an opportunity to see him regularly and build a friendship with a romantic twist. The venue was not perfect, seeing that my uncle owned the place and could drop by at any time. We tried to be careful not to get caught sneaking kisses in the back room.

In between sessions, Tommy would teach me some simple words in sign language. We went through the alphabet too. If I didn't know the word for something, I'd spell it out. That took a long time though. He assured me that with continued practice, I would speed up.

I couldn't wait to see John again to practice all I had learned. Tommy appreciated my efforts to build a friendship with his brother.

After a couple of weeks of singing and meeting up with Tommy, I knew I had to tell Uncle Vince. I couldn't keep this a secret much longer. This was his club. Someone was bound to tell him that Tommy has been hanging around, especially around me.

I never told anyone I was Vince Russo's niece because I didn't want special treatment, but his employees know who I am. My uncle may have told them to watch over me and report back to him. Well, if he had told them to spy on me, he would've already had a fit about Tommy dropping by so frequently. His gray eyes barely blinked as he watched me perform on the stage.

Chapter 7

January 17, 1971

UNCLE VINCE AND Nancy planned a romantic week away in Reno. My uncle said it was a business trip to expand Spritz to that area. An entire week with no curfew! Katie was happy to have some freedom too. We went on a shopping spree, and wandered along the Vegas Strip instead of our typical Sunday "family" dinner.

Tommy wanted to see more of me. He was making plans for us all week. I knew he was tired of hiding and meeting in secret. The time had come for me to tell my uncle we're seeing each other. I believe I love Tommy. No, I had already fallen.

Tommy brought me to the Montgomery, the hotel and casino he inherited because of his pop's illness. The fabulous hotel was sectioned into three main wings with European themes of England, Ireland, and Scotland. Large flags of these countries adorned the lobby.

The Montgomery was named after one of Tommy's grandmothers who was from England with British roots. Although Tommy's pop is half Italian, he decided to honor his late wife, whose family was from Ireland. The color schemes and murals across the ceilings and walls made you feel as if you stood atop the Cliffs of Moher, overlooking the Atlantic Ocean in Ireland; bask in the glory of the rolling hills throughout the Scottish Highlands; and unearth the mystery of Stonehenge in England.

Tommy was quite pleased with some recent upgrades, especially adding the traditional British, red telephone boxes in the lobby. I was amazed and impressed by the décor. I'd never visited any of these countries, but the Montgomery allowed me to escape to these exquisite sites through the essence of my imagination.

The lights, the sounds, and the excitement of the casino never got old. People greeted Tommy with big smiles and handshakes. After all, he was the man in charge. He walked beside me without his affectionate hands clinging to me. No hand holding or kissing for luck at the tables and slots like at Caesar's Palace. I had to get used to the fact that in some circles, people knew he was still married.

God, what if she were here? What if I were face to face with her? I shook my head, ridding those horrid thoughts from my brain. He's getting divorced, I reminded myself.

As I sat at a slot machine, pulling the handle down with hopes of winning, Tommy excused himself. He returned a few minutes later, helping me collect the few coins in the tray I had left. He put his hand around my arm and nudged me to follow him. I was surprised he weaved his arm through mine for anyone to see. He swept me across the marble floor to a set of elevators. The elevator doors closed behind us. Tommy squeezed my body in tight, then offered his lips and tongue generously.

The elevator operator seemed to know exactly what floor to press to take us to. The doors flung open at the twentieth floor.

"Good night, Mr. Cavallo," the elevator operator said.

"Good night, Ollie," Tommy replied. He led me down a hallway to a corner room, opened the door, and turned on the lights. The room was beautifully decorated with an amazing view of the Strip from the balcony. The flashing lights brightened up the whole street. The town looked magical from up high, like Disney Land.

I also knew why he brought me here. My uncle's out of town for the week, and my boyfriend brought me to a hotel room. My hands crossed, clasping my arms as shivers flew through my entire body.

"Would you like some champagne?" he asked, lifting a bottle up from the ice bucket.

I didn't respond immediately. But soon I nodded. A drink might settle my nerves.

"Would you like anything else? I can order room service. Whatever you want." He poured the champagne into a crystal flute, and handed the glass to me before clinking the rim with his, and toasting to our night together. Those seductive eyes of his stuck to mine like glue.

After a brief sip, I shook my head, refusing anything from room service. As he stepped closer to me, he placed his glass on the counter and took mine from my fingertips, setting it next to his.

His lips lightly touched my shoulder, neck, and cheek then he whispered softly, "I love you, Angie." His lips pressed firmly against mine before I could respond.

I couldn't breathe. I pulled away for a mere moment.

"I mean it. I never felt like this about any woman before."

His kisses were irresistible as his hands flew up and down, exploring my body, feeling every silky curve with his fingers.

"I want to make love to you." He stopped and stared longingly into my eyes.

Could he sense my hesitation?

He brushed away a few long, dark strands from my face. "What is it?"

My head lowered. I couldn't look into his eyes, feeling awkward, like a child. "I don't want to… disappoint you."

"Disappoint me? Why would you think that?" His fingers lifted my chin, drawing my head up so our eyes would meet.

"I'm not very… experienced," I whispered.

He tilted his head and gazed at me with softer eyes. "Baby, that's okay. You couldn't disappoint me," he said, studying me and my obvious discomfort.

I thought I might pass out. My hands gripped his arms to steady my body.

"Are you a virgin?"

My hands trembled. I felt so embarrassed, but managed to nod, making no eye contact.

His strong arms wrapped me closer to him. His heartbeat pounded quickly against my cheek, allowing me to feel safe and protected in his grasp.

"Do you want to be with me, Angie?"

"Yes," I responded, looking upward, directly into his eyes now.

"We can take it slow," he promised.

And slow and tender he was. His fingers lightly touched my arms, turning me around with my back facing him. He brushed my long layers away from my back, flipping my hair across my shoulder. Gently, he kissed my neck while pulling down the zipper of my cream-colored dress. In what seemed like a split second, the polyester garment hit the floor, leaving me vulnerable in my underthings.

Somehow I found the nerve to turn and face him, helping unbutton his shirt. I lost my breath for a moment at the sight of his broad chest and powerful arms that always held me so tightly. With sweet, subtle movements, his lips kissed away my anxiety.

Tommy released the belt from his gray slacks. With no inhibitions, he removed the rest of his clothing as my eyes wandered, pleased with all aspects of the man standing so confidently before me. His hands pulled my body closer to him, feeling every naked part against my flesh.

Distracted by the fiery touch of his body, I barely felt his fingers unhook my bra. Within seconds, my panties dropped to the floor. Tommy quickly scooped me up and carried me to the king-size bed.

"You are so beautiful, Angie."

I couldn't wait anymore. My hands pulled him on top of me while my lips met his. I wanted to kiss every inch of his glorious physique. He turned me over, atop him, granting me access for deep exploration with my mouth and tongue. Moans left his lips when I greedily consumed his instrument.

His powerful arms tugged my body upward to kiss my lips, wasting no time tasting and teasing me. When he found my pleasure point, the rush went through me, causing my body to quiver uncontrollably. Never in my life had I felt anything so pleasing. I heard myself call out his name while my body throbbed.

Slowly, he crawled to the top of the bed and kissed each one of my eyelids and my nose. Then he nipped on my lip and caressed my cheek. "This may hurt a little at first, sweetheart."

My lips reached for his. I didn't care. I wanted him. I wanted to feel him inside me. I couldn't wait any longer. My legs spread around him, allowing him to enter over and over, again and again, until he shuddered, sighed, and collapsed on top of me.

Afterwards, room service brought up a fruit platter with cheese and crackers. I nibbled on some red grapes.

My body trembled slightly, still excited yet nervous with some awkward feelings mixed in. I always imagined what my first time would be like. Being with Tommy here in this spectacular hotel room, feeling loved and desired, surpassed any fantasy I could create in my own vivid mind.

Tommy stood from the bed and treaded to the bathroom. The hissing sound of running water echoed. He returned to the bed to swipe a strawberry from my fingers with his teeth. "How do you feel?"

I couldn't find the words to describe how I felt. I merely said, "I'm fine," with a huge smile I felt appear across my face. I purposely neglected to explain the burning and mild stinging effect from his large phallus.

"Fine? That's it? Just fine?" He grabbed my body and playfully tossed me on my back.

"Okay, okay, I feel unbelievably satisfied. Is that better?"

"Much better." He stood and lifted my naked body up from the bed.

"What are you doing?" I shrieked.

He carried me to the bathroom where the tub was filling up, and he carefully placed me inside, causing me to screech as my flesh hit the warm water. He seemed to take pleasure soaping up a wash-cloth and massaging the suds against my fair skin.

"Why don't you join me? I'll make room for you," I teased.

At my suggestion, he slipped into the warm water and pulled me atop him, holding me closely with those muscular arms wrapped around my waist.

"You know I can't stay here tonight with you. I want to, but I can't. I'm sorry," he whispered.

Disappointed barely described how I felt, but I chose not to display anything negative. "I understand."

He sent me a bright smile before kissing me.

He drove me home, long past midnight, with my head resting gently against his shoulder.

Katie may not be awake. I'd have to contain myself until I could speak with her in the morning.

Tommy walked me to the door, pulling me into his arms. "You are so special to me. You're my girl now." He tenderly lifted my chin toward his lips for a sweet kiss. "I love you."

"I love you too."

Chapter 8

January 18, 1971

IN THE MIDST of a fabulous dream about Tommy, a continuous ringing disrupted my fantasy. I turned to see the clock on the night-stand. Eight o'clock in the morning. Is that the phone, I wondered.

A light tap on the door was heard with Katie's voice calling out to me.

I jumped out of bed, grabbed my bathrobe, and let her inside.

"The phone's for you." Her brown eyes were wide and bright.

"Who is it?" I asked quietly.

Her brows raised with delight, so I raced down the stairs to answer the phone.

"Hello."

"Good morning, sweetheart. Did I wake you?"

Pure happiness was triggered by the sound of his voice. "Good morning. I'm awake. I didn't expect to hear from you this early."

"I have a surprise for you."

"A surprise? What is it?"

He chuckled. "I can't tell you what it is. But since your uncle is out of town this week, can you pack a bag and let me take you away for a few days?"

"Huh? Away? Where?"

Another laugh, thrilled to tease me. "I have a business trip and will be gone a few days. I want you to come with me. Can you be ready in an hour?"

I was silent. An hour? That doesn't give me much time, but how could I say no to such a tempting offer? "Yes, I can be ready in an hour."

"Good. I'll pick you up by nine-fifteen."

"Wait! What should I pack?"

"A bikini." He hung up, sounding very pleased with himself.

I barely had time to talk to Katie, but when I told her I'd be gone for a few days, she seemed genuinely happy for me and told me to have fun. She'd cover for me if Uncle Vince called to check on us. I didn't have time to ask her about Brett, or share the details of my romantic night with Tommy. I had to shower, get dressed, and pack quickly. A bikini? Where could he be taking me? Obviously, some-place warm in January. I threw together a few different outfits, some casual and others more on the dressy side for dinner.

Tommy picked me up right at nine-fifteen. He seemed to be a stickler for punctuality, and I was not completely ready for this spur of the moment getaway. He tapped his Swiss watch strapped to his wrist, alerting me to hurry. He snagged the suitcase from my hand and opened the door, eager to leave.

Katie gave me a bear hug before I strolled out the door behind him.

Chapter 9

WHEN WE ARRIVED at the airport, we were escorted directly onto the runway. I merely followed Tommy, who seemed to be a pro at traveling. Lifting my eyes upward, a small airplane sat before us with the door opened, and a staircase plunged from out of its side for us to climb up into.

The breeze outside whipped my long dark hair around, tangling the ends. It was a cool day that made me feel grateful to be headed somewhere warm.

The pilot departed the plane and greeted Tommy by name and with a quick shake of hands. He turned to me and offered his hand to shake as well. I was delighted to return the greeting when Tommy introduced me to Captain Roy.

"Is this the plane we're taking?"

"Yes, it's the company jet. Captain Roy takes me wherever I need to be. Are you ready for an adventure, Angie?"

Could he see the excitement beaming from my face? A company jet? His own pilot?

Tommy swooped me up the stairs quickly.

Inside the plane were several seats. There were also a few swivel chairs, colorful with a purple and green swirled pattern. The position of the chairs reminded me of a lounge area.

"Have you been on a plane before, Angie?"

"Yes, a few times. Not like this, though." I instantly thought about my father. "My dad took us skiing in Denver a few times. He loved the cold weather."

"Really? You like to ski?"

"I had fun when we were a family. We stopped being a normal family after I was about eight years old."

"I thought your father died three years ago."

It took me a moment to respond. "He did. Life changed for me when I was about eight." I shook my head. Now was not the time to bring up the past. "I'd rather talk about where we're going." It was easy to change the subject. All I had to do was sit upon his lap, run my fingers through his brown, shaggy hair, and kiss him hard on the mouth.

The pilot entered the seated area, announcing our departure time, and blushed as he realized he intruded on a private moment.

I slipped off Tommy's lap into my own seat, slightly embarrassed by the disruption, but Tommy placed me right back onto his lap.

Before takeoff, Captain Roy slid the door closed behind him. Tommy encouraged me to take a seat and wear the safety belt. As soon as we were up in the air, I slipped out of the seat and nestled into his strong arms. I loved that feeling of security his glorious muscles offered.

"Are you gonna tell me where we're going now?" I whispered as my teeth tugged at his ear lobe then moved down to his neck.

He shook his head.

My hands wandered down his chest as my lips parted his, and our tongues lightly danced. "Will you tell me now?"

"Not yet, baby."

With ease, my fingers released the clasp of his belt before reaching inside using long, delicate strokes.

"Okay, I'll give you a hint." A groan escaped from his lips. "The Caribbean."

Without a moment to waste, and after a generous hint of our destination, he removed my panties from beneath my mini skirt, and placed me on top of him upright in the seat. Our bodies glided in perfect rhythm, connected in every way. I was quickly learning how to use sex as a weapon to get whatever I wanted from him. Powerful was how I felt at that moment.

Chapter 10

THAT AFTERNOON, WE landed in Aruba. White sand beaches, a beautiful blue sky, and a dazzling, tropical sun beating down on us when we arrived at the hotel. Tommy pointed out the pool and hot tub. The beach was a few steps away.

"I have another surprise for you," he said, pointing in another direction inside the hotel.

"There's a beauty parlor back there. Why don't you have your hair done, paint your nails, whatever you want. I made the arrangements to charge my account."

"What? I thought we'd spend the afternoon together at the beach."

"We will. I told you this is a business trip. I have to meet with some people right now. You can spend time in the beauty parlor or sit by the pool while I work, okay?"

He surely sensed the disappointment from within me.

"Baby, come on, I brought you with me to this beautiful island. I have work to do then we'll be together tonight. I'll plan a nice dinner out for us. I promise. I have to go." He plopped the key to our room in my hand, and requested the bellman take our luggage. I received a quick peck on the cheek as he walked to the lobby where he met a group of men all wearing expensive-looking business suits.

I unpacked our belongings, carefully placing shirts and slacks on hangers or in dresser drawers. I decided not to spend the remainder of the afternoon inside getting my hair and nails done. The day was too sunny and warm to stay inside. I packed bikinis, and I planned to wear them.

I wasn't comfortable walking to the beach alone, so I strolled out to the pool area and found an available lounge chair. The warm sun felt good against my skin. Normally, I don't take a lot of time to sunbathe in Vegas. Summer temperatures are too hot, and my fair skin tone can be easily abused by the sun's rays.

I don't remember falling asleep, let alone closing my eyes.

A gentle tap was felt on my shoulder. A man stood before me, wearing a bright yellow swimsuit and a big smile. His lips lightly gripped a long, brown cigarette.

"Hello" was the only word I managed to say to him.

"Have you been out here long?" he asked, mumbling his words through the cigarette clenched between his teeth.

I really wasn't sure since I fell asleep, and I didn't bring my watch. I just stared at the man for a few moments.

"You look like you're getting sunburn."

My body popped up in the chair to catch a glimpse of my arms. I couldn't tell if they were red.

"I have some extra suntan lotion with me if you'd like some."

"Thank you. That would be nice."

He wiggled a tube of suntan lotion before my eyes, then squeezed the creamy substance into my hands. "I can get your back if you'd like."

Hmm, now I saw where this was going. "That's not necessary, but thank you."

"Angie."

I heard my name called, but my eyes were still slightly blinded by the sun. I turned my head both left and right before I saw Tommy approaching with a stern look worn upon his face.

"I thought you were going to the beauty parlor?" He bent down to kiss my cheek, then turned toward the Coppertone man. "Who's your friend?"

"Oh, I'm sorry, I didn't catch your name," I asked the man.

He grabbed his lotion and towel, never told me his name, and merely said, "Have a nice evening," before offering his chair to Tommy.

Tommy gratefully took his seat over. "Your skin looks red, Angie. Why didn't you go to the beauty parlor?"

"Why do you want me to get my hair done? Is there something wrong with my hair?"

"No, I just thought it'd be a nice treat for you, and I'd like to know how the services were here."

"It's a beautiful day. I wanted to enjoy the sun. You told me to pack a bikini."

"Let's go inside before you turn into a lobster."

He was right, my skin was red, and we had a couple of more days here to absorb the sunshine.

"What did that guy want?"

"Nothing," I answered nonchalantly. "He noticed my sun-burned skin and offered me tanning lotion."

"Is that all?" His jaw stiffened.

"Yes. Why are you angry?"

"I'm not angry. I went looking for you in the beauty parlor, and they said you never showed. Then I find you by the pool with some guy."

I took his hand and stopped him in the middle of the lobby. "It was nothing," I whispered. "I fell asleep in the chair. He woke me and said my skin looked burnt. That's it." I may not have had relationship experience before Tommy, but I easily recognized jealousy.

"I didn't know who he was or what he wanted."

"Are you finished with your meeting now?"

"Yeah, I made us a reservation for dinner. We should get ready." He tossed me a wink, showing me everything was all right. Then he took me by the hand, and we enjoyed the rest of our night together.

Tommy had a business meeting every day in Aruba. I asked him what his meetings were about. He had a plan to expand the family business and purchase more hotels. He may be buying the hotel we're staying in, hence the reason he wanted me to spend time at the beauty parlor. He wanted my opinion about the staff and amenities offered.

Since I understood his reasons now, I had my hair and nails done while he was working the next day. I also spent time shopping for souvenirs or swimming in the pool. We had breakfast in bed each morning, ate dinner out at fancy restaurants, and made love through the night. He promised he'd make time on our last day together to join me at the beach.

Visiting the serene beach was the best day yet. The water was so clear, we could see our feet no matter how far out into the ocean we swam. The sand was white and silky smooth between our toes. After a few days having him almost all to myself, how do I go back to Uncle Vince's house, and Tommy returns home… to his wife?

Chapter 11

January 22, 1971

WITHIN NO TIME at all, our getaway was complete. Our plane landed back in Las Vegas. The smile was wiped off my face. As we headed for his car, I couldn't help but shed a few tears.

Tommy pulled me close to him and dabbed the drops from my eyes. "I have another surprise for you, but you have to stop crying."

I nodded. All I wanted was to have him to myself. That would be the best surprise. I shrugged my shoulders and stepped into the Camaro. He drove past the turn that would have taken me back to Rancho Circle. "Where are we going?"

He sent me a wicked smile without a word uttered.

We arrived at an adorable ranch home with a gated entrance and perfectly manicured landscaping in Paradise Palms, a neighborhood not too far from the Strip.

"Where are we, Tommy?" My eyes wandered around the outside of this luxurious-looking home and piece of land.

Tommy jumped out of the car, opened my door, and helped me out. Taking hold of my hand, he guided me to the main entrance. He slipped a key into the lock and stepped right inside. "What do you think?"

"About what?" I asked.

"This." His arms stretched outward. "This house. Isn't it amazing? The kitchen is enormous with brand-new appliances. The bedroom has these really big closets you can walk inside. It's a great home only a few years old. What do you think, Angie?"

I didn't know what to think. "It's lovely, Tommy. Who lives here?"

"We do! I bought it for us."

My heart skipped a beat, maybe two. What was he saying? Was he leaving his house with Sadie? "Our home? You and me?"

"Yes, baby." He picked me up and swirled me around. "I told you. You're my girl. I'm going to take care of you, of us."

"Did your divorce go through?" I asked, beaming with joy.

The smile he once wore turned, and he released me from his grasp. "What? No, Angie. I told you that's going to take a while."

"How is this our home if you're not divorced?"

"I bought this place for us. You can move in here. You don't have to live with your uncle anymore. I will take care of you. And I'll be here all the time. It's the only way we can be together right now."

My arms crossed, unsure what just happened. He bought a home for me to live in and for him to... visit me?

"Baby, we had an amazing few days in Aruba. Look at this place. It's incredible, right? When my divorce is final, this will be our home together... you and me."

"Can you afford all this, Tommy?"

He laughed. "I can afford anything you want. Do you know how to drive? I'll have a car parked out front with the keys in it for you. You can see your family anytime."

"I never thought about moving out. My uncle doesn't even know about us yet."

"And you're concerned he won't approve. You're eighteen, Angie. You don't have to live with him. He can't forbid you to see me if you're living here." He grabbed my hand and led me down the hallway. "I'm putting a desk in this room over here. I can make an office out of it. As long as I can use the phone to make calls, I can work from here sometimes or half days. I just need to bring some paperwork and files home with me. You can travel with me on business trips too, just like this week."

My head spun. In so many ways, this sounded wonderful. The step of moving out also meant I needed to tell Uncle Vince about Tommy and me. That would not be easy.

Chapter 12

January 23, 1971

THE BED FELT so empty without Tommy's arms draped around me. How I missed him already.

Uncle Vince will be home later today, and I'll be singing at the club tonight. At some point, I have to tell him about Tommy and me before he heard the news from someone else. A knot formed in my gut, knowing today was the day.

I wiped the sleep from my eyes, took a long stretch, then hopped out of bed to neatly fix the sheets and drape the peach quilt over the pillows. A few decorative pillows were propped back into position next to my childhood stuffed bear. "What should I do with you, Teddy? Should I give you up so another little girl somewhere can snuggle with you at night as I used to?" This lovely white bear was a security blanket of sorts for me whenever Mom and Dad were at each other's throats, or when Connie was high and stealing money from Daddy's wallet.

Footsteps were heard outside my room. I felt like I hadn't seen Katie in a week. In fact, I hadn't. I carefully placed Teddy back in his rightful spot on my bed, and headed to the kitchen for some much needed caffeine.

Katie sat at the kitchen table, making a peanut butter sandwich.

I snuck up behind her. "Good morning."

"Oh, hi. Glad you're back. Dad called every day asking to talk to you." Her tone seemed displeased to cover for me all week.

"I'm sorry. I didn't mean to put you in such an awkward position."

"No, it's fine. I told him you were either in the shower or shopping. He believed me."

"What's wrong, Katie?" She didn't seem to be her usual cheerful self. I felt awful making her lie to her father for me. It's more than that. The color in her face was gone with no trace of a smile. Her eyes were pink and a little swollen.

Tears burst from her brown eyes as my brain made the connection that she was upset about something.

Moving a chair closer to her, I sat and placed her head on my shoulder, allowing her to bury me with the stream. "What's wrong?"

"Brett's been avoiding me at school and stopped returning my phone calls."

"Oh, I'm sorry, Katie."

"I thought everything was fine, but he moved on to Sherry Cagney, the blonde-haired, blue-eyed, princess type with big boobs and no brains."

A sigh left my lips and a lump formed in my throat. I can only imagine what that felt like. Heck, the man I loved had a wife, but he was in the middle of a divorce. I wanted to cheer my dear cousin up so much. "This is Brett's loss. You'll meet another boy. How about we go to a movie before your dad comes home? Or shopping? Tonight, you can come to the club to hear me sing. There are a lot of single young men there, you know."

"You don't have plans with Tommy?"

"I haven't heard from him yet, and besides, I need to tell your dad about Tommy and me tonight. Maybe I need a distraction today too." I stood up from the chair, pulled a tissue from the box, and wiped the liquid from Katie's face. "Come on now, let's get cleaned up and go out for the day."

The only phone number I had for Tommy was his office number. I had no way of contacting him anywhere else. I hoped he would have called me before Katie and I went out for the afternoon. He knew I was singing tonight. I'd have to wait to see him then. My first priority was to cheer up my cousin.

Katie asked me a million questions about Tommy's surprise getaway. I didn't want to go into too many details about the fabulous vacation we had together, followed by him buying me a house after the boy she was so infatuated with dumped her for another girl. However, if I didn't tell her about the house, she'd find out later when I told her father. Naturally, she was surprised and even happy for me. Of course, the real issue came to light—his wife.

We saw the movie, *Love Story*—a huge mistake, seeing that Katie was trying to forget about her own love story, and I felt a minor connection because Tommy's wife and my uncle were the obstacles to our very own love story. But nobody died in my real-life drama. We both cried so hard at the end of the movie, we started to laugh at our absurdity. A comedy would have been a better choice.

Pulling up in the driveway, Tommy's Camaro was parked off to the side. No sign of Uncle Vince being home yet.

Katie parked the car, and I jumped out to greet him.

The Camaro door opened, and Tommy catapulted toward me. "Where were you? I was worried." His arms wrapped around me, then he nodded his head hello toward Katie.

"We didn't have plans, did we?" I asked.

"I called this morning and no answer. You've been gone all day."

From the corner of my eye, I watched Katie gingerly inch her way inside. I felt grateful for the privacy.

"Katie and I spent some time together." I accepted the kiss he offered, his eyes displaying relief to see me. "I don't know how to reach you if you're not at your office, Tommy."

"Well, we won't have this problem when you move in. Did you pack?"

"Pack? Tommy, I haven't even told my uncle yet. He's not back, but he will be home soon. Remember, I'm singing tonight. I'll see you there."

"I'll try to make it tonight. I was hoping to have you packed and ready to go."

"I need to speak with Uncle Vince first. I don't want him to see you here. Wait. What do you mean, you'll *try* to come tonight?"

"Sadie's mother is visiting unexpectedly." His eyes rolled back with great discouragement. "Outside of going to work, it will be difficult for me to get away from home while she's in town."

"I thought you slept in separate bedrooms."

"We do."

"How do you explain that to her mother?"

"She is aware we have problems, Angie. She's only here for a few days." His eyes glanced at his watch. "If I can't meet you at Spritz tonight, I'll call you in the morning from a payphone down the street. I want to know when you'll be moving in."

"Tommy?"

His lips pressed against mine firmly. "Sorry, baby, I have to go."

I had so many questions as Tommy's sports car fled the driveway. Some I was afraid to ask. Others I was afraid to know the answers to. I don't question his love for me, but I do wonder about Sadie. Does she suspect he's seeing someone? Does she want the divorce?

Chapter 13

"HELLO! WHERE ARE my girls?" Uncle Vince's voice nearly shook the house. His deep, loud tone was as large as his personality.

Katie and I were dancing in her bedroom, listening to Crosby, Stills, Nash, and Young's, *Déjà vu* album. "Teach Your Children" was one of Katie's favorite songs. That's when we heard his voice over the peppy melody. We ran down the stairs to greet him with big hugs. He looked so happy. Whether the happiness came from a week's vacation with Nancy or to be home with us was uncertain. He had so much joy on his face, I didn't have the heart to drop the bomb about Tommy, but I needed to tell him before I left for the club at eight o'clock.

I waited for my uncle to unpack and become settled. When he reached for the bottle of bourbon and poured a glass for himself, the moment had arrived.

"So Angie, where were you all week? I talked to Katie, but you were never home when I called. You look... tan." He sniffed the bitter scent of bourbon before sipping from the glass while I paused, desperately searching for the right words to say. "I know, Angie, and I'm happy," he added with a delightful smile.

"Happy?"

"Yes. You're dating."

Slight confusion followed by perplexed relief, eased my tension.

"How is Louis? Where did you kids go?"

Oh no, Louis Maroni. Poor Louis. Katie told me he called a few times while I was away with Tommy. I never once thought to return his calls. That was terribly rude of me. "I didn't see Louis, Uncle Vince."

"What do you mean? His father told me he was going to call you. He didn't call?"

"It's not that. I've been wanting to tell you something for a while now."

He released the glass onto the bar counter and turned toward me, arms crossed. "What is it?"

Somehow the words escaped. "I've been dating someone, but it's not Louis. Someone who makes me very happy, Uncle."

"Really? Who? I mean Louis is going places. He's a fine, young man. He'll make a good husband."

"I don't love Louis, Uncle. I'm in love with someone else."

"In love? With who, Angie? Why the secrecy?"

The smile across Uncle Vince's olive complexion showed genuine happiness, until I uttered Tommy's name.

"That's out of the question, Angie. End of story. What are you thinking? What is he thinking? No. No, he's not the man for you!" His back turned away from me and his fist slammed the counter of the bar.

"Uncle, please. I can't stop seeing him. I love him. He loves me."

"Oh, he loves you? Really? What does his wife have to say about that? You do realize he already has a wife." His black eyes were wild with anger. That loud, dark voice of his echoed throughout the main floor of the house. Katie surely heard our conversation from her bedroom.

"Yes, I know he's married right now, but he's getting divorced."

"Divorced? And that makes this okay? It's okay for him to treat my beautiful niece like some kind of tramp?"

"He doesn't treat me like that. He loves me!"

"I thought you were not only beautiful, Angie, I thought you were smart too." He approached me cautiously, arms opened and placed his hands upon my shoulders. "Don't be his mistress. If he loves you, he'll make you his wife. He'll end his marriage now if he loves you."

"He wants me to move in with him."

"Oh? Where is he going to put you? In the guest room, so he can take turns sleeping with you one night and his wife another night? Or will he sleep in between the two of you?"

"Stop it. Don't talk like that, please."

"You can't see him, Angie. That's it. It's over. I'll make sure he doesn't bother you ever again."

"No! You can't control who I love. You can't make me love Louis, or marry someone you think is a better choice for me. I love Tommy, and I want to be with him. I love you, Uncle Vince, and I appreciate everything you've done for me. You're like a father to me."

"My brother is spinning in his grave right now! I made a promise to him. I said I'd protect you if anything ever happened to him. You are *my* responsibility, Angie."

"I'm eighteen. I have to be responsible for myself. I'm going to move in with Tommy. He bought a house for us."

"You're making a big mistake. Don't do this."

"If that's true, it's my mistake to make. I'm sorry if I disappointed you, but I want to do this. I hope you don't hate me."

"Hate you? Angie, I love you like my own daughter. I want the best for you and trust me, Tommy Cavallo is not it. He's not good enough for you. Will you think about this?"

"I have."

"People are going to talk. Do you really want to be known as a homewrecker? The other woman? His mistress? Because that's what you are and everyone will know it."

"Tommy planned his divorce before he met me. We fell in love. It just happened. I want to be with him."

He chugged the rest of the bourbon and slammed the glass on the counter, turning his back away from me. "You're family. You will always be my responsibility."

"You can't stop me from leaving, Uncle."

It took him a few moments before he finally nodded, realizing I was serious about moving out. "When he disappoints you, because I know he will, Angie, you call me."

I recognized those somber eyes. He wore them at Daddy's funeral. Breaking his heart was not my intent, but somehow, I felt free.

Packing my room was harder than I expected. Not because of the work it took to gather my belongings. There were so many good memories in this enormous house. Uncle Vince provided a life for me. Although he was as overprotective as Daddy was, I loved the family aspect. A real sense of family. I lost that because of my sister's addiction and Mother's failed attempts to resemble a good parent. I stared at Teddy, propped up against my pillow, flicked his ear, and placed him back upon the peach quilt before leaving the security of this home.

Chapter 14

February 11, 1971

REGARDLESS OF MY uncle's objections, moving in with Tommy was so exciting! He made sure I had everything I needed in the house. A color television, 8-Track Player, swimming pool, and did I mention a car?

A 1970 white Cadillac convertible sat in the driveway. What a beauty! Luckily, Uncle Vince taught both Katie and me how to drive. Although I didn't have a lot of experience behind the wheel, I did have my license.

Tommy let me drive around the neighborhood not too far from the Strip. I only scared the hell out of him one time, trying to parallel-park, nearly hitting a black Ford Mustang. Besides that one incident, I thought I fared well.

Life with Tommy moved at such a quick beat. I barely had time to catch my breath, keeping up with his vivacious energy.

Tommy came to the house daily. He's a hotel owner. His business operates twenty-four hours a day. I stopped asking what excuses he gave Sadie for not being home. All I cared about was having him to myself, even briefly. With the car, I was able to do my own shopping.

I wanted to cook more. Tommy bought me a cookbook and all the ingredients to make a variety of meals and desserts. He left me money to stock the pantry and refrigerator. I had my own money from singing at Spritz, but Tommy insisted on paying all of the household expenses. I never saw the bills.

The room at the end of the hallway was turned into an office. He had a desk and a small file cabinet put in. The phone company hooked up another phone in the office so he could make calls to clients or business associates when he worked from our home. I loved having him here, even if he sat behind a closed office door.

If Tommy had to stop by the Montgomery along the Strip, I'd often take a ride with him. People always treated me with respect because I was with him. At first he didn't hold my hand, but within a short period, he did. They knew I was his girl, and I didn't care what the grapevine thought or said behind my back.

A brief trip to Hawaii made the agenda, a project Tommy had been talking about since I moved in. I couldn't wait to go! Even though he had business to conduct, we spent full nights together, passionate as always.

Each morning, we would hit the gorgeous, white sand beaches with inviting turquoise water, bathing beneath a clear blue sky, as palm trees danced to a light breeze. We witnessed an active volcano, puffing smoke and spitting fire from the mouth of its large, black, mountainous terrain. Streams of hardened black lava surrounded the area. In the evenings, we'd relax while enjoying a magical dinner show, or experience delicious island food and drinks at a luau.

This summer, he planned a trip for us to New York City! His eyes were focused on a specific hotel there. No casino, but New York had a lot of traffic and a large market for people taking vacations or business trips. A good investment for sure. He hinted about targeting Europe soon. I begged him to look at Italy and France. I always dreamed of going to big, antiquated cities like Venice, Rome, and Paris. Tommy promised he'd show me the world. This was just the beginning.

Chapter 15

Valentine's Day 1971

A BOX OF long-stemmed, red roses was delivered, along with chocolates and a note from Tommy wishing "the love of his life" a happy Valentine's Day—the first of many!

I decided to make one of his favorite meals, a beef roast with mashed potatoes and gravy, followed by a chocolate fudge cake for dessert. Tonight at the club, I planned to dedicate a song to him, "At Last" by the sultry Etta James. At last, my love has come along—it's the perfect song to sing to him on this romantic holiday. I hummed the melodious tune all week.

Tommy came home for lunch and enjoyed the savory meal I cooked for Valentine's Day. I thought the roast was a bit tough, but I'm still getting a handle on cooking. He said he loved dinner and that's all that mattered to me.

Cooking was one thing my mother did well. I do have some fond memories of her. A kitchen cupboard door stuck, making a popping sound whenever she opened it to pull out the pans and mixing tools. Every time I'd hear that cupboard open, I'd run to the kitchen, pull up a chair to stand on, and watch her work her magic with anything she prepared. She used to make these elaborate meals every night—when we were a happy family.

I spent some of my club earnings on a very sexy, black nightie. As Tommy helped clear the dishes from the table, I changed into the sheer fabric and presented him with the chocolate cake. I don't think he even noticed the cake. Here we were in the middle of the day, pawing at each other like animals.

I strolled into Spritz that night as planned. My eyes wandered around to see if Tommy had arrived.

Richie, the manager, introduced me to the crowded room, filled mostly with couples exchanging sensual glances and holding hands. Lights were dimmed. Candles sparkled in the center of each table. Hearts and flowered décor hung throughout the walls and from the ceiling. The air reeked of romance for everyone there.

Where was my love?

The audience applauded when my set was finished then carried on with their conversations and drink orders.

Richie handed me a glass of wine on the house. We sat at a corner table near the stage and sipped the Merlot from fluted glasses. He told me his sob story. His girlfriend dumped him last week, so he was pretty down on Valentine's Day.

I was feeling a little melancholic myself, unsure where Tommy was. He completely missed my song dedication.

Through the crowd, I recognized his stature, the brown hair, and those muscular arms. I was so happy to see him. I watched his eyes search the room, obviously looking for me.

I pushed myself out of the chair to stand, but Richie took hold of my arm and moved me in close to remind me of a schedule change for next weekend.

"Get your hands off her."

Richie's head slowly moved upward meeting eyes with Tommy. He quickly let go of my arm and stood up, a good three inches taller than Tommy. His attempt to say a pleasant hello to Tommy failed.

Tommy took me by the hand and marched me across the smoke-filled room through the crowd of couples and out the door.

"What's the matter with you?" I wiggled my arm from his grasp.

"Me? Why do I walk in here to find him touching you and whispering in your ear?"

"We were just talking. He's the manager here. You can't treat him like that. Not to mention you embarrassed me."

"I see the way he looks at you. This isn't the first time I saw him touch you while talking to you. You're my girl, Angie. He can't put his hands on you like that."

"It's not like that, Tommy. Will you please calm down? Fighting with you is not how I wanted to spend Valentine's Day." My legs carried me closer to him. My red painted fingertips stroked his cheek lightly. When his eyes met mine, I watched the stress and anger diminish.

Using both hands, I massaged his temples and ran my fingers through his thick, shaggy hair. I'm not sure why he needed so much reassurance from me. My lips reached up toward his for a quick nip. I tasted the liquor and smelled the harsh scent of whiskey on his breath.

His arms wrapped around my waist, drawing me in closer. "I'm sorry, Angie. I don't want to lose you."

"I'm not going anywhere. You can't come down here like this, Tommy. This is my job."

"You don't need to work. I told you I will always take care of you."

"I know you will, but I love to sing. I want to sing."

"How about you sing at the Montgomery? Bigger place. Larger crowds. More money."

The offer was rather enticing.

Chapter 16

March 25, 1971

I TOOK TOMMY up on his offer to sing at his hotel in the lounge a couple of nights each week. The pay was better, and he controlled the schedule. He wanted to ensure my ability to travel with him on business trips. If he planned a last-minute rendezvous for us, he would simply make a phone call to easily find a replacement act.

Everyone at the Montgomery knew I was the boss's girlfriend. I just wanted to sing. Where I sang and who the audience was didn't matter.

The doorbell chimed around eleven in the morning. Before I saw her face, I noticed Katie's blue Dodge in the driveway. I was ecstatic to open the door and see her standing outside my home for the first time since I moved here. My arms stretched outward for a big hug. Instantly, I sensed something was wrong. Her arms were limp, and she didn't utter a word. "Hey, are you okay?"

She shook her head as tears began to fall.

"Come inside. Let me take your cape." I folded the navy blue, knitted cape, and draped it over the armchair in the den. Taking her by the hand, I nudged her to sit beside me on the sofa. "Talk to me, sweetie. What's wrong?"

A few moments passed for Katie to catch her breath and wipe her tears before she could answer me. "I'm pregnant."

My eyes widened, surprised to hear this news. I didn't even know she had sex. She never told me. I took a second to process this information. "Brett? Did you and he…?"

"Yes, but he says it's not his! I know it's his baby. I wasn't with anybody else, I swear."

"Shh, I believe you. Of course I believe you. How can he do this to you?" Visions of Brett's demise floated through my head. Driving his Volkswagen Beetle off a cliff, rattlesnake bite, drowning in the Pacific, or being abducted by aliens to name a few. Then I thought about my dear cousin having a baby. I couldn't believe she was going to be a mother.

Becoming a mother was something I always dreamed about for myself. I didn't have the best role model, but my heart was so full of love to give a child someday. Now Katie would experience this, even if it wasn't planned and she wasn't married.

"Did you see a doctor?"

She nodded. "I wasn't feeling like myself. He told me I was pregnant after the examination." She stood up, paced the floor, folded her arms then unfolded them. "I want to graduate high school. There's only a couple of months left of school. What do I tell my father? What if he sends me away?"

"Send you away? No, Katie, he wouldn't do that. I think Brett may have something to worry about," I said in jest, well sort of.

"Oh God, you're right! He'll want to know who got me… knocked up. Then I have to tell him Brett wants nothing more to do with me."

"Do you want me to be there when you talk to him?"

"No, but thanks. He's been a little sad since you left. Now I have to tell him this."

"You know I'm always going to be here for you. You can count on me." I grabbed a tissue from the bathroom to wipe her eyes. "You're going to be a mother, Katie. That's truly a gift. He or she can count on me too. We're family."

Uncle Vince respected family. He'd be surprised when she told him this news, but I couldn't imagine he'd send her away or stop her from finishing high school. I needed to see him. I didn't want him to think I abandoned our family. Maybe if he saw Tommy and me together as a couple, he'd understand how much we loved each other. It was a nice dream or wishful thinking.

Katie was still on my mind later that afternoon when Tommy stopped by to work at home for the rest of the day as he often did. What will she do without a husband to support her? Uncle Vince would never throw her and her baby out. That's a fact.

My mind wandered. What if this happened to me? Tommy loved me, but we can't be married until his divorce is final.

"Angie? Did you hear me?" Tommy asked, pushing himself off the floor after fixing a leaky pipe beneath the kitchen sink.

"Huh? Oh, I'm sorry. Did you say something?"

"I asked you to hand me a towel." He walked to the cabinet and grabbed a towel from the shelf. "Where were you just now?"

I blurted out, "Katie's pregnant."

Slowly, Tommy turned toward me with raised brows from my outburst.

"She told me today."

"Who's the father? That kid, Brett, she was seeing?"

Shifting my weight from left to right, I nodded. "He told her it's not his."

"What? He bailed on her? I can only imagine what Vince had to say about that?"

"I don't think she told him yet. She's afraid. She told me first." I welcomed his hug. "Tommy, what if I... we?"

"What? You won't get pregnant as long as you're taking your pill. You are taking it every day, right?"

My eyes drifted away from him.

"Angie? You're taking that birth control pill every day, right?" His eyes were wide, nostrils flaring with concern.

Slowly my eyes met his again. "I do, when I remember. I forgot a couple of times."

"Jesus Christ, Angie! You can't forget to take your pill. Shit!"

I felt a tear stream down my cheek. He's never yelled at me before.

"You can't get pregnant, Angie. Not now! Do you understand? That can't happen."

"I just forgot a couple of times. It wasn't on purpose."

His hands covered his eyes and face in distress. He took a few deep breaths then leaned against the kitchen counter, appearing calmer. "Okay. You need to remember. I'll have to remind you."

"I don't need you to remind me. I'm not a child."

"Stop acting like a child then. I take care of everything here for you, but I can't swallow that damn pill for you."

I turned my back on him, stormed to the bedroom, and closed the door behind me, pushing in the lock. This is not how I thought we'd spend the afternoon. I could have stomped my feet and slammed the door, but that would be acting like a child.

The front door slammed hard behind Tommy as he left our home, angry and frustrated with me.

The phone rang at least ten times that afternoon. I called Katie to check on her. She said she hadn't called me. I imagine it was Tommy trying to reach me. No one else called our house. I didn't want to talk to him, still upset about the way he spoke to me.

Taking the pill every day is important to remember. He was right about that.

Chapter 17

April 2, 1971

LAST NIGHT I baked a couple of pies. The refrigerator drawer was filled with ripe apples. I thought I'd bring John a pie since baking was not his forte.

I arrived just as his nurse was leaving. She's a tall, attractive blonde, all in white. I'm sure he flirted relentlessly with her. I sent her a wave. She returned my friendly sentiment with an elusive smile.

As I opened the door, John rolled toward me in his wheelchair with a grin plastered to his face.

I'd been practicing my signing with Tommy. He loved that I enjoyed visiting John while he was at the office.

I placed the pie down on the counter and turned to face John without saying a word. I don't want him to read my lips. I want him to understand my signing. He was a stickler for perfection like Tommy, and corrected me if I placed a finger in the wrong position. I so enjoyed this budding friendship we developed.

I used my hands to inquire about the sexy-looking nurse who just left.

He blushed some. I didn't need to know sign language to understand his symbol that described her large breasts.

We laughed a lot together. Yes, I made apple pies. However, I had an ulterior motive for seeing John without Tommy. This may be incredibly improper, but I wanted to ask John about Sadie. Tommy did not like to discuss her with me, nor his divorce. Whenever I brought it up, we'd end up arguing. He started to drink more. He warned me from the beginning, the divorce could take time. I needed to understand why.

While waiting for the right moment to bring up Sadie, John captured my attention with his hand gestures. I was a little slow still to keep up with him, so I requested, with a chuckle, that he go easy on me.

"I can tell something is wrong, Angie."

"I hate to put you in a bad position." I paused, fiddling with my fingers, and I wasn't signing. "Can I ask you something? In confidence."

He nodded in agreement.

"Tell me about Sadie."

His eyes closed, and his head turned from me.

"I'm sorry. I shouldn't have asked."

"No. I understand. What do you want to know?"

"Why is this divorce so difficult? Does she want the divorce? Does she love Tommy still? Does she know about me?" My hands moved so fast and furiously with so many questions, John could barely get a word, or sign, in.

"It's complicated. What has Tommy told you?"

"He hasn't said much lately. I upset him when I bring it up. He's been drinking a lot. I'm worried." My dark brown eyes filled up.

John took my hand and gently pressed it against his cheek. "Sadie was a mistake. Their marriage was an arrangement. Not so much about love."

"I don't understand."

"Our father was a family man. Very traditional and old-schooled. He believed you aren't a real man if you can't manage a home and a wife. Tommy had to prove himself worthy to take over the business. Sadie was chosen for him, in a sense."

"An arranged marriage?"

"Yes and no. Tommy and Sadie liked each other. They were friends. Pop put pressure on Tommy to get married. Pop would have never handed Tommy the business through the power of attorney or his will if Tommy were single. Pop really liked Sadie and thought she would be good for him. Sadie liked the money. She will fight for the dough in court when Tommy divorces her."

"Does she love him, John?" I held my breath, waiting for his answer.

He shrugged. "Maybe. I'm not sure if her love is for my brother or his wallet."

"Does she know about me?"

"She's sharp enough to figure out Tommy might have something going on. Maybe she doesn't care. As his wife, she has access to millions."

I knew the Cavallos had a lot of money. Heck, my family has money. I have an inheritance from my father that I don't touch. I was always accustomed to financial security and probably took it for granted.

"Pop has a ton of money to leave behind. Tommy inherits the business and the family estate. Since Pop had the stroke, Tommy already has access to it, and he's making more with the new hotels he started to buy. Sadie won't walk away with nothing."

"If he has so much, why can't he just give her some money then leave?"

He shook his head. "I don't know all the specifics. This was an arrangement, and I stayed out of the details. There are legal agreements involved that tie into their marriage. I know Tommy has lawyers working on disputing the language in the paperwork."

My head was fuzzy. My feet paced against the tile floor. I started to speak instead of signing, forgetting John only knows I'm talking if he can see my lips. "Tommy said there wasn't a prenuptial agreement."

"I don't know what agreements were a part of this exactly. He may not be able to divorce Sadie for a long time, Angie. But my brother loves you. He adores you! I see it in the way he looks at you. When you're not here, all he does is talk about you. You have to understand he is under a great deal of pressure from everyone. He's expanding the business. I think, no, I know, he doesn't want to go home to Sadie. He wants to be with you. Building the business throughout the country and overseas is keeping him away from home. You are a part of that world now. He plans to take you everywhere with him. He doesn't love Sadie, but he may not be able to walk away very easily. I hope you're a patient woman, Angie. He needs you. Don't push him. He has enough stress."

God, I love Tommy, but I hate knowing this divorce could take a lot longer than a year.

"People look at me and feel sorry for me because of this chair and because I can't hear."

I shook my head and tossed him a smile. "They just don't understand you."

"True. Yet I'm the lucky one. I'm free! No pressure to marry any one particular woman. I'm not involved with the business. I don't need all that money. I have all I need right here."

I smiled at him, inspired by his wisdom. "You've got me as your friend too."

He held my hand and kissed the palm then nodded his head in agreement. He searched through a kitchen drawer and pulled out a knife and spatula, an indication he wanted some pie.

Chapter 18

April 4, 1971

I CALLED KATIE to see how she was feeling. She told Uncle Vince about the baby. He blew his top at first, but this was his precious daughter and first grandchild. I knew he would accept the situation. What he can't accept is the baby's father walking out on his daughter. Unfortunately, an unwed mother is frowned upon. People gossiped. Katie would be labeled a tramp by society. My dear uncle cared what people thought. That's why he was hurt about my decision to be with Tommy. I needed to see him. It was time. I wanted him to see that I was okay.

Sunday family dinner always started at one o'clock. It took some convincing for Tommy to agree to join me. I heeded John's advice, and backed off asking him questions about Sadie and the divorce. Still, I'm so curious what was going on; and I hoped he would soon confide in me.

We arrived at Uncle Vince's home about ten minutes early. The usual guests were already inside, sipping on wine or bourbon when we walked into the parlor. Conversations stopped completely, and all heads turned toward us when they noticed Tommy was with me.

"Hello, Uncle." I approached him cautiously for a hug.

He opened his arms and kissed my cheek. A hint of a smile showed.

I didn't let go right away. I really missed him more than I anticipated.

Tommy stood behind me, and out of respect, he offered his hand to shake.

My uncle accepted his hand then turned to me. "Angie, introduce Tommy to our family."

We strolled around for formal introductions. Tommy already knew Sal Maroni and Benny DeLeone.

Katie sat in the corner speaking with Louis. Ugh! I never returned his phone calls, nor did I tell Tommy my uncle wanted me to date him. Hopefully, he'd never find out. I disrupted their conversation to say hello and introduced Tommy.

Louis was cordial. Why would I think differently? He was the perfect, young gentleman, after all.

Soon, a large tray of chicken parmigiana atop mounds of spaghetti marinara was carried to the dining room table. Roseanne, the housekeeper, scrambled to set an extra place setting.

I'm sure it was a surprise to my uncle that I brought Tommy with me. When I called Katie to tell her I'd come to Sunday dinner this week, I never thought to confirm Tommy would be joining me. That sentiment should have been assumed.

I sat in between Katie and Tommy. Louis quickly took the seat on the opposite side of my cousin. I wondered if Louis was here to court Katie. But she's... ahh.

I wasn't sure how I felt about my uncle playing matchmaker for his pregnant daughter. He always tried to find a suitable man for Katie. Did Louis know she was expecting?

Uncle Vince stood in front of the whole "family" with a glass of bourbon in hand. "I have some very exciting news to share. Louis asked me for my approval to marry my beautiful daughter, Katie. I was beyond pleased to give him my blessing. He's a fine, young man. Someone who I know will always respect my daughter and cherish her."

His eyes wandered toward Tommy and me for a brief moment. I knew he thought the exact opposite of Tommy as he did Louis.

"My daughter accepted his proposal, and I wanted to be the first to congratulate them both. Salute!"

Everyone raised their glasses in their honor except for me. Instead, I managed to find Katie's hand beneath the tablecloth and squeezed it tightly. She squeezed my hand back, but she wouldn't look at me.

I knew my uncle arranged this. He planned a future for Katie and her baby.

Chapter 19

June 26, 1971

THE WEDDING WAS planned after Katie's eighteenth birthday and her high school graduation. Her pregnancy was definitely showing because of her naturally slim build. She wore extra-large sized clothing to conceal the baby while she finished school. For her wedding, she wore a simple white gown with a large enough gap at the waistline to hide the precious bundle.

Thrilled to help with the wedding plans, I worked with Alice Maroni to reserve a room at Amici's, a nearby restaurant, and selected the menu. I couldn't resist thinking about the kind of wedding I would want someday.

Katie helped to make some decisions, but she didn't seem to have her heart in it. I asked her if she was happy.

Uncle Vince convinced her she needed a husband. The Maronis were considered family; and Louis already had a job at city hall. Within no time, my uncle was convinced Louis would run the town, even the state someday. Royalty, he believed. He wanted that for his daughter. He wished that for me as well.

Tommy was uncomfortable attending the wedding with me, but he didn't trust my uncle. Seeing how he planned a marriage for his daughter, he wondered if my uncle would attempt to fix me up with another up and coming, younger, single man. He was not going to let me attend Katie's wedding without him. He had quite a jealous streak that heightened when he drank.

A limousine brought Katie and Uncle Vince to the church. I drove with Tommy in the Cadillac.

The sky was gray. Rain threatened the afternoon. People arrived and quickly took their seats inside before the storm let out its massive burst of thunder and lightning.

A woman stood outside near the church entrance. Dark curls in a bouffant hairstyle atop a small frame, wearing a sky blue, silk dress and black heels. As she turned toward me, I recognized the face of my Aunt Dolly. I whispered to Tommy who she was then slowly approached her. "Aunt Dolly?"

"Angie?" She opened her arms and gave me a hug then studied my face carefully, taking in every feature. "You look lovely!"

"I'm happy to see you. So glad you could make it." I turned toward Tommy, grabbed his arm, and leaned him in to be a part of our conversation. "This is Tommy. Tommy, my Aunt Dolly." They exchanged smiles and handshakes.

"I was so surprised to hear she was getting married, Angie. She never mentioned Louis before. Although I knew his parents, Salvatore and Alice."

I secretly wondered if Katie informed her mother that she was becoming a grandmother.

"Can I escort you ladies inside?" Tommy asked.

"Thank you, dear, but I'd like to wait for my daughter to arrive."

I glanced at Tommy, offering a look that suggested we wait outside with her. Katie would appreciate my welcoming her mother and keeping her company.

Within a few minutes, the limousine arrived and parked out front. My uncle stepped out first, proud as a peacock, opening the door and helping his daughter out. He smiled big and bright until he glanced up at the top of the church stairway, and saw his ex-wife waiting with Tommy and me. We all noticed his faded expression.

Aunt Dolly turned her petite frame and gazed at me with a nervous grin. I didn't know what the friction was between the two of them, but the tension resembled my parents' marriage toward the end.

When Katie saw her mother, she darted toward her, beaming. This was the first time I recognized happiness on her face in months.

Uncle Vince followed Katie up the stairs, marched passed all of us, and waited inside. The moment was very uncomfortable.

Tommy glared in my direction, hoping to slip inside, but I couldn't leave Aunt Dolly alone.

As maid of honor to Katie, I needed to stay with her until she made it to the church altar. I whispered to Tommy, asking if he would escort my aunt inside and sit with her. He did just that. She took her seat in the second row on the bride's side of the aisle. The first row was designated for Uncle Vince.

I wore a pale pink chiffon gown with a sash around the bodice and pearls at the neckline. As I sauntered down the aisle, my eyes focused on Tommy. We looked at each other as if the day was ours. Oh how I envisioned I would have a day like this! Gliding up the aisle to the altar with Tommy waiting for me. But today was Katie's day.

She gracefully stepped across the white carpet runner, carrying a very large bouquet of white flowers with hints of baby pink carnations and greens. She held the bouquet low to cover any trace of the baby she carried. She wept a bit, seeing her mother smile with tremendous pride and delight.

Uncle Vince never made eye contact with Aunt Dolly.

Louis was a bundle of nerves, hands quivering and legs shaking in his black tuxedo as Katie approached him at the altar. Uncle Vince lifted her veil, kissed her cheek, and gracefully placed her hand gently into Louis's palm. That was the first time I saw Louis display a half-smile.

The ceremony was delightful. Alice Maroni sobbed with joy so loudly, the priest jumped during the exchange of vows.

The weather was not agreeable as rain poured in droves from the sky. Las Vegas didn't see much rain in the summer months. Was this a sign of sorts? A sign that Katie was making a terrible mistake? I didn't dare share my personal thoughts with Katie. She did what she had to do for the sake of her baby. She gave her baby a good father.

We posed for photographs before driving to Amici's for an elegant dinner.

Katie spent an inordinate amount of time with her mother. When I saw my aunt place her hand upon Katie's belly, she knew she had a grandchild on the way. It was a shame she moved so far from her daughter. Katie may need her mother. I never understood my aunt and uncle's divorce, but Aunt Dolly always kept in touch with Katie.

My mother was dead. Dead to me anyway.

Chapter 20

The Summer of 1971

THE SUMMER MONTHS came and went quickly. Tommy bought hotels in New York City, Venice, and Rome. Every week we found ourselves with Captain Roy on the company jet. This summer was the most time Tommy and I spent together since we first met.

In some places, people assumed I was his wife and referred to me as Mrs. Cavallo. I never corrected them. Neither did Tommy. It was a little fun for me to play that part. I was his wife in many senses, except in the legal sense; the one that mattered. I could play the game all I wanted, but I knew the truth.

New York in July was exciting! Time Square was thrilling, and seeing a few Broadway shows like "How the Other Half Loves" and "No Place to Be Somebody" were on the itinerary for our trip. We climbed to the top of the Empire State Building. The skyscrapers blew me away. The city's excitement mirrored Las Vegas but on a different level. We took a ferry ride to Ellis Island, and saw the sensational Statue of Liberty. The city had a story to tell, filled with charm, eloquence, and history.

Tommy got us into some nightclubs. He arranged for me to sing on stage for one song with the band until the lead singer grabbed my ass. That was all he had to see. He completely lost it!

Tommy ran onto the stage, knocked the man down, and continued to beat his face until blood was splattered everywhere. He had too much to drink. He didn't even feel the pain on his knuckles from the beating he gave that guy. The man was okay overall. He probably had a broken nose. Tommy kept screaming at him to not touch his girl, even when the fight was over.

I met our driver by the curb. He helped me drag Tommy into the car where he soon passed out.

After the trip to New York, Tommy believed we needed a bodyguard. He had the money to pay for the service, and he didn't want to get his hands dirty again. He also wanted to make sure no man put his hands on me. Frankly, he was lucky that crooner didn't press charges against him.

Tommy hired Jim, a security manager from the Montgomery. He had the largest biceps, even bigger than Tommy's. Jim didn't talk much. He was discreet and kept confidences. In other words, Jim knew Tommy had a wife, and he knew I was his girl. Jim also had connections. He knew Tommy's drink of choice, Jameson Whiskey, and his occasional dabble with cocaine. Jim supplied Tommy with whatever he wanted whenever he wanted it.

Everyone smoked pot, used coke, or LSD. People weren't even discreet about it. Drugs and the sexual revolution were a part of the sixties culture and still going strong in the seventies.

In August, we flew to Rome. Never in my wildest dreams did I imagine seeing such beauty. St. Peter's Basilica was the most marvelous cathedral I ever entered. Michaelangelo's famous Pieta welcomed us as we walked inside. However, the church was as eerie as it was beautiful. Numerous tombs invaded the space, haunting my mind and spirit. Europeans of notable status were buried inside churches.

The Roman Colosseum ruins left a lot for my imagination. The structure stood in all its magnificence, yet filled with demons from the past. Imagining the gruesome battles that occurred with men fighting to the death was harsh. A lot of pain and torturous events took place within the degraded walls of the building.

The Trevi Fountain was positively remarkable. Envision strolling down a small street of little significance then suddenly, an enormous, marble monument with tremendous detail in the sculptures appears, dominating the vicinity. The water in the fountain sparkled, as the sun radiated a colorful rainbow above the scattered statues.

Visitors gathered about, tossing coins into the brilliant water, which is rumored to ensure your return to this amazing city. The stunning masterpiece didn't seem to fit in with the location, yet this trivial road was its home.

Tommy wanted to buy a hotel within walking distance of Vatican City. The current owner was not interested in Tommy's offer, which made Tommy really upset and insulted. I asked him why, but he wouldn't tell me. He never liked to talk in great detail about the business with me.

The deal may have fallen through, but we stayed a few extra days in the city anyway. Jim was with us, but he always kept his distance to give us privacy.

One night after a few whiskey glasses in our hotel room, Tommy confided that Sadie kept tabs on the company jet. She knew when he was away on business, and she'd know when he returned. He dreaded going home to her. He didn't share much with me for obvious reasons. I knew when we were together, he loved being with me. I knew he loved me. Back in Vegas, he only spent time at Sadie's home to sleep. Every other waking minute was either at the hotel office or with me.

I never brought myself to ask him this question, but I wondered how Sadie could stand being married to Tommy. How could any woman be married to a man who was only home for a few hours during the night? What was it like to be Sadie Cavallo?

After we left Rome, we took a short flight to Venice. The hotel deal went through in Venice. We celebrated with a trip to St. Mark's Square. We climbed to the top of the clock tower to witness spectacular views of the water ways Venice was famous for. We tasted gelato, and watched the people breeze by while we sat at the café in the square, taking in the antiquated beauty.

I picked out a lovely, red, leather pocketbook for Katie, and a few baby trinkets for the little one when he or she arrives in October.

The pale pink structure of the famous Doges Palace didn't impress me to be honest. However, the inside was filled with many treasures, marble décor, and extravagant sculptures.

That evening we were serenaded in a gondola beneath the moonlight along the canals of Venice. This was one of the most romantic places we ever visited. I was thrilled we'd return in the future since he purchased the hotel he had his eyes on.

On Thursday, the jet landed in Milan. Tommy rented a car and sped us up north to Lake Como. His Pop had taken his family here once on vacation when his mom was still alive. He was eager to share the breathtaking scenery with me.

Homes were built into the mountain. The crisp, clear water sparkled in the sunlight. Seas of many bright yellow, red, and pink flowers covered the landscape. We ate lunch at a quaint restaurant in Bellagio, overlooking spectacular views of the lake.

For at least two hours we sat in silence, staring out into magnificent splendor. I moved my chair closer to Tommy and placed my head at the base of his neck. He wrapped his arm around my shoulder and held me tightly. The lake had a calming effect on the both of us.

Chapter 21

October 8, 1971

ON OCTOBER 8, 1971, my sweet cousin, Katie, became a mother. She gave birth to a precious boy named Michael Vincenzo at eleven-ten in the morning. Michael weighed seven pounds, eleven ounces, and was twenty-one inches long.

Katie confided in me that Louis wanted to name the baby after him, but she couldn't do that. She knew Louis would be a good father to Michael, but he wasn't his biological father. Naming her son after Louis didn't feel right to her.

Tommy came with me to the hospital to see them.

Michael was pink and perfect with a lot of thick, black hair that stood straight up. Holding him in my arms was like a dream come true.

Becoming a mother was so important to me. Bringing this subject up to Tommy was challenging. We couldn't discuss the subject of children when we weren't married. And we couldn't discuss marriage when he wasn't divorced yet. A tear of joy was shed when this little one opened one of his dark eyes to see me holding him, as I glanced down with a smile plastered to my face.

Katie laid back in her bed and closed her eyes for a few minutes as I held Michael. She knew her baby was safe in my arms. Turning on her side, she looked at me with sadness. I expected her to tell me she wasn't happy with her arranged marriage to Louis, but Louis stood in the room. That wasn't it. Clearly, she had something on her mind to share with me.

Louis asked Tommy to join him in the hospital cafeteria for some coffee.

I carried the baby to the bed and sat beside Katie.

"Angie, you know I love you like a sister."

I smiled. "Of course I know, Katie. I feel the same way about you."

Sniffling, she grabbed a tissue and wiped her nose before speaking further. "We asked Louis's sister and her husband to be Michael's godparents."

My head snapped quickly away from the baby toward Katie's sad eyes. "I see." To be chosen as a godparent is an honor in Italian families.

"I wanted you to be his godmother, but the Maronis pushed for his godparents to be a married couple. Louis agreed with his parents. You know how my father feels about Tommy, Angie."

A nod was about all I could muster. "I understand."

"I hate to disappoint you."

"No, it's fine. We're still family. Michael is my cousin."

After a few glasses of wine later that evening, I cried upon Tommy's shoulder.

Chapter 22

Christmas, 1971

DECEMBER 23, THE day before Christmas Eve. We were invited to Uncle Vince's for the Feast of the Seven Fishes, an annual tradition in the Russo household. As a little girl, Daddy would drive us up to Uncle Vince and Aunt Dolly's home for Christmas Eve dinner. Fish was not my favorite meal as a tot, but as I grew older, I loved it. Uncle Vince would go all out with the menu and presents, followed by Midnight Mass. I asked Tommy if he would join me. Much to my dismay, he said no.

"It's Christmas Eve. You won't spend the holiday with me?"

"I can't, baby. I'm sorry. You know I'd rather spend the holiday with you. I'm with you all the time!"

"Are you telling me you're spending Christmas Eve with Sadie?"

He rubbed his chin then ran his hand through his thick mop of hair before carefully answering me. "Sadie's family visits every Christmas. I can't say I have business to do. Not on Christmas. I don't have a choice."

"You have a choice. You just won't divorce her. It's the end of the year. You told me last year around this time that it could take a year."

"Yes, I told you it could take a year, but I really don't know when the divorce will be final. I have a lot of responsibilities to a lot of people, Angie."

"What about me, Tommy? Don't you have a responsibility to me?"

"You live in this house. I support you. I take you on every business trip. Hell, I make up business trips just to spend more time with you! I work down the hall to be near you!" He held in a deep breath then released it with a sigh, calming himself. "I just can't get away for Christmas."

My back turned away from him in an effort to hide my anger and tears. His brother, John, told me I needed to be patient. I'm trying very hard, but my heart ached.

Tommy's tone softened further as he approached me. "Baby, please. Christmas is not important to you and me. New Years is our holiday. A trifecta. It's your birthday, our anniversary of when we first met, and New Year's Eve." I felt his firm hands grip my shoulders then massage my neck.

I wiggled from his grasp and moved away, my back still facing him. "I have no say?"

"I hear what you're saying, but I'm stuck," he pleaded. "Look, spend Christmas at your uncle's house. You'll get to see Katie, Louis, and the baby. Know that I'll be thinking about you constantly, wanting you, and loving you... always." He squeezed my waist and kissed my neck as his hands wandered to my breasts. He took hold of my hand, spun me around, and placed my hand against his heart. "You are always right here." He tapped my hand against his heart. "Forever in my heart, Angie."

Chapter 23

New Year's Eve, 1971

TOMMY STAYED AWAY a lot this week since Sadie's family was in town. He snuck away for a little while here and there after Christmas Day to see me. He knew how upset I was with him. He hated when I cried. Two days ago was the last time I saw him.

He told me he had a big surprise for me in honor of the holidays, my birthday, and our first anniversary. I packed a bag, according to his instructions, and collected my passport and money from the safe nested within the wall of his office. I merely bought him a couple of neckties for Christmas. After all, what can I buy for a multi-millionaire? It's not like I can compete with his gifts.

Jim drove us to the airport. He accompanied us on most of our trips since the New York incident. He was a very quiet man. I often forgot he was with us. His job was to keep his eyes and ears opened for our safety, and to keep Tommy in line sometimes too.

We landed at Charles De Gaulle airport in France. Tommy wasn't kidding when he said he would make up for Christmas. My stomach was in knots from all the nervous energy.

A taxi took us for a drive around the town where we saw the Palais Garnier, also known as the opera house, Notre Dame Cathedral, the Arc de Triomphe, and the magnificent Eiffel Tower. What a sight to see! The Eiffel Tower was taller than I ever imagined.

Tommy paid the driver extra money to wait for us as we stood in line for a turn to be carried up in the elevator to the top of this impressive building. The scenery was breathtaking from up high, but the cold wind was unbearable. We couldn't stay up there too long. December in Paris was a cold month. We spotted horse carriage rides around the Eiffel Tower, but it was too cold today. We were not prepared for such frigid temperatures.

There was so much to see and do in Paris. I loved Italy, but something about Paris was extraordinary. We visited museums like the spectacular Louvre and Museé d'Orsay. French theatre was quite risqué. The women there flocked to Tommy. Whether it was his good looks or the way he spent money, I wasn't sure.

The bitter cold forced us to buy winter coats, scarves, ear muffs, and gloves; much needed purchases if we wanted to explore the city on our own. I enjoyed strolling along the Champs Elysees, entering stores and ordering croissants at a nearby café. Tommy didn't hesitate to buy me French perfume and lingerie. I picked up a bottle of French perfume for Katie too.

We stayed at a hotel Tommy had his mind set on to purchase. However, the owner had a change of heart and decided he was not interested in selling. Tommy was so annoyed, we packed our things and left the hotel in the middle of the day.

He drove me to an antiquated building with black iron gates and a large archway to walk through to reach the entrance passed a courtyard. The ornate courtyard consisted of water fountains and lavish statues scattered throughout. The outside displayed numerous balconies with beautifully designed wrought iron railings, bursting with remnants of frost-bitten plants. I envisioned colorful flowers overflowing from the pots in the warmer months. Wherever we were, this was an upscale building.

"Do you have a business meeting here?"

"No, this is another surprise. I was going to wait another day or two, but since we need a place to stay now, it's time you saw this." He paused then spun his head back and forth to gauge the lobby area. "Wait right here."

I watched him stop and speak to an older man in a dark business suit. Tommy's French was awful! From where I stood, I witnessed his attempt to converse with this man. His hands were moving as if he were signing with John. The display was amusing to observe. This man escorted Tommy into another room.

After several minutes, Tommy returned, taking me by the hand and guiding me to a set of elevators. Eventually, the old-fashioned elevator doors opened and slowly rode us up to the top floor of the building. The loud screeching and sluggish movement gave away its old age.

"Why are we in an apartment building?" I asked. There were various doors on the floor with personal decorations and welcome mats at our feet.

Tommy merely smiled the way he did when he wanted to surprise me. That wicked smile he wore so well. He stopped in front of a door with the number 1150 on the outside, took out a key, and unlocked it. He fussed with the light switch to turn on.

As I entered the large, empty space that smelled of fresh paint and new carpeting, at first glance was the Eiffel Tower seen from miles away through the partially opened blinds that hung from a large window. "Wow, where are we, Tommy?"

"Our home in France. Do you like it?"

"What? Our home? You bought this?"

"Yes. My realtor assured me it was an excellent investment with a spectacular view of the tower."

"Oh my god! Are you serious? This is ours?"

"I told you I'd show you the world, babe. This is just the beginning. I know we can't live here full time, but anytime we return to Paris, this will be home. Our second home." His eyes gazed about the expansive, empty space. "I think we need furniture though. Let's go shopping tomorrow and you can pick out whatever you want to decorate."

Suddenly, I felt a bit overwhelmed. I strolled around, observing the rooms and the open space. Then we discussed his vision for each one. This was the first time I saw it. It's not a terribly big space. The ambiance and city view are what sold Tommy on buying this for us.

"We will come back here every year to celebrate New Year's Eve together. This is our holiday. Our anniversary and your birthday." He drew me in for a sensual kiss. "Happy birthday, Angie."

Chapter 24

May 11, 1972

THE MORNING WAS as dark as my mood. Cloudy with some raindrops falling outside. Inside, I felt miserable, waking up with terrible cramps. I wasn't expecting my period, yet the cramping continued. My monthly cycle always raged like an angry beast preparing for battle. Today's sharp pains were much more fierce than usual.

My appetite was fine. I managed to eat a bowl of Cheerios with a cup of coffee. After a long, hot bath, I threw on a yellow sundress with the thought of visiting John today. At the last minute, I decided it would be best to stay home and rest. Tommy was in a meeting when I called the office.

The cramping became more severe as the day progressed, which frightened me. Driving myself to the doctor's office was out of the question, fearing the constant, throbbing pain would cause an accident. Katie had a baby to care for. Uncle Vince would surely make a fuss and somehow blame Tommy for my discomfort. I called the operator for an ambulance. Although it seemed a bit extreme, the pain was too much for me to tolerate.

A fire engine and ambulance arrived moments apart from each other, and I cautiously walked to the door to let the paramedics inside. I was doubled over in agony at this point, and grateful these trained professionals didn't flash their lights or use their loud, blaring horns to tell the entire neighborhood I wasn't feeling well. Could I be pregnant? Having a miscarriage? Horrendous notions clouded my brain. I was desperate to find out what was happening to me.

Much to my chagrin, I allowed the men to help me inside the ambulance and drive me to the hospital.

I did my best to describe the pain I was experiencing to Doctor Blake in the emergency room. He had to be more than six feet tall with fiery red, wavy hair and blue eyes. He asked me a lot of questions about my health and when my last period was, which I couldn't remember exactly.

Maybe I was pregnant. There was a part of me very excited about having a baby. The timing may not have been right, but maybe my being pregnant would drive Tommy to divorce Sadie faster, even if he had to let the money go.

Doctor Blake poked and prodded at me before performing an internal examination. He smiled at me. "Angie, I want to order some more tests."

"Could I be pregnant, Doctor?"

"No, Angie. You aren't pregnant, but I want to run some tests to get to the bottom of the pain you're experiencing."

A part of me was disappointed to hear I wasn't pregnant, while another part was relieved. I knew Tommy wouldn't be happy if I were pregnant right now. If I wasn't pregnant, what was happening to my body? The pain increased to a higher level. I tossed and turned on a stiff mattress, searching for a comfortable position to lessen the stabbing blows that beat against my side.

Between the tests and nurses checking on me from time to time, hours passed. The staff gave me some medication for the pain, which helped eventually. I asked a nurse if I could use a phone. I wanted Tommy to know where I was. He usually worked from our home in the afternoons. Surely, he'd arrive and find my car in the driveway, and I'd be nowhere on the property.

Standing before me opening the privacy curtain was Doctor Blake reading some papers in a folder wiping away his red waves from his brow. "How are you feeling, Angie?"

"The pain medicine is helping. Do you have my test results?"

"Yes. You had a cyst on one of your ovaries that burst. This is fairly common in women, and it can be very painful when the cyst ruptures."

"A cyst? What does that mean?"

"It may mean nothing. You may never experience another cyst rupture again. Some women have cysts that dissolve on their own without feeling anything."

"Can I go home?"

"Not yet. I want to run another test to confirm something I noticed."

"Confirm what exactly?"

"Let's see what the next round of tests say, Angie."

"It's not cancer, is it, Doctor?"

"I don't believe you have cancer. Don't worry about something like that. Let me schedule these tests, and someone will be in shortly to take you to radiology."

My head nodded, feeling a bit worried.

At some point in between tests, I fell asleep. Around three o'clock, I awoke to see Tommy sitting in the chair next to me.

He saw my eyes flutter open, then moved his body to sit beside me at the edge of the bed. "Hey, baby, how are you feeling?" His fingers smoothed against my cheek and entwined in my hair.

"How did you know where to find me? I have no phone here to call you."

"Shh, it's okay. I went home and you weren't there, but your car was in the driveway. Mrs. Nielsen from across the street told me you were taken away by ambulance. I called the local hospitals to track you down. You gave me quite a scare." He kissed my forehead then my lips with a delicate touch. "What happened?"

"I was in pain, and I didn't know why. The doctor told me I had a cyst that ruptured."

"What? Are you okay? Are you still in pain?"

"They gave me something for the pain, but the doctor had more tests taken. I don't know why." I felt his hand squeeze mine for support. Having him at my bedside was a relief.

"You rest. I'll be right here."

Maybe it was the medication they gave me, but I felt really tired. I barely remember my eyes closing.

I heard Doctor Blake's voice introducing himself to Tommy. I tried to sit up in the bed to hear what he had to say, but the effort was more trouble than what it was worth. I remained lying down.

"How are you feeling, Angie? I know we put you through a lot of tests today."

"I think I'm okay. I'm very tired."

"Well, the pain medication they gave you may cause drowsiness."

"Doctor, what's going on with her?" Tommy asked.

"We ran some tests, Angie. The cyst shouldn't cause you anymore trouble. I'll prescribe you some pain medicine to take for the next day or two. The pain should subside. But no driving while you take those pills."

"Okay, that sounds good, Doctor, thank you," Tommy answered with relief.

"Is that all, Doctor Blake?"

The doctor wheeled a squeaky stool closer to the bed and sat beside me. "Angie, there's a large amount of tissue outside your uterus and blocking your fallopian tubes. This is unrelated to the cyst, but it can be problematic for you."

"How? What does that mean?"

The doctor's blue eyes were heavy. I braced myself for bad news. Cancer maybe?

"It's possible you may have a condition called endometriosis. I'm having a specialist review your records, and we'll schedule other tests to confirm my suspicions. You could experience painful menstrual cycles and heavy bleeding at some point, if you haven't already. What may be more concerning to a young woman of your age is infertility. The condition could prevent you from having a baby."

After hearing those words, I completely tuned him out. The doctor kept talking, but I heard nothing except blah, blah, blah.

Chapter 25

The Summer of 1972

AFTER MY VISIT to the emergency room, I struggled with day-to-day activities. Sometimes just getting out of bed was a challenge. Hearing the doctor tell me I may not be able to have a child someday was a devastating blow. I dreamed of having several children with Tommy. My future was all planned out in my head the moment Tommy's divorce was final. To take that dream away from me was cruel.

I saw my regular physician and asked him to run more tests. He came to the same conclusion as Doctor Blake. He tried to give me hope, telling me the chances were slim, but not impossible. I met with several specialists who unanimously confirmed the same dreadful result of infertility.

Why was I taking birth control pills? If it was nearly impossible for me to get pregnant, there was no reason for me to take these stupid pills anymore. I threw the supply in the trashcan.

Tommy tried to cheer me up. He really did. Once a week, he would pick up John and bring him to our home to see me. I wasn't getting out much and I had no desire to socialize. I knew Tommy was worried. I caught him signing with John about me. He told John he was beside himself, unsure what to do to make me feel better. He hated leaving me alone at night. At night when he would leave me to sleep at his home with Sadie. I didn't even seem to care about that anymore.

I used to cry, but I stopped. I stopped feeling. Is this what grief feels like? I experienced grief when my sister died, then again when Daddy died. This was different. I didn't lose a child, yet knowing I can never experience having a baby growing inside me, giving birth, or raising a child, made my heart ache so deeply. Sadness invaded my mind. I felt defective and hopeless.

Katie would come by with Michael to check on me from time to time. It was always good to see the baby. Katie's son was the closest I would ever come to a child of my own, it seemed.

Uncle Vince called me every day when he heard I was "moody." I wore a mask when they visited; not literally of course. I didn't want them to worry about me.

Katie brought me some books to read. I hadn't been able to focus for too long on anything. Although I tried to read.

The newspaper listed an ad for classes at the University of Nevada right here in Las Vegas. If I can't be a mother maybe I need to think about a career. Women were being hired for higher paying jobs more than ever. We're not just housewives anymore, thanks to the women's liberation movement. I needed something to concentrate on. Something to enjoy and be proud of. Tommy talked about taking me away somewhere to have fun. I loved that he wanted to take care of me, but I needed more out of life.

I could tell by the sour expression on Tommy's face he wasn't happy I wanted to take college classes.

"Angie, I take care of you. I have money to support you. You don't need to do this. Why do you want to be sitting in a classroom for hours every day?"

"I can take classes in the morning when you're at the office. I need to do this. I want this, Tommy." I insisted, yet uncertain if this endeavor was possible, considering my mood swings.

"How are you going to manage? Last week, you slept throughout the day, every day. What makes you think you can handle school right now?" He argued with me, but he made good points.

"Before my diagnosis, it was challenging enough to deal with the fact that you're still married to another woman. Now I learn that I can't give you a child in the future. Don't you know how much that hurts me? Your father wanted you to have children to leave the family business to. He didn't want you to sell it to strangers. How do I know you won't leave me for a woman who could give you a child?"

His arms wrapped around me as he kissed my temples. "I don't want anyone else, Angie. If we can't make our own baby someday, maybe we can adopt a baby."

Did I hear him right? Was he serious or pacifying me? "Adoption? You'd consider that?"

"I know you'd be an excellent mother someday, when we're both ready, but you need to get out of this funk you've been in. Maybe you need to talk to a doctor or something."

"I've been to my doctor."

"I mean a head shrink kind of doctor." His voice was low, nearly a whisper, attempting to be delicate, but seeing a shrink was not what I needed to hear.

"What?" My hands balled into fists, and I punched his chest hard. "You think I need a psychiatrist?"

"I don't know. You're moody and you sleep a lot. You have no energy. Now all of the sudden, out of the blue, you want to go to college? You never talked about that before. That's a big decision to make."

"I'm not crazy!"

"I never said you were crazy, baby. Stop it."

"You just want me to sit home all day, wait on you, clean the house, fix your lunch, look pretty, and have sex!"

"What's wrong with that?"

I picked up a glass jar from the kitchen counter and threw it at his head. Lucky for Tommy, my aim was terrible.

Chapter 26

September 1972

CLASSES BEGAN. FEELING undecided about a major, I chose general classes like English and college writing. I loved to read and write, hence why I keep a journal to document important life memories to reflect upon. Two classes was enough to start. I still had a home to take care of.

Tommy begrudgingly agreed for me to take classes. He was adamant the time away from home, hours of studying, and typing papers would be too much for me. But I stood my ground, extinguishing his pessimistic insecurities, despite my feeling overwhelmed, nervous, anxious, and excited simultaneously. My emotions raced from high to low or low to high in mere minutes.

I convinced him that having a worthwhile goal to achieve like a college degree would be a positive experience that might make me happy again. I knew I hadn't been myself lately, and I wanted to get back on track. I wanted to be the woman he fell in love with. She's still in this broken body somewhere.

Managing school and the house became easier in time. Tommy pitched in to clean up after himself. He surprised me with school supplies. He bought me a typewriter and a small desk to work on in his office. That was his way of saying he supported my decision.

Staying up late to write papers for school became a challenge though. I struggled with fatigue and some sadness still, but getting out of the house really helped me. I'm almost twenty years old now, still of college age as the other students. I met some really interesting people, other classmates and professors.

Mrs. Redding, a middle-aged female teacher, was my favorite. She inspired me. She enjoyed reading my papers and liked my writing style. Her praise encouraged me to want to write more… if I had the energy.

Chapter 27

October 5, 1972

KATIE AND MICHAEL came to the house to have lunch with Tommy and me. I can't believe this little tot will be one year old in a few days. I could still pick him up and nibble on his chubby thighs, making him laugh.

Tommy liked it when Katie dropped by with Michael. Maybe he liked it because their visits put a big smile on my face, and he liked to play ball with Michael in our living room. Little Michael followed Tommy around, tugging at his pants, vying for attention. Tommy felt special. I could see his eyes light up whenever Michael chased after him with wobbly legs, dragging his green and white crocheted blanket behind him.

"I'm so glad you're doing better, Angie. I can tell by looking at you," Katie said.

My face felt flushed, slightly embarrassed my moodiness caused her and others to worry about me.

"Do you like school?"

"I really do. It's harder than I thought. I try to stay up late to complete all of my homework. I've been so tired. I can't keep my eyes open sometimes."

"Well, I'm proud of you. I never imagined going to college."

"Beauty school was your calling, Katie. Have you considered going?"

"Oh, I couldn't do that. Who would take care of Michael? It would be too much."

"It's something you always wanted to do."

"Louis wouldn't allow it. He'd be embarrassed. His wife working when we have kids at home to take care of."

"Kids? Are you planning on another baby?"

Her cheeks turned rosy, and her head lowered. Her dark eyes blinked excessively. "I didn't want to tell you after everything you've been through." She took a sip of lemonade from her glass before responding, "I'm pregnant again."

"Oh." A forced smile displayed. "That's wonderful, Katie. I'm happy for you." I was happy for her. Truly happy. Somehow, I felt sad for me again. My younger cousin was on her second child at age nineteen, and I won't ever have a child of my own.

Tommy stood in the hallway with Michael listening to our conversation. I was convinced he recognized the sadness in my eyes. I know I felt it.

I couldn't stop the tears from shedding that evening. My unhappiness had nothing to do with Katie's pregnancy. I'm glad she's growing her family. She appeared to be happy with Louis. Life threw me a curveball, taking away my ability to conceive.

Tommy stood from the couch, sprinted to the office, and returned with a vial in hand. I recognized the cocaine he used recreationally from time to time, but I didn't realize he kept a supply in the office. "Listen, this will make you feel happy and will give you more energy. I hate watching you suffer like this, baby."

"No, Tommy, I can't." Thoughts of my sister's addiction to heroin entered my mind. "After what happened to Connie..."

"This isn't heroin. No needles." He opened the vial, sprinkled the white powder onto the coffee table and cut it up into a straight line. "It's easy. Watch."

"I've watched you snort that shit before, Tommy, just not in our living room."

"I'll clean up. I promise."

My head hurt and my eyes were sore from crying. After some more coaxing from Tommy, I clumsily sniffed up a line he laid out for me with a short straw. Oh, how it burned my nose and throat. What was the attraction to this? Although I must admit, soon my energy increased, and my mood was up and positive.

Chapter 28

April 29, 1973

KATIE GAVE BIRTH on April 3, 1973 to another boy, this time naming him Louis Jr. She and Louis were proud parents again. Louis's face beamed with excitement. Michael was pleased to have a little brother. Aunt Dolly came to town to attend the christening.

Louis's older brother and his wife were asked to be godparents. I didn't let it bother me. In fact, nothing bothered me. No more tears shed about not having a baby. I can't remember the last time I sang at the Montgomery. I had Tommy and coke. That made me happy.

Uncle Vince opened his home after the ceremony. He hired a caterer to bring in a wide variety of food and alcohol for the guests. I was shocked that Aunt Dolly was invited to the house. My uncle still won't speak to her directly, nor does he look in her direction. He was extra flirty and very hands-on with Nancy too. I was sure he tolerated the situation with his ex-wife for Katie's sake—whatever that situation was.

Tommy was eager to leave the reception. We were flying to France that night for a business opportunity in Nice. We started to make our rounds, saying goodbye to everyone to depart quickly. Katie was busy with her guests and the baby, but she seemed to avoid speaking with me today. Uncle Vince was pouring Sambuca into Nancy's coffee cup when we approached him to say goodbye.

"You're leaving already? Dessert is just being served."

"I'm sorry, Uncle, but we're flying to France tonight."

Uncle Vince studied my face carefully with hardened eyes. "I need to talk to you, Angie." He glanced toward Tommy. "Alone."

He wrapped his arm around mine, escorting me down the hallway and into the library, then slamming the door closed.

"Are you all right, Angie?" he asked, still studying me, glaring practically through me.

"Yes, I'm fine," I responded with a smile.

"Really? You don't look fine to me. What has he done to you?" His dark eyes grew cold as they wafted up and down my face.

"Tommy? He hasn't done anything."

"Look at you! You're pale and thin. Distracted. I didn't see you hold the baby or play with Michael today."

"I'm fine, Uncle, really."

"I know how disappointed you were with what the doctors told you last year. Tommy isn't divorced yet, is he?"

Annoyed, hands on hips, I shook my head and stomped toward the large picture window, turning my back on my uncle to stare up at the stars.

"I'm worried about you, sweetheart. It's been more than two years. If he loved you, he'd be married to you by now."

"Please don't go there."

"Doesn't that matter to you anymore? He should've left his wife. There's no reason for him to be married and have you as some kind of side dish. You're better than that!" His voice became louder with each syllable spoken.

"I need to go."

"You don't need him, Angie. You need your family!"

I kept walking.

Chapter 29

April 30, 1973

WE ARRIVED IN Nice at nine o'clock the next morning, France time. We were burned out and exhausted. Tommy's meeting was at noon, so we laid down to catch a couple of hours of sleep.

When the alarm buzzed, Tommy jumped up and got ready to meet his business associates. I didn't have the energy to get myself out of bed yet. He kissed the top of my head before leaving.

I quickly figured out that coming down from a coke high wiped me out. I needed another hit just to keep going. I've known this for the last few months. This wasn't right, and I knew it. I wasn't like my sister. I could stop. I'd stop when I was ready. At that moment, enjoying Nice with my love was more important.

Later that afternoon, Tommy returned to our hotel room, ecstatic about the deal he just made. He was bouncing off the walls with excitement and couldn't stop bragging about his ingenious transaction. We planned to celebrate with a night out on the town at a club not far from the hotel. First, we needed a bump.

After picking on some appetizers at the club with Jameson shots, we were dancing the night away. Tommy traced off to the bar to refill our drinks. I had enough between the drugs and booze. My brain was really fuzzy, but the high felt so good. This upscale, expensive club was loud and busy with the French elite all in attendance. The blinking lights blinded me as a zippy, French song vibrated through the speakers with a rock-n-roll beat.

While Tommy stood at the bar, waiting for another drink, a svelte, attractive blonde, wearing a thin, white spaghetti-strapped dress and clearly no bra, slowly approached him. She spoke to him for a couple of minutes. He looked back at me, grabbed our drinks and returned to our table.

"Who's that woman?"

"She's pretty, don't ya think?" he said casually.

"What?" A hint of jealousy displayed.

"Don't you think she's attractive? I mean, look at her."

My jaw dropped, arms crossed. "I thought I was the only woman you had eyes for."

"You are, babe." He leaned in and kissed my lips then my neck before taking out another vial right there, out in the open for another hit.

"Baby, maybe you've had enough." I warned him.

"Look around. Everyone's getting high." He handed me the straw for a turn. I don't think I had ever taken that much before in one day.

"That blonde at the bar—she wants to come back to our room with us."

"For what?" My temper flared. "You're not having sex with her!"

"No. No. No. She likes *you.*" He smirked in that sexy way he mastered.

"Me? What are you talking about?"

"She said you're very beautiful."

"You're joking."

"I swear to God. She's not interested in me and my dick. She wants you." He put his arm around me and kissed me again. "Come on, baby, this could be a lot of fun. I'd be there the whole time and I'll only be with you." He signaled the woman over to join us at our table before I could absorb all of this.

Shannon was her name. She sat right next to me, practically on top of me.

I took another hit, so much more than I needed. I was really jacked up.

In a slightly aggressive manner, she grabbed my hand and coaxed me onto the dance floor while Tommy stayed at our table, watching our bodies glide together. Usually he was very jealous when a man touched me or looked at me. Perhaps because Shannon was a woman, it was less threatening to him. I had to admit, it was fun witnessing him become hot and bothered as his eyes conveyed pleasure observing us dancing closely.

There was something very erotic about the way she moved and touched me on the dance floor. Her fingers melted into my dark hair and explored the curves of my body. Between the drugs and alcohol, I feebly agreed to let Shannon into our room.

Chapter 30

WHEN WE ARRIVED at our hotel room, Tommy poured us all a drink, but Shannon set her sights on me immediately and kissed me hard on the mouth. I was nervous to have this assertive woman fondling me with playful hands. It didn't matter how many hits I took or shots swallowed. My heart beat fast and furiously to a rhythm we could've jived to.

Tommy removed his tie and placed it over my eyes, tying a knot at the back of my head. Without vision, I could only go by the senses of touch and hearing. I felt Tommy's hands on me. His caress was familiar while another pair of hands removed my clothing.

Her floral scented perfume blended with Tommy's cologne. I couldn't see anything, but the sensation of four hands stroking my body, two sets of lips tenderly kissing me everywhere, stimulated every erogenous zone. I could tell by her perfected movements she had done this before, satisfying a woman.

Tommy lifted me to the bed and lowered the tie from my eyes so I could watch Shannon ravish me with those soft lips and expert tongue. He unzipped his pants and slid my hand down to please him. Despite the amount of drugs and alcohol in his system, he didn't last long.

The night never seemed to end. She didn't stop.

Instinctively I reciprocated, gratifying her in a way that was familiar to me, knowing how Tommy pleasured me so many times.

As soon as she caught her breath from the smoldering encounter, Tommy ordered Shannon to leave. She was as high as we were and didn't reply. He yelled at her again, demanding she leave our room. He wanted me all to himself now.

With Shannon at the edge of the bed, he stripped off the rest of his clothes, pounced atop my body and thrust himself inside me while Shannon watched us, smiling elusively.

Chapter 31

May 1, 1973

I AWOKE TO the bright sun shining through the window. My eyes wouldn't open instantly. Slowly, I pushed my body up. When my eyes finally widened, a mop of blonde hair was in my view. Shannon lay naked beside me on the right, her arm limp across my stomach. She must have passed out before leaving our room per Tommy's instructions. Searching for the clock in the room, it was two in the afternoon. We slept the day away.

To my left lay Tommy, out cold, snoring.

My head throbbed, my body was numb, and my skin felt sticky and dirty. God, I needed a shower, slowly remembering everything that happened last night. Remnants of the evening floated into my mind. A part of me was mortified. I could blame the drugs and alcohol. I could blame Shannon, even Tommy. But I let this happen. I brushed Shannon's arm off me, then pushed the tangled sheet away from my legs, and scooted to the end of the bed, freeing myself from between the others.

I stumbled to the bathroom, used the toilet, and turned the shower on. My legs and hands were jittery. My toothbrush sat on the sink. I used it to vigorously clean my mouth, teeth, and tongue. My feet carefully stepped into the shower to soak in the hot beads of water. A bar of soap was wrapped in paper in the soap dish. I tore the paper off the bar and soaped up a wash cloth to clean my flesh. I couldn't get clean fast enough.

The creak of the door caught my attention. "Tommy?"

No response.

Staggered footsteps were heard.

I opened the shower curtain and witnessed Shannon sitting on the toilet. I closed the drape to quickly finish washing my hair, hoping she'd go away.

The shower curtain opened abruptly. Before I could say a word, Shannon stepped into the tub and helped herself to the warm sprinkles of water… and me. "Good morning," she said with a sensuous grin, then she pushed me against the tile wall and kissed me softly with little warning.

I pulled away, only to hear the door burst open, and saw Tommy standing in the bathroom naked, staring at Shannon and me in the shower—together.

The calm before the storm. I recognized the stern expression he wore. He snapped!

Tommy grabbed strings of blonde hair from Shannon's head and pulled her from the roots, dragging her out of the shower, and onto the tile floor.

She screamed, pawing at his arms to release her.

"What the hell are you doing? I told you to leave last night!" By the hair, he tugged her limp body from the floor, now wet from the shower water. He pinned her to the wall with his hands clenched around her throat.

"Tommy! Stop! Let go of her." I stepped out of the tub onto the wet floor, sliding in the puddle.

"I'll deal with you later!" He screamed and pushed me away with a free hand, causing me to slip and fall onto the cold, wet tile floor on my side. He turned to Shannon. "I told you to leave last night. Angie is mine! You don't fucking touch her again! Understand?"

I jumped back up and grabbed his arm, trying to pull him off of her so she could breathe. "Tommy, you'll kill her. Stop, please! You'll go to jail!"

He released his hands from her throat.

She coughed and gasped for air.

I knew he was jealous, but he was a different person. Memories of the New York incident flashed through my foggy mind.

Tommy grabbed Shannon by the arm and dragged her out of the bathroom. He scooped up her dress and pocketbook, then threw her naked body out into the hallway of the hotel, tossing her shoes at her, one by one.

"What are you doing? Let her get dressed at least."

"Oh, I'm sorry, did you want to kiss your *girlfriend* goodbye first? Did you want to finish what you started in the fucking shower?"

His voice was so loud, Jim came running out of his room from across the hall. He saw Shannon flinging her dress over her bare body, staggering down the hallway.

A few hotel guests opened their doors to observe the dispute, then quickly slammed their doors behind them while Tommy continued yelling, standing in the nude, enraged.

I picked up Tommy's shirt from last night off the floor to cover my naked body in front of Jim, who stepped inside our room, elbowing Tommy back inside. Tommy was still screaming at me about the shower. I couldn't comprehend what he was yelling about.

Jim cautiously approached Tommy without touching him. He spoke slowly and softly. "Tommy, man, calm down. What can I do for you? You want me to take that woman home?"

Finally he stopped shouting at me long enough to take in a few deep breaths. "No, I don't give a shit about her. I'm glad she's gone." He rummaged through his suitcase.

I knew what he was looking for. Thank God there was nothing but empty containers.

He threw a vial at Jim. "Get us some more."

"No. No more, Tommy. Jim, don't you get him anymore," I ordered.

"What did you say? After what I just walked in on, you're giving me and Jim orders? Who the fuck do you think you are?" He inched closer to me and for the first time since I met him, he frightened me. I ran into the bathroom, slamming the door behind me, locking it.

He banged on the door, yelling relentlessly that I cheated on him. He was going crazy!

I sat on the floor, scrunched between the toilet and the wall and cried. I listened to Jim try to calm him down. He told Tommy security would be there to arrest him if he didn't control himself.

"Angie! Angie, let me in," he hollered, kicking the bathroom door.

I wanted him to go, but he broke through, entered the bathroom and saw me crying on the floor, my arms clasping my folded legs, rocking in the corner. A glass must have broken during the struggle with Shannon. I stepped in the debris, cutting my foot and leaving a thin trail of blood across the checkered tile. I was too numb to feel the pain.

When Tommy saw me shivering and the blood on my feet, a change seemed to occur in him. He collapsed on the floor and covered his face. His tone improved and his voice was smooth. "Are you okay? Did you cut yourself?"

It was like watching a Hyde to Jekyll transformation. I couldn't answer him. I was frozen in that spot on the wet floor, quivering from head to toe. I realized the shower was still running, water everywhere.

Tommy slowly drew himself up and eased his way out of the bathroom. Movement in the other room sounded as if he was putting on clothes. He mumbled something to Jim. Then I heard the door slam.

Jim entered the bathroom only to witness my body rocking steadily on the tile floor. He quietly drew near me, offering his hand to help me stand. I couldn't control the trembling. Tommy's shirt fell off me. I didn't even care if Jim saw me naked at that moment.

Jim grabbed a towel from the rack and draped it around me, helping me out of the bathroom. He walked me into the main room and brought me to the blue, floral sofa where I took a seat. Then he offered me a shot to calm my nerves.

I shook my head. No more alcohol. No more drugs. I couldn't live like this anymore, a slave to such vices. I wanted to go home.

"I'm gonna wait outside, Angie. Why don't you get cleaned up and dressed?"

As soon as Jim closed the door, I looked for my suitcase and began tossing my clothes inside. I threw my green-printed dress over my head and found a matching pair of flats. As I passed a mirror, I stopped and looked at myself. I didn't recognize the woman in the mirror. My arms were thin, face sullen, and eyes red and puffy. I couldn't take a second glance. My hair was still wet. I combed it out, grabbed my pocketbook and searched for a credit card. As long as I had a credit card and my passport, I could get home. Home was where I wanted to be.

I picked up my suitcase and opened the door to see Jim standing in the hallway. I didn't say a word, but his eyes focused on my suitcase. I moved quickly to scoot around him, but he stopped me, taking hold of my arm.

"Angie, wait." Soft spoken Jim, polite and respectful as always.

"I need to go, Jim. You need to stay and take care of Tommy. I'm going home." Tears flooded my eyes.

"I have to take care of you too, Angie. I can't do that if you leave by yourself."

"You don't understand," I pleaded. "I need to leave before he comes back. He's so angry."

"He won't hurt you, Angie. I promise I won't let anything happen to you."

"You can't stop him. You saw him. He went crazy!"

"If I thought you were in any danger of him, I'd take you out of here right now. He took a walk to cool off."

"What if he gets more drugs? He has to stop. We both have to stop."

"I hear you, Angie. I'll take care of it. He listens to me."

Jim was right. Tommy listened to Jim. He used to listen to me.

Chapter 32

MY FEET WORE a path in the rug of the hotel room. My nerves were shot. I felt like a prisoner in this room. I craved a hit of coke, but I kept thinking about what the drug really did to me. The powder gave me a false sense of reality; a temporary relief from the pain and grief I bore when I learned I couldn't conceive. It took my mind off of Tommy's marriage. I didn't care he hadn't divorced Sadie anymore.

The door opened and Tommy sauntered in. He appeared calmer, but I noticed his trembling fingers. I stood up from the bed to face him, still fearful. I took a step away from him for every step he crept closer to me.

"I want to go home. Jim won't let me leave." My voice was shaky.

"Jim's doing his job."

"Keeping me prisoner?"

"I want to know what happened this morning while I was asleep."

I stared at him, unable to speak.

"What happened, Angie?" He was becoming impatient, but his voice was calm for the moment.

"Nothing happened, Tommy."

He shook his head at me in disbelief. "You're gonna lie to me right now? Really? I know what I saw."

"I woke up and saw she was still here. The two of you were sleeping. I got up by myself to take a shower. I heard someone come into the bathroom. I thought it was you, but it was her. She stepped inside the shower with me and she… kissed me… once. That's it."

Tommy nodded and scratched his chin before the accusation. "That's it? There was no replay of last night?"

"Last night was your idea! You wanted her here."

"I wanted her gone last night too!"

"Then you should've made sure she left before you passed out!"

He plopped his body at the edge of the bed near me. I stopped moving away from him. He reached for my hand and held it, but I shook it away.

"I'm sorry if I scared you. But what if you woke up and found her in the shower all over me like that? You wouldn't like that. I know you wouldn't."

"You liked watching us last night." A lump nested in my throat as I said that, hating that I agreed to it. Angry he suggested it.

"Last night I was with you. You didn't sneak off to another room to be alone with her."

"That's not what happened. You could have killed her, Tommy! What if she were really hurt? What if she goes to the police? You could be arrested!"

"She's not going to the cops, Angie," he stated matter-of-factly.

"You don't know that! If it were me, I'd go to the police."

"No, she won't call the police. She's some dignitary's wife who likes women. If anyone found out she was here last night, cheating on her husband, it would cause a scandal." Tommy glanced down and saw my foot with a few minor cuts and some blood seeping through the bandage. "Are you hurt? Do you need a doctor?"

"I need to go home. Now. I can't stay here. I don't ever want to come back to Nice again. Ever!"

"Baby, we have three more nights together. I don't want to leave now."

"Then you can stay. I'm going home!"

"Things got really out of control last night." His hand wiped across his forehead, thinking. "Too many lines and too much booze…"

"No more. I can't do it anymore. No more drinking. No more drugs. I'm done. I'll take a regular flight home. I'll take a taxi to the airport," I rambled, anxious and jittery.

"Why are you talking crazy like that? You're not going home alone. Okay, you want to leave Nice, I understand. Let's fly to Paris to our loft."

"You are not listening to me. I'm going home, whether I leave with you or without you."

He stepped away from the bed, picked up his suitcase and begrudgingly started to pack.

Chapter 33

THE FLIGHT HOME was intense, yet quiet. I couldn't look at Tommy without thinking about the last twenty-four hours. How I wished I could wipe away the entire incident from my memory. He tried to talk to me. I had nothing to say.

When we arrived home, Jim dropped us off. Tommy tried to follow me inside, but I stopped him cold. "Go home." I placed a hand upon his chest.

"What do you mean *go home?* I am home."

"I need space."

"Angie, I know you're upset…"

"Upset? I watched you nearly squeeze the life out of a woman! I was afraid you were going to strangle me!"

"I'd never do that to you! I was jealous, and I didn't know what I walked in on. But I didn't hurt you."

"You scared me."

"Don't. Don't cry, baby. I'm sorry." He attempted to approach me for comfort, but I backed away.

"I don't want any more drugs in our home. Last night was too much. It's a problem now. I don't want to end up like my sister."

"That won't happen. I wouldn't let that happen."

"I can't stop you from using the drugs. But if you don't stop, I will move out."

"What? You can't leave me, Angie." He tried to enter the house. Again, I stopped him.

"I will, Tommy. I swear I will. You have to choose between cocaine and me, because you can't have both. I'm done. And I'll be done with you if you keep using."

I slammed the door shut behind me.

Chapter 34

The Road to Recovery, 1973–1974

I CRAVED COKE constantly, or maybe it was the high I desired. Desperation set in. I actually ransacked the desk in Tommy's office to see if he left any vials behind. Anytime I felt the need for a bump, I thought about Nice, Shannon, and Tommy's rage. How could I allow myself to get out of control? I was so ashamed. I criticized my mother for being an awful parent, and my sister for killing herself with heroin. I'm no better than they were.

My headaches were tolerable, but the nausea was severe for a while. I lost more weight. The scale struggled to reach one-hundred pounds. When would this end? I dropped out of school. I had every intention of earning a college degree when I felt better. My recovery was a priority now.

Tommy seemed to be okay. He had the desire to get high, but not the "need" to get high like I did. He used the drug more often than me, yet his cravings were not nearly as severe as mine. Guilt consumed him, knowing he was the one who encouraged me to use. The decision was mine. I could have said no. Every day he praised me for staying sober. Having him with me, loving me, and encouraging me helped. I needed him to help me get through this. No one else understood how much I was suffering.

Uncle Vince and Katie called from time to time. I didn't want to talk to them, but Uncle was getting upset anytime Tommy answered the phone and told him I was fine but busy. He even showed up at the house one day to see me in person. I wouldn't answer the door. Tommy wasn't home. Maybe that was the reason he dropped by at that time of day, to try to see me alone. I couldn't allow him to continue showing up unannounced. I made the call.

It was so difficult for me to hear my uncle's voice and not cry. He heard directly from me that I was doing well, although I wasn't. He thought I was still taking classes at school, or at least I led him to believe that. I couldn't bear to tell him I was tired, unable to eat much, sick with nausea, and my body ached miserably.

Tommy stopped using completely. I knew he wasn't sneaking a hit. It was easy to tell when he used. I saw it in his eyes, disposition, and temper. I was more important to him than coke. Jim never supplied either of us with any drugs after Nice.

Tommy backed out of the deal with his prospective business associates in Nice. I meant what I said about never returning there. The thought of reliving that night with Shannon, or the way Tommy and I were when we were high, was intolerable. Because I wouldn't travel with him to Nice, he refused to buy a hotel or any property there.

Paris was a different story. Paris was special to us, our second home. He was committed to our spending every New Year's Eve in Paris together.

Becoming sober was a difficult road to walk along, but after several months, Tommy and I were back on track as a couple and as human beings again.

I reluctantly spoke with my doctor about the drug use and cravings. He told me about withdrawal symptoms, and offered me tips for controlling them. We discussed what made me turn to drugs as a remedy. It's still difficult to discuss infertility, but I did.

I brought up my sister's death to the doctor. Heroin use was on the rise and highly addictive, he explained.

My poor sister. I had been so angry with her for overdosing, and I blamed my mother for Connie using drugs in the first place. Connie was a child of sixteen years old when she started using. I was an adult. My choices were my own fault and no one else's. Connie was young and innocent. If her cravings were more severe than mine had been, I could understand how hard it was for her to stop with no one around who understood her pain. I hoped my dear sister was at peace.

Now that I'm sober, I thought back to little Louis's christening. The way my uncle glared at me, studying my face and body language. Did he know what was happening to me? The babies must be getting so big. I missed my family terribly.

Chapter 35

July 28, 1974

MY APPETITE RETURNED when the nausea subsided. I managed to gain five pounds over the last couple of months. The color was back in my cheeks. My immediate life goal was to see my family today, then register for classes later in the week. I promised myself I would finish school, and I wanted a college degree. One step at a time, I told myself daily.

It was Sunday, and family dinner started at one o'clock sharp. My plan was to show up at Uncle Vince's at noon. Early enough to determine if I'm welcome before the others arrived. I considered calling ahead, but I would acquire a real, honest reaction seeing them in person versus a voice on the other end of a telephone.

Tommy kissed me goodbye. He wanted to come with me for support, but this was something I needed to do on my own. It had been a while since he visited his father. He dreaded going to the convalescent home to see him. Often, Pop didn't know where he was or why he wasn't at home. He'd tell Tommy he needed to go to the hotel to sign off on some important papers. His mind was not the same. As I would be attempting to make peace with my family, Tommy had to do the same with his.

Driving up to the house, Katie's Dodge was parked in its usual spot, close to the front door. She left me messages over the last few months, but I rarely responded. My heart raced ninety miles per hour. I rang the doorbell instead of walking inside as I normally would.

Katie's voice was heard on the other side of the door, telling my uncle she'd answer it. I didn't know if I should smile, cry, or run to my car and drive off before she saw me.

"Angie?"

My fingers twisted terribly as I fumbled for something to say. I couldn't even utter a simple hello.

Katie grabbed my fingers, preventing further twists, and pulled me in for a hug. "I'm so glad you're here." She cried before yanking me inside.

We both took a moment and wiped our eyes.

"I wasn't sure you'd want to see me," I said, happy my twisted fantasy was off-base.

"I've been worried about you. We all were. You're not with Tommy?" Her neck stretched behind me to see if Tommy was in the driveway.

"I thought it would be best for me to come alone. It's been so long since I've seen you. I can't tell you how much I missed you."

"Angie?" Uncle Vince stood beneath the large chandelier hanging in the corridor. He eyed me up and down before showing me a hint of a smile and approaching, ever so slowly.

I stood completely still, frozen in that one spot for a moment. "It's good to see you, Uncle. I hope you don't mind that I stopped by." My voice was shaky, praying he would welcome me.

He stared closely at my face, lifted my chin with his thumb and forefinger, and studied my eyes specifically. "You're not using that shit anymore, are you?"

Damn, he knew. "No," I mumbled softly, embarrassed by my irresponsible actions.

He lowered his face to mine and planted a soft kiss on my cheek.

I wrapped my arms around him tightly and sobbed.

"There, there, my sweet girl. I'm glad you're home."

"Grandpa!" Michael came charging in to find his grandfather.

I couldn't believe how much he'd grown in a year. The first thing I noticed was his blonde hair, a trait he surely inherited from Brett, his biological father, because the Russos have jet black hair. Young Louis stumbled in after Michael, barefoot, wearing overalls, trying to keep up with his big brother. They both looked up at me and stared. Surely, they don't remember me.

"Hi, boys." I knelt to their level, looking them both square into their big, brown eyes. "I'm your cousin, Angie. I can't believe how handsome you both are. What big boys!"

They both smiled and nodded.

I requested time alone with Katie before the Maronis, DeLeones, and Franciscos arrived for dinner. She asked Louis to watch the boys while we took a stroll outside around the property.

I forgot how pretty the backyard was. Nancy helped Uncle Vince with the landscaping sprays of various colorful plants, flowers, and palm trees. I never had a green thumb. She worked hard to keep these plants looking so lovely in the Las Vegas desert.

"I'm sure you want me to tell you what I've been doing for the last year, Katie."

"Do you want to tell me?"

I laughed half-heartedly. "Not really, but I'm sure you have questions."

"I could tell you were… lost. High on something. We never gave up on you, Angie. We hated to back off, but you refused to see us. It was all I could do to keep my father from sending a SWAT team in to rescue you."

We sat upon the bench swing overlooking the vegetable garden with what seemed to be tomatoes and squash begging to be picked.

"I was stupid. Really stupid. I tried to fix one problem and started another one. If you knew, you never said anything to me, Katie. Why?"

"A part of me wanted to shake you senseless. I was worried. Worried you'd end up like… Connie."

A tear fell from my eye at the sound of that comparison. "I'm sorry I worried you. I think about Connie all the time now. More than ever. I was so angry with her for her addiction. For dying on me. I've no right to judge her anymore."

"Please, whatever you do, don't start that again. That day at your house upset me so much."

"What day?" I attempted to recall what she could possibly be talking about.

"The last time I was at your house was before Louie's christening. You just weren't yourself. Tommy was sleeping in the middle of the day, which was odd. Michael was running around your house looking for him. I chased after Michael and found him in your bedroom. Tommy was sound asleep. On your dresser was a mirror with white residue all over it. I wanted to blame Tommy, but your whole demeanor changed. I knew you were using that shit too."

I cringed at the thought of her witnessing something so deplorable that became an everyday occurrence in my home. My palms covered my eyes, sick with shame.

"What if Michael got into it while at your house? I grabbed the boys, made some excuse to you, and we left."

"I can't apologize enough, Katie. Neither one of us were thinking clearly then."

"I was going to ask you to be Louie's godmother that day. I felt awful not asking you to be Michael's godmother, and I knew it hurt you. But after seeing the drugs, I couldn't..."

"You were right to not ask me." I shook my head with disgrace. "I didn't deserve the honor. I am better now, Katie, and so is Tommy. No more drugs. It's been fourteen months and 28 days of sobriety for both of us. I'm finally feeling... normal. I hope you and I can get our friendship back and be a family again."

Katie hugged me with sincere acceptance.

Chapter 36

May 27, 1975

I WAS LISTENING to the morning news on the radio. Reporters were still talking about the Watergate scandal and Nixon's impeachment from last summer. I barely paid attention to politics last year, given my condition. Since Nixon's actions were highlighted on every news channel and paper, naturally I knew what was going on in the country. President Ford attempted to put all of our minds at ease. Our country was still at a low point, however. The media implied that Ford wasn't entirely trustworthy after pardoning Nixon for his crimes. I should specify "alleged" crimes.

Sunday dinners at Uncle Vince's turned into political debates. Sitting in a room with a bunch of Republicans, some still supporting Nixon, while others thought he was a disgrace, was monotonous. I offered no opinion, not as though anyone ever asked for my opinion.

Louis had been pro-Nixon since he met the man in person several years back. My dear cousin surely must be exhausted listening to his defense of our former president.

If I ever told them I supported the women's liberation movement and the equal rights amendment, I'd probably be banned from Sunday dinners altogether.

It was early on Tuesday morning when I heard Tommy's BMW pull up. Typically, Tommy would drive to the office early then he'd come by for lunch and work from our home in the afternoon. I had to stop by the university this morning to register for classes in

September, keeping my commitment to my education. He knew my schedule better than I did. Maybe he needed something from the office, I wondered.

When he stepped through the door, his eyes and nose were red. My first thought was he was using again; how I feared that. But his eyes were curved, filled with sadness it seemed.

"I wasn't expecting you so early. Is everything okay?"

His brows lowered before reaching out for me, drawing me close to him. He held me tightly, sobbing. "It's John. He died last night."

I pushed him away from me to see his face. "What? No! How?"

"I don't know yet. It happened last night. I got the call too late to tell you. I needed to see you and tell you face to face."

My arms wrapped around him. I didn't want to let him go. John meant so much to him. The bond they had as brothers and friends was genuine. Taking his hand, I led him to the cream-striped sofa and sat beside him. I looked at his face and held his flushed cheeks gently. "Are you going to be okay? How are you dealing with this? This is a major loss for you and for me too." I began to study his face, his eyes and nose especially.

"Why are you looking at me like that?"

"I'm worried about you. I don't want you to fall back into any… bad habits."

He knew exactly what I meant and merely shook his head. "I won't. I promise, I won't." His hand grasped mine tightly.

"You can lean on me for anything." I had to be the strong one now. He needed me to support him. I was concerned he'd go on a drinking binge, or worse, score some coke. "Do you know what happened to him? How did he die?"

"The doctors haven't given me the results of their examination yet. I demanded an autopsy. His body is in the morgue. I need to go there. Would you come with me?"

"Of course I will. Anything you need. Who found him?"

"A woman. A friend," he stuttered as his eyes turned away from me.

"Who? He never mentioned a female friend. One of his nurses?"

Tommy smirked. "Yes."

"Why was she there late at night? Couldn't she have done something to save him? She's a nurse. Or was he already... gone?"

"Well, um, she's not a nurse. Not a real nurse."

"What do you mean 'not a real nurse?' I ran into a couple of his nurses several times."

He chuckled through his tears a bit. "Baby, John wasn't sick. He was always independent."

I stared at him, unable to comprehend.

"John was in a wheelchair, but he wasn't sick. He was a man, just like me, with physical needs. He liked these women to dress like nurses to avoid any gossip from the neighbors. People always looked at him like he was weak and feeble because of his disabilities, but he wasn't sick, and he didn't need a nurse for *medical* reasons."

"Wait. They were hookers?"

Tommy nodded, expressionless, until I burst out laughing. Then we both laughed.

He showed me some old family pictures of him and John as babies and as teenagers with their parents before their mom passed away from breast cancer. Anyone could tell Tommy and John apart because of the wheelchair. That chair made people look at John differently. Hell, he was different, but the chair and being deaf weren't the reasons. He was a good, kind, smart, and funny person. He didn't let the wheelchair dictate who he was as an individual. Those who thought John was different didn't take the time to know the kind of man John was outside of that chair. But I did.

We drove to the morgue together and were escorted to the room where John's body laid on a table with a sheet covering him. Tommy squeezed my hand so hard it felt numb.

The sheet was removed from his head, and was pulled down to his chest for us to view. Tommy moved the sheet slightly to find John's hand to hold.

I touched John's pale cheek and kissed his forehead. He felt so cold and clammy, but he looked peaceful, as if he were asleep. I wished he'd open his eyes, sit up, and tell us this was a cruel joke. Still, I couldn't cry. How could I be in denial of his death when his cold body lay before me, hard evidence that he was gone?

Chapter 37

May 28, 1975

THE NEXT DAY, I helped Tommy pick out a casket, the flowers, and all of the other funeral arrangements. He didn't want a major public announcement because he didn't want his father to hear the news. Pop was ill and would never get better. The last thing he needed to hear was that his first born son was dead. The services would be tasteful but small and simple.

"I need to buy a black dress for the services," I said.

Tommy's head whipped quickly in my direction. "No, that's not necessary."

"I know I have a lot of clothes, but nothing really appropriate for a funeral."

"That's not what I mean." He paused, stared at me then looked away and sighed. "Shit. I know how much you loved John, and you know how much it meant to me that you sincerely developed a bond with my brother. But Angie, you can't go to the funeral."

"Of course I'm going, Tommy. How can you say that?"

"How can I explain who you are to John? We can't be at the funeral like this... together."

"Because of Sadie? Sadie, who never visited John, is going to be by your side at his funeral, and I have to sit here and do nothing?"

"I'm sorry." His eyes showed sincerity while his words stung sharp and deep. "I knew this would come up. Please understand the position I'm in." He moved close to me for a hug.

I punched his chest hard and moved away from him. "I loved John. He was my dear friend. You're really telling me I can't say goodbye."

"You came to the morgue with me. You planned his funeral with me."

"Exactly. I did this. I did this for you and for John."

"And he knows you loved him. He loved you too. Wherever he is, he knows you were a part of his... send off. I need you, and you are here for me like you always are. I love you for all you've done. I will take you to the cemetery after the services and we'll have our own private moment with him."

What could I do? I forget sometimes that I'm not Tommy's wife.

Chapter 38

May 31, 1975

THE DOCTOR HAD confirmed John died from a heart attack caused by atherosclerosis. We were shocked to learn that John struggled to keep his blood pressure and cholesterol levels under control. John never shared his health issues with Tommy. He knew Tommy had enough stress with managing the hotels and recovering from addiction. Today, he will be buried.

I wanted to be at the funeral. I don't have to sit with Tommy. Of course, then I'd see Sadie, maybe even meet her. He would be so angry at me for going there when he asked me not to.

I remembered what John told me about being patient and the amount of stress Tommy was under. Losing John added to his stress level. If I wanted to be supportive of him and not send him spiraling into a drug or alcohol binge, I needed to stay put. But I didn't like it.

Tommy called Katie, apparently, and explained the situation to her. She and the boys came by to keep me company. He also had Jim sit outside our home. He knew me very well, and must have thought I'd want to sneak into the services, or attend the cemetery vigil.

The truth is, knowing Sadie would be there was what made me stay away. Naturally, I'm curious about her. What does she look like? What is she like with Tommy? Does she put on a show in public as if they were some happily married couple? I didn't think I could handle that.

Katie, Michael, and Louie filled my afternoon with bubbles, Play-Doh, and Sesame Street. We put swimsuits on the boys and took a dip in the pool since the day was so warm. I was grateful for the visit and interruption of my conspiracy to crash the funeral.

Tommy called me from the convalescent home Pop was living in. After the services, he needed to see his father. I didn't see Tommy until about eight o'clock in the evening. No binge drinking or drugging, thank goodness. Day by day. It was a process to continue for the rest of our lives. John would want that for us, and Tommy always wanted to honor his brother.

He donated money to John's childhood school, the Utah School for the Deaf and Blind, in John's name, so they could continue to support the needs of people with hearing disabilities. These services were so important to help people like John learn to communicate in the world around them and live independently. Tommy sent regular donations in John's memory.

Chapter 39

June 5, 1975

ONCE ALL OF the legal arrangements were finalized after John's death, Tommy needed to escape. He had his eye on a hotel in London. A hotel that was going under and needed an investor to salvage it. In no time, we were packed and ready to fly. We hadn't traveled too much since Nice, except for our annual New Year's in Paris. Our recovery was a priority.

Tommy thought we were ready for another adventure. School was on break for the summer, and I wanted something to do to keep myself occupied. I liked to stay busy. I needed to.

London was wonderful! A different vibe than Paris. The weather was quite cold for June. People talked about an unpredictable snow falling a few days before we arrived. I was glad we missed that.

We strolled by Buckingham Palace, Big Ben, Westminster Abbey, and took a ride on the London Eye. What a remarkable view from this enormous Ferris wheel! Theatre in London was amazing. Many eerie tales about the escapades of Jack the Ripper were told. We shopped at Harrods. I wanted a Beatles t-shirt and Tommy chose a Rolling Stones tee. The best thing about London was everyone spoke English!

Tommy brought me to the hotel he planned to purchase. The building was off the beaten path, but not far from some of the main attractions near Hyde Park. This hotel was more affordable for the average person. Usually he invested in large, high-end hotels with many first class amenities. This would be a different approach, but he liked it, and had a vision for improvements while keeping the per night cost down for tourists. I rarely heard him talk business. Listening to his brilliant proposition for the hotel was impressive.

The current hotel owner offered us the week at a luxury residential building he owned not far from Regent Street. An adorable two-bedroom flat with large rooms and an incredible view of the hustle and bustle of the city below. Still, the location was close enough to pubs and entertainment, and far enough away from the noise and crowds. We loved it!

As the week was ending, I felt sad to leave London so soon. I stopped at a nearby bakery to pick up scones with clotted cream, a rich, thick and delicious cream popular in England. Something to snack on for our trip home.

Tommy was late from his final meeting with some lawyers. I stayed behind to straighten up the flat and pack our bags. I snapped a few pictures of this adorable little nest with our new camera. When he returned, he had another surprise. He bought this flat for us! God he was impulsive and generous, and I loved him so much.

Chapter 40

New Year's 1976

NEW YEAR'S DAY in Paris. Every time we returned to Paris, Tommy planned something new, fun or unique. He loved to surprise me.

For instance, this year we took a drive to Versailles for the day to see the famous Palace of Versailles. The palace was gorgeous as one would expect. In particular, the Hall of Mirrors was a spectacular sight, with its luminous chandeliers gleaming beneath a ceiling of wondrous murals with gold trim and marble walls. Rays of sunlight bounced off of the original, seventeenth century mirrors that occupied the left side of the lavish room, filled with sumptuous artifacts from the era of the scandalous King Louis XIV.

The gardens outside the palace were positively remarkable! From a distance the terrain appeared like a green-printed quilt, with perfectly clipped grass forming specific patterns. Numerous fountains throughout the grounds, each with a different style and sculptures like Neptune, the four seasons, Apollo, and many more spouting water in an enchanting exhibition. Walking around hand-in-hand with my love was incredibly romantic.

I snapped a lot of pictures of the area. Tommy kept taking pictures of me. As we were leaving Versailles, a couple was having their wedding photos taken with the palace in the far background. We stopped the car to take a peek at the lovely bride and her groom with the exquisite scenery behind them.

"Someday," Tommy whispered. "Maybe we should have our wedding in Paris."

"Are you trying to tell me something, honey?" I wanted to ask when his divorce will be final, but I controlled myself.

He simply smirked at me with those delicious lips.

Another surprise Tommy had for me was a trip to Lake Como. We said goodbye to Paris and planned a few days around the Lake we were so fond of.

After driving through the narrow roads with the beautiful lake and alp-like mountains at our side, we stopped in front of a large complex.

"We're here!" He parked our rental car, then hopped out to walk me around the outside of the building. Lake Como was simply enchanting. We stood before its beauty for a few moments in silence enveloped in each other's arms. The lake continued to have a calming effect on the both of us.

He tipped the bellman to help with our suitcases.

"Is this where we're staying?"

Again, he smiled. He was definitely up to something.

We rode in the elevator to the top floor, the penthouse. I expected the view to be delightful, but we had a balcony to sit out on with a table and chairs for breakfast with such an extraordinary scene to keep us company. Tranquil was the best word to describe this apartment and the area.

"Are you buying this building or something?"

He chuckled. "I love how well you know me. No, I'm not buying the building. It wasn't for sale." He grabbed my waist from behind and pulled me in for a squeeze and kiss. "I did buy this penthouse for you though."

"What? Why?"

"Because I love to see that smile on your face. I think we need to pick a special time every year to come back here."

I peeled the sapphire blue dress from my shoulder tips, sliding it down until it hit the floor. "I think we need to celebrate. Any ideas how?"

Chapter 41

January 8, 1976

WE WOKE UP early and sipped coffee on the balcony of our gorgeous new Como penthouse.

Tommy arranged a quick flight to Venice to meet with the manager of his hotel to discuss an unexpected issue. Because we were in Italy, he wanted to deal with the situation in person. It was so early, and since we needed to travel home in a couple of days, I chose to stay behind to admire the lake and do some shopping in lovely Bellagio. Besides, when he is in business mode, I'm usually left on my own to shop or explore the area while he worked. I didn't need to travel to Venice with him for that. I hated to leave this place. Life seemed so peaceful and perfect here.

The telephone rang a funny tone compared to the American devices. Assuming it would be Tommy calling, I playfully answered, "Ciao, amore mio."

"Hello. I'm looking for Mr. Thomas Cavallo."

I recognized Mrs. Arden's voice, Tommy's secretary. "Hello, Mrs. Arden. Tommy isn't here right now. Can I give him a message for you?"

"Angie, I need to find him right away. Do you know where he is?"

"He flew to Venice this morning."

"I called the Venice hotel and couldn't reach him."

"Is everything okay?"

"There's been an accident." Her voice was strenuous, yet firm. "Mrs. Cavallo was badly injured. I need to find him and make arrangements for Captain Roy to fly him home. Do you have another phone number I can call?"

"Let me see what I can do. If I can get a hold of him, I'll have him call you immediately."

Sadie was in an accident? He should know about this. I suppose we'd be leaving Italy today. I had a phone number for the Venice hotel and dialed the number to reach the office. I mentioned Tommy's name, but the woman wasn't certain how to track him down. I advised this was an urgent situation, and I needed to speak to him immediately. Fortunately, she spoke decent English, and her tone was soft and kind.

I paced the floor until the phone rang about fifteen minutes later. "Hello."

"Angie, what's wrong? I was handed a message in the middle of a meeting to call you right away."

"Mrs. Arden has been trying to reach you. She said Sadie was in a bad accident. You need to call her for the details and fly home ASAP."

"What? What else did she say?"

"Tommy, I wasn't comfortable asking her questions about your wife. Will you call her then let me know what's going on? I'll get us packed and ready to fly home."

I detected the sound of a heavy sigh through the phone.

"Yes, I'll call her right now." The phone clicked.

Staring at the telephone, I willed it to ring. At least a half-hour passed before I heard from Tommy, who sounded panicked.

"Sadie's banged up pretty bad from this accident. I'm sorry, baby, but I have to fly home today."

"Okay. I understand. I started to pack our things. When will you get here?"

"I can't get back to Como. Roy is flying me home immediately."

"Can't you stop in Milan to pick me up?"

"Listen to me. You have the credit card. Buy yourself an airline ticket home. Take the car rental back to the airport."

"How will I get in touch with you?"

"Call Mrs. Arden when you get home. She'll know how to reach me."

I couldn't speak. I have to communicate with him through his secretary?

"Angie? Are you there?"

"I don't know how to get to the airport or drive this car. It's a stick shift."

The frustration in his voice was evident. "All right. Leave the car. Can you call the rental company? I'm sure they can take care of it for an extra charge or something. Take a cab to the airport please. I have to leave now."

"Okay. I love—" The phone clicked.

There wasn't a flight available with an open seat until the next evening. I sat in this penthouse alone all day and night, waiting to hear from Tommy. He didn't even call to see if I managed to get a flight home. It isn't like him to not check in with me.

I didn't bother Mrs. Arden, although she might have given me some details. This was such an awkward situation. What if she was close to Sadie? I never gave that a thought before. She was always pleasant to me. Mrs. Arden is in her fifties and appeared traditional and old-fashioned. I couldn't call her with questions about my boyfriend's wife.

My uncle warned me I'd be the mistress and not receive the same respect as a wife.

I called the car rental office and explained the emergency situation about the rental car left in Como. They agreed to have someone retrieve it for a nominal fee, of course. I left the car key with the building manager before calling a taxi to pick me up and take me to Malpensa Airport in Milan.

Chapter 42

The Winter of 1976

ON JANUARY 11, I finally returned from Milan. It felt good to be home. I was worried about Tommy still. We've never gone this long without talking to each other. The taxi driver helped me with all of our luggage, and dropped it near the doorway. Fortunately, I still had some American money on me to tip him well.

After lugging the suitcases to our bedroom, I jumped in the shower then brushed my teeth. The flight was long and crowded, and I sat near a smoker. I despised the smell of smoke in my hair and on my clothes. I couldn't wait to throw on a simple night gown then unpack.

The phone rang. I jumped up to answer it and heard Len Stein's voice. I met Len a few times while out with Tommy. He was Tommy's attorney and friend.

"Angie, Tommy wanted me to ensure you arrived home safely."

"Is everything okay?" I asked, curious why his attorney was calling me.

"Tommy was arrested. He's being held at the police station."

"Arrested? Why?" I hated where my mind traveled because my first thought rushed to drug use.

Len asked me to explain everything that happened when we were in Paris and Italy. I told him all I knew, but I needed to understand why he was arrested.

"Sadie accused Tommy of the car accident that almost killed her."

"Len, Tommy wouldn't have done that. Not to mention the fact that he was in Europe the entire time with me."

"Yes, but we have to keep you out of this if we can. We know he was conducting business and met with his associates. They need to be his alibi along with the pilot, Roy."

"Alibi? How can she accuse him of this?"

"Relax, Angie. There is no evidence yet that anyone tampered with her car at all, but Sadie made this accusation, and the police have to explore it. I'm working on getting him released."

"Is he all right? Is there anything I can do? Can I see him?"

"Stay put. He was very concerned about you flying home from Italy. He'll be relieved to know you're home and you're safe. I've been trying to reach you for hours."

"I couldn't get a flight home until last night."

"I'll keep you posted about his release."

I couldn't help where my mind wafted. Tommy wasn't a murderer. He wouldn't try to kill Sadie. What if people thought he did this because of me? I mean, we haven't been discreet at all about our relationship unless Sadie would be around like at John's funeral.

Eventually, Tommy was released. The police never charged him with attempted murder. Sadie's brake line was damaged, which caused the crash. They had no evidence that anyone tampered with her vehicle. The event was ruled as an accident. Tommy proved he was out of the country when the incident occurred. No one had to ask me any questions. My name never came up.

I didn't quite understand why Sadie thought he tried to kill her. Tommy explained she had suffered a head injury and was unconscious for several hours before she awoke in a hospital bed and made the accusation. Still, he continued to go home every night. If she really thought Tommy tried to kill her, why would she allow him in her home? Why would she want him there at all? Is the money that important to her? John told me she was greedy and wanted the money.

Much to my dismay, I only saw Tommy for a short time in the afternoons each day. We couldn't travel together until all of this non-sense blew over. We stayed inside while he was here with me. From time to time, he would join me at family dinner at Uncle Vince's house, but not every Sunday.

Chapter 43

August 1976

BECAUSE TOMMY AND I were not traveling much, I filled up my days, taking extra classes during the spring and summer months of 1976, and finally earned a business degree. I had some idea as to what I wanted to do. Observing Tommy buying hotels and properties, my interest was in real estate.

I needed to take classes and pass a test to become a licensed realtor. Not only could I make a decent salary with this career, I would meet interesting people, and maybe assist Tommy with his realty needs when he wanted to purchase property. How cool it would be to work with him! He already worked with a man who helped him with his real estate investments, but I thought I could persuade him to work with me to launch my career.

I shared my idea with Tommy about my career choice. Excitement beamed from within me as I explained my plans to obtain a license. He listened patiently with no reaction. No facial expressions. He just let me speak. "Tommy, are you listening? What do you think?"

"It's not going to be easy for you, you know. Men may not be too eager to work with you."

"Because I'm a woman? Seriously?"

"I'm sorry, but yes. You have no experience. Just because you could get a license doesn't mean you will be able to get buyers."

"You wouldn't want to work with me?"

"Me? I have a guy I've worked with for years. I can't drop him."
"Wow, it's nice to know you have no faith in me."
"Don't put words in my mouth. I never said that."
"I will prove you wrong."

Chapter 44

April 1977

ALTHOUGH WOMEN HAD already made their mark in this industry, I was the only female in the classroom to learn about the realty business. After a lot of prep work and attending classes, I passed both the national and Nevada State licensing exams. Some of the men in the class didn't even pass the tests.

Unfortunately, passing the tests was the easy part for me. Finding an agency to work with a brand-new, young female was more of a challenge. Although there were openings at several agencies, I didn't seem to fit the bill as a new employee. As discouraged as I was, I didn't give up, and I refused to ask Tommy for help.

He saw the disappointment I felt, especially when I shut down and refused to talk to him about it. I really wanted to prove him wrong, but I was failing miserably in that respect.

Although I never asked for his help, Louis contacted me with an opportunity to work at his friend's realty office. Louis became a state representative. Katie was so proud of him. As the Maronis and my uncle predicted, he was moving up in the political ranks at a young age and had a lot of connections to a variety of businesses. His friend's name was Jerry Apple, like the fruit. Jerry was looking for some new blood in his office. There were no other female agents working there, but Jerry was willing to meet with me.

Jerry was a good-looking, polished man in his forties at least. Salt and pepper hair, olive complexion, and medium build. He smoked at least four Marlboro's during our forty-five-minute interview. I tried not to hack while speaking with him through the thick wall of smoke between us. Oh, how I hated the odor of cigarettes and the stinging effect it had on my eyes, but I needed this job.

At the end of our meeting, surprisingly, he offered me the job. I was overwhelmed and excited. I shook his hand with such gratitude and thanked him at least a dozen times. It was all I could do to prevent myself from hugging him.

To thank Louis for this opportunity, I sent him a box of Italian pastries filled with his favorites, bocconotto, zeppole, and sfogliatelle.

Jerry had me start work the next day. He showed me the ropes about both residential and commercial sales, and offered me some important tips to remember for making a sale. "Know your clients well. Listen to their needs. Focus on the positives of all properties and make a correlation of the buildings or houses to your clients. Communicate with clients often. And be honest. Honesty establishes trust."

As I was learning a lot from Jerry, Tommy seemed distant. I wasn't sure if he was upset that Louis helped me to find a job when he didn't, or if I was spending way too much time telling him "Jerry" stories at work. My job kept me busy and away from our home. He missed that I wasn't home in the afternoons when he was here. I wasn't making his lunch, doting on him, or available for sex as often as I used to be.

Then I made my first legitimate sale! I sold an industrial building to a baker who was looking for a new location. I remembered everything Jerry taught me about knowing my clients and their needs. The building was not initially used as a bakery, but I had a vision of the space and prime location that would work to transform the place into a bakery. My first sale after only a few weeks working with Jerry. He was proud of me and gave me several new clients who walked through the door to build up my client list. I sold two homes and one other industrial type building in six weeks' time.

Tommy started to show up at the office to see me and watch me work. The place was crawling with men hungry for sales. He was concerned my colleagues may be hungry for me. I saw that familiar look on his face that I knew all too well. Jealousy.

He asked for a moment alone with Jerry in his office. I didn't understand what he was up to. I hoped he wouldn't give Jerry a hard time. After about fifteen minutes, Jerry called me in.

"Angie, you're doing well. You've made quite an impression as the new girl around here. Clients like you, and you have an amiable, hospitable nature when working with them. Maybe it's because you're female, I'm not sure. Maybe that makes you appear more trusting. In any case, Tommy requested working with you exclusively."

My head whipped toward Tommy. "Did he?"

Tommy smiled, proud as a peacock.

"How do you feel about that, Angie?" Jerry asked. "You still have a lot to learn in this business, but I think you've got what it takes to succeed. You'll have to be licensed in multiple states."

I brusquely interrupted Jerry. "May I speak with Tommy outside alone first, Jerry?"

Jerry nodded and Tommy followed me past a row of office desks, where my male colleagues were either speaking on the phones, smoking cigarettes, or typing excessively. I led him into a private conference room, closed the door behind us, and shut the blinds.

"What are you doing?" I asked suspiciously.

Tommy's smile faded. "What do you mean? You're doing great here! Why wouldn't I want to work with you?"

"I thought you had a realtor you didn't want to drop."

"I'd rather work with you. Come on. You wanted my full support."

"You should have talked to me before going to my boss, Tommy. Why did you do this here, like that?"

"You don't want to work with me? What the hell, Angie? I thought you'd like this. Jerry said if you work with me exclusively, you could even work from our home."

"What? You have no right making those arrangements for me!"

"Jerry liked it. He knows who I am. He knows the kind of business I'll bring him, but I'll only work with you."

"I didn't ask you for any favors, Tommy. Frankly, you never even offered. You're upset because I'm succeeding! And you want me home!"

"No, that's not true."

"Oh, yes. I know it's true. You were happy no one would hire me because it kept me home. But now I'm going out and meeting people and doing really well at this job, and you can't handle it."

"I just want to be a part of it! I miss you, okay. I admit that. I miss not having you around. Don't you miss not seeing me as much?"

"This is my job, Tommy. Maybe I'm not around all afternoon like I used to be, but I want to do this. I like having a career."

"Well, Jerry liked the fact that I can guarantee him nationwide business. As your client, I can expand your network. This will help you make an even bigger name for yourself. If I walk, I don't think Jerry is going to like that."

"I don't like that you manipulated my career."

"I'm sorry, baby. I will always support you. You proved you could do this on your own without me, and now I want to support you in a big way. You should be proud of yourself for accomplishing this. I'm proud of you. I love you."

Chapter 45

July 8, 1977

ONCE I BECAME licensed in multiple states, Jerry loved the idea of my working exclusively with Tommy. He never once questioned our relationship. He worked to promote his agency for buyers and sellers outside of the standard homes and businesses.

More training was needed on my part as well. Hotel realty is a little different than residential, especially working internationally, and I was still pretty green in the industry. Legal agreements and laws differed in various states and countries. Jerry and I developed a list of international realtors to collaborate with overseas for every whim Tommy visualized. I must admit, I was feeling the pressure, and I didn't want to fail at my job or fail Tommy, who was now counting on me.

We loved New York City, and we visited Manhattan a few times each year when we could. Tommy wanted me to find an apartment for sale in the city for us to use, or for him to rent out to clients who may be visiting. He often would rent out the homes we weren't using overseas to his business associates for a fee; another way to make money on these investments.

We landed at John F. Kennedy International Airport and hailed a taxi to drive us into the city. Our appointment with the realtor in New York to see the available apartment was on Saturday. Tommy had to meet with Todd, the New York hotel manager, about business then we would have dinner out. We loved the Italian restaurants in Little Italy.

Todd told us about some great new discotheque on Fifty-Fourth Street near Broadway. He often sent prime guests to the club to get them in the door or through a back entrance. He "knew a guy." I loved how New Yorkers talked about knowing important people for extra benefits. We decided to check out this hot spot. A little music and dancing was always fun. Neither of us had been to an actual discotheque before.

The night was warm with a light breeze in the air. The disco wasn't far from the hotel, so when we returned from dinner, we walked. The street outside the club was packed with people trying to gain admittance. The line went all the way down the street. Tommy gripped my hand tightly to stagger through the maze of people to reach the doorman. The music from inside was blasting loudly enough to hear Donna Summer's "Love to Love You Baby" from a block away.

At first the man or *guard dog* wouldn't let us inside. He turned away a lot of people, but he eyed us up and down. Tommy explained again who we were and that our names were on a list for entry. After a few minutes, the doorman signaled us to follow him. He opened the door and we slipped inside.

The place was enormous and seemed to hold a couple hundred people. Strobe lights flashed. The music was so loud, I felt the rhythm beating in my throat. Wall-to-wall people were packed in like sardines. Theatre seats were high above the dance floor. I noticed a few folks gathering together in the balcony section. It was easy to see this once was an extraordinary theatre.

Male bartenders were topless, serving alcohol and drugs to the customers from a bar shaped like a diamond. Drinks and drugs were being licked off people's bodies. Some people danced in their underwear. This place was really wild!

Tommy ordered us club soda. I was relieved he didn't drink Jameson anymore. One could get out of control in a place like this. He asked the bartender for Billy, the man Todd knew, who allowed us inside.

The blonde-haired, green-eyed, bartender with bulging biceps said Billy was in the VIP lounge, but he'd have him find us.

I was impressed this place had a VIP lounge.

Soon we glided through the sea of customers and hit the dance floor. K. C. and the Sunshine Band's "I'm Your Boogie Man" played loudly as we danced up a sweat. There were too many people moving and grooving on the dance floor.

After a few numbers and a solid attempt to perform disco moves, Tommy took my hand, and we grabbed a seat. One seat. He sat down, and I plopped upon his lap.

The couple next to us was going at it pretty hot and heavy. I thought she was going to mount him right there on the seat beside us.

In no way am I a prude, but this couple was really outrageous, and they were as high as kites. I remembered that feeling, and I didn't miss it.

A short man with a thick mustache, wearing blue jeans and no shirt, tapped Tommy on the shoulder. "Are you Cavallo?"

Tommy moved me off his lap, stood to his feet, and shook the man's hand. "Yes, you're Todd's friend, Billy?"

"That's me. He told me you'd be coming. What do you think?" He stretched his arms up and out, referencing the outrageous club.

"Thanks for getting us in. This place is pretty wild."

"Steve, the owner of 54, doesn't let just anyone in. Todd said you were a hot couple and would fit in here." Billy's eyes wandered, checking both of us out to a degree that made me uncomfortable. "Todd also said you're a good man to your employees. Is this your wife? Girlfriend?"

"Yes, this is Angie," Tommy replied.

I smiled and offered my hand to shake.

Billy lifted my hand for a gentle kiss.

Swiftly, I jerked my hand away and glanced at Tommy's face to make sure he wasn't going to flip out, but he doesn't drink anymore. His demeanor and jealousy were under control.

"Follow me. I'll show you the rooms upstairs." He tossed me a wink as he said that.

Billy pointed in the direction up, and we followed. I remembered the bartender mentioning a VIP room. I couldn't escape my own curiosity, wondering if Billy was taking us to this special room for elite guests.

"Anything you want, let me know." He opened the door to what he referred to as the "rubber room."

Tommy and I gazed inside only to see people snorting powder like coke or heroin and drinking shots. Some people were completely passed out, partially naked. I nudged Tommy's arm. He knew I wanted to leave.

In another room, there must have been six people swinging without a care in the world about onlookers viewing their sexual exploits. Tommy grabbed my hand, and we left the area fast.

"Where are you going?" Billy asked. "Nothing up there you liked? I can…"

"We're good, Billy. Thank you." Tommy politely nodded at Billy, and we found our way out the door to the street. We took in a deep breath before laughing pretty loudly.

No wonder hundreds of people wanted to enter this place. Most likely because it was a privilege just to be accepted by the door monitor. As long as you looked good, pretty women and handsome, clean-shaven men, you would be welcome to enter. Those desperate ones who were refused entry may have felt shunned by this exclusive society. Yet they continue to try to gain admittance, dying to know what went on inside Studio 54. Curiosity could be maddening.

We strutted back to the hotel that night, hand in hand, still laughing at the absurdity. Imagine, we were allowed inside to mingle with celebrities and other A-list types, yet we chose to leave after about an hour. The desperate ones standing in a herd by the front door would have killed for the opportunity. I must admit, the evening allowed for some good conversation later, once the element of surprise passed.

The next day, we looked at a few apartments available in the city. I helped Tommy make a decision based on the expense of each apartment, the use we'd have for it, and of course location. New York apartments were not cheap no matter how much money one had. I encouraged him to go with the least expensive apartment because the area around the building appeared safe for walking, far enough from the noise of the main city streets, but easy to access transportation. He actually listened to me and took my advice. I suggested he rent it out by the week or month when we wouldn't be using it.

Chapter 46

March 11, 1978

TODAY, TOMMY TURNED thirty-five. Because my career had been going well, I managed to buy him a special gift, a Rolex Submariner with a leather strap and stainless steel base with a black face. He will love it! First, dinner at Palmieri's, where we had our very first date more than seven years ago.

The cleaners had his best suit cleaned, crisp shirt collars and a new button that matched perfectly where one fell off. He kept some jewelry at our home. I found his diamond tie tack with matching cuff links on the cherry dresser in our bedroom; a gift I bought him last Christmas when we celebrated our anniversary at our Paris loft.

Tommy upgraded my '70 Cadillac to a '77 Oldsmobile Cutlass for Christmas. I missed the Caddy, but he gave me a lot of mechanical reasons why the change was needed. What do I know about cars? I just stopped at the gas station once in a while to fill it up. To be honest, Tommy took care of the gas too.

My black cocktail dress was a good choice for the evening. The neckline was low, which Tommy liked. The long, Italian gold chain with a diamond heart dangling between my breasts was a perfect accessory, along with my gold charm bracelet.

The gift was wrapped. Dessert was in the refrigerator. Everything was in order. All I needed was Tommy.

Four o'clock sharp, and Tommy's BMW pulled into the driveway. He's always punctual. When he walked inside the doorway and glanced at my outfit, his brows lifted, eyes widened. "Why are you all dressed up?"

"Happy birthday!" I approached him, arms opened for a big hug, followed by a sensual kiss.

"That's the best birthday greeting I ever received. You look beautiful."

"I told you I had a surprise for you."

"I assumed my surprise would be less formal... if you know what I mean," he said, displaying that sexy smirk I loved to see.

"I made us dinner reservations. First, you need to change."

"Change? Really? I wanted to hang out here with you tonight."

Admittedly, I was disappointed with his lack of desire to celebrate his birthday. "Tommy, I planned a really nice evening for us. You're thirty-five!" Grabbing his arm, I pulled him down the hallway. "Come on. Your suit and accessories are waiting for you."

After a quick shower and change, he was a new man. He looked sexy in that dark suit! He insisted on driving, my control freak of a man. He hated surprises. He hated anything he had no control over. So I was forced to tell him our reservations were at Palmieri's.

We'd been to Palmieri's several times since our first date. For tonight, I requested the same table in the back near the fireplace where we sat New Year's Day 1971.

Always the gentleman, Tommy held my chair out to sit. Once he took his seat, he picked up my hand from the table and lightly kissed my palm. "I remember the first time I brought you here. You wore that short, sexy, orange dress. Did you have any idea how badly I wanted you that night?"

Smiling, my head shook, and I nearly blushed. He had that effect on me back then and seven years later.

"You really have no idea how beautiful you are, Angie. That makes you even sexier to me."

"I wanted to come here tonight to celebrate your birthday, yet you're making this day about me."

"You make it hard to concentrate on my birthday or anything else in that dress. Besides, you know I'm not a fan of celebrating my birthday."

"Why is that? You never like it when I fuss about your birthday, yet you bought us a loft in Paris for my birthday."

He took a swig from his water glass and avoided eye contact with me.

"Tommy? What is it?"

"My mother died a few days after my birthday. I don't like to talk about it." His voice was cold and dry.

I knew he lost his mother to cancer, but for as long as I've known Tommy, I never asked the date of her death. "I'm sorry. I didn't know your birthday made you think of her in a tragic way. What if you thought about the wonderful times you had with her instead of her death? From all the amazing stories you've shared with me, she sounded like a really loving and caring mom."

"She was. She was really sick on my birthday. She should've gone to the hospital. Kept her illness and her pain to herself. It was my birthday, and she didn't want to spoil my day because she was sick. The next day, she was so ill, Pop took her to the hospital, and she never came home after that. I guess I never cared to celebrate my birthday after that year."

I reached out for his hand and squeezed it. "Your mom put your needs above her own. She didn't want you to miss out on your birthday then. I'm sure she wouldn't want you to stop celebrating your birthday now."

His eyes stared down at the breadbasket.

"Do you want to leave? We can go if you want. We haven't ordered yet."

"No. We can stay. There's something I've been wanting to talk to you about, and now is a good time to bring it up."

Gosh I hoped he would tell me his divorce was final!

"Since we're talking about my mother, let's talk about yours."

Well, this conversation went in a completely different direction than I expected. "My mother?"

"You talk about her like she's dead, Angie. Where is she? Do you even know?"

"I don't want to talk about her. I can't."

"My mother died… for real. I wish I could talk to her again. Hear her voice. Smell her perfume. Eat her famous roasted chicken dinner with scalloped potatoes. I will never see her again. I don't want you to have any regrets. Don't be angry at me for bringing this up, but I think you need to see her. Maybe you can make amends with her."

"Make amends? My mother was not like your mother, Tommy. She was a junkie! She cared more about her drugs than she did her family. It's her fault Connie got hooked on heroin. She wrecked our family, and it wrecked my life. My father was so overprotective of me, I couldn't leave the house. I was homeschooled. He only allowed me to take singing lessons if my teacher came to our house. I loved my dad. I adored him. But since I met you, I now see all that I was missing in life. I didn't know how to really live until I met you."

"Your father was over the top, and I get it. He didn't want you to fall down the same path as your mother and sister. You were still young. He had every right to want you to be safe, and I believe he thought he was doing right by you. You never wanted for anything."

"Friends. I had no friends because I couldn't go anywhere. That's no way to raise a child." I dabbed my tears with a red linen napkin.

"Don't cry, sweetheart. I hate it when you cry. I'm sorry. Now that you're an adult, it's your decision if you want to see her. Even if you can't make amends with her, you can tell her how you feel instead of harboring all of this anger toward her. I bet your uncle knows where she is, if she's still alive."

Seeing my mother was not something I thought about—until now.

Chapter 47

September 24, 1978

SINCE TOMMY'S BIRTHDAY, I couldn't help but think about my mother on occasion. Betty Russo, expert baker, magnificent cook, skillful Bridge player, drug addict. What happened to my mother and where she was today was a mystery. Blatant memories of her always sleeping behind a locked bedroom door struck.

Daddy would tell me not to bother Mommy while she was resting. We weren't allowed to go into her room. I can't recall when she changed. One day she would help me with my homework and bake Anginette cookies. Suddenly, she did nothing but sleep.

Connie would sneak into her room. She was always so curious, my big sister. What was the attraction to our mother sticking a needle in her arm? Instead of listening to Daddy, she fiddled with the needles lying in a box by the nightstand and started to prick herself. I didn't tell Daddy. He'd be so angry with Connie. Maybe I should've snitched.

By the time he knew what Connie was doing, she couldn't stop. When he cut her off from the supply in Mother's room, she left home and found other ways to get her fix.

Soon after, Mother was gone. Daddy blamed her for Connie's addiction. She never said goodbye to me. I was glad she was gone though. When we learned of Connie's tragic death, overdosing on heroin, the aversion I owned for Mother turned to hatred.

Tommy joined me for Sunday dinner at Uncle Vince's house, as he's done so many times. This time was extra special because Katie asked me to be godmother to her third son, David Mark. This little one weighed in at nine pounds, five ounces. He really wasn't little at all. I had no idea how my petite cousin pushed this large, precious, baby bundle out of her. These three boys meant the world to me, but David Mark was my godson, so he had a very special place in my heart. Although I'm their cousin, Katie referred to me as Aunt Angie.

The Maronis, DeLeones, and Franciscos all arrived for dinner. Nancy hadn't attended a family dinner in a couple of months. Uncle Vince never discussed the situation with Katie nor me. I was saddened to hear this because she seemed to make my uncle very happy for several years. He had a right to his privacy, so Katie and I didn't ask him what happened between them.

After dinner, the boys raced outside to play. Tommy and I often spoiled the boys by bringing them a little something from time to time. Today, we brought Michael and Louie Nerf footballs. Tommy insisted they each have their own to prevent a fight. It was a good idea.

Tommy and Louis played with the boys tossing the soft balls back and forth while the rest of us sat on the patio observing all the action. The kids adored Tommy but they didn't refer to him as their uncle.

Uncle Vince, a very proud grandfather, held David's little head up to watch his brothers and told him he'd be running around with them this time next year.

"Uncle? I want to talk to you about something."

"What is it, Angie?"

"Do you know where my mother is?"

Naturally, my question shocked him. I seemed to have a knack for shocking him.

"Your mother? Angie, why would you ask me that?"

"There's not much my father didn't share with you. You were the executor of his will. She was his wife. Did he leave her anything? Surely, my mother had to be mentioned in his will, even if it stated not to leave her anything, not even me."

The rest of the family listened in, as eager for a response as I was.

"This isn't the time or place, Angie."

"When can we talk about it?"

"Your mother was not well, Angie, you know this. She's not someone you should worry about or think about. We are your family." He pointed to everyone sitting on the patio with us, even precious David.

"Will you help me find her?"

He shook his head from side to side. Without glancing in my direction, he simply said no then handed David to Katie and walked inside alone.

Chapter 48

January 1979

AFTER THAT DREADFULLY hot September day at Uncle Vince's, Tommy and I talked about my mother. For once, I opened up to him about everything I knew. He understood why I hated her and blamed her for Connie's death. He also reminded me of our abuse of coke. He still blamed himself for getting me involved with drugs, but I'm responsible for my actions, not him. Our situation was different than my mother's careless actions with two young children in the house.

Remembering when I suffered through withdrawal, I realized I should not have judged Connie or my mother for choices they made under the influence. Whatever led Mother to use heroin, I may never know, unless I saw her. Maybe seeing her would help me heal and stick with my own recovery plan. Maybe I'll continue to hate her. Maybe she's dead.

Tommy didn't want me to have any regrets where my mother was concerned. He had a fabulous relationship with his mother, and he still grieved her.

I asked Tommy if he could hire someone to find Elizabeth "Betty" Barbuto-Russo born November 1, 1927, in San Francisco, California.

"Of course," was his answer.

I didn't tell Uncle Vince.

My mother was found after several weeks of searching. Then Christmas was here, and our New Year's getaway to Paris followed quickly thereafter. Okay, I admit it. I was procrastinating! I had an address. I knew Mother was alive, but I couldn't make the commitment to see her. Tommy didn't push.

She haunted me, my mother. If I were to ever have a decent night's sleep again, I needed to face her. What would I say? I had no idea.

Chapter 49

February 7, 1979

MOTHER LIVED IN a nursing home in New York on a floor that specialized in mental health services.

As soon as I told Tommy I was ready to see her, he made arrangements for Captain Roy to fly us to New York and ensured our apartment in the city would be ready. No one was scheduled to rent the apartment this week. The holidays were over, and it was very cold and snowy in the city this time of year. Renting that apartment out in the devastatingly frigid month of February was a difficult feat.

Flying to New York allowed Tommy to meet with the New York hotel manager in person as well. It became a business trip for him.

Why was my mother on some mental ward of a nursing home? Tommy's private investigator told him she had been there since 1963, the year Connie's heroin abuse began. I was about ten years old. Daddy told me Mother was sick, and she had to leave us to get better.

Connie had the same sickness, but she returned home once in a while to steal from us when Daddy wasn't around. I used to beg her to stay. She was nice to me when she visited, but she was different. Now I understood what she was going through with her addiction. I missed her, the healthy version of Connie.

Tommy asked Jim to fly to New York with us and rent a car for the drive to the nursing home in Long Island. I was a bundle of nerves on the drive there, still thinking about what to say when I saw her for the first time in fifteen years.

The parking lot appeared busy for a Wednesday at eleven-thirty in the morning. I took a good look at the cold, brown, brick building. It appeared old, as if it sat here on this property for a hundred years. The grounds were snow covered, so I couldn't tell if the lawns and gardens were kept up with. No bright-colored leaves on the trees. Everything was dead. I hated this place before I walked through the door.

Jim stayed with the car and Tommy grabbed my hand, tugging me to go inside—not to rush me, but because it was a mere eighteen degrees. I propped up the collar of my fur coat and pulled the white scarf around my face to block the whistling wind.

As we entered, there was a small sitting area near an empty reception desk. Tommy pointed to a white wall with a cork board hanging from a nail. There were notices pinned to the cork. Bingo at two o'clock. Music at four o'clock. Daily movie at six o'clock. An upcoming Valentine's Day dance. At least there were activities for the patients.

"Can I help you?"

We turned to notice a woman with an afro, wearing a long, tan-colored dress with a wild leopard-print pattern, staring at us. I stood frozen until Tommy gave me a gentle push forward.

"Hi. I'm here to visit someone."

"Sign in please." She handed me a clipboard with paper asking me for my name, the patient's name, room number, did I bring any food for the patient, and the time of my visit. The question about bringing in food surprised me, but since I had none, it was irrelevant. I did, however, wonder if I should have brought flowers or something.

"I don't know her room number, ma'am."

"Who's the patient?"

"Elizabeth Russo."

The woman stared at me as if she were confused, and lowered her glasses to the rim of her nose. "I'm sorry, who?"

"Elizabeth Russo. She goes by Betty. Is there a problem?"

Tommy stepped closer, wondering if something was wrong.

"I know who you mean. Mrs. Russo hasn't had a visitor in… oh… at least twelve years! For as long as I've worked here anyway."

Embarrassment suddenly took over.

The middle-aged woman with a medium-brown skin tone opened a large book. She used her pointer finger to scroll through the pages until she found my mother's name listed. "She's up in room 512, elevator down the hall on the left to the fifth floor. Excuse me, who are you to Mrs. Russo?"

I paused. "I'm her daughter."

Her eyes flew up and down my body, paying extra attention to the fur coat that warmed me and the jewels securely placed against my neck, wrists, and fingers.

"Thank you," I said politely before sprinting down the hall to find that elevator. Tommy could barely keep up at my pace. "Tommy, can you wait down here for me?"

"I hate for you to do this alone, Angie."

"I'm not alone. I know you're here with me. I don't know what kind of condition she'll be in. Let me see her by myself, at least this time."

He nodded as the elevator door opened with a brash screech to carry me up to the fifth floor. The ride seemed to take forever. This had to be the slowest, ancient elevator I ever used. It made a loud thump as it stopped on floor five.

As I stepped off the elevator, I turned right to see an open room with several people in wheelchairs inside, listening to a record player with Sinatra's "Witchcraft" blaring. The smell was awful; a combination of urine, feces, and disinfectant with every breath I took.

Most people were elderly, at least eighty or older. An elderly woman, thin and short with very long white hair, walked passed me, holding a baby doll in her arms, stroking the doll's matted, blonde hair, while chanting words in a language I couldn't place. Another woman barked at me. A gentleman grabbed my fur, petting my coat, referring to it as his dog, Sam.

What a horrible place my mother lived in! How could she live here? Was she anything like these other disturbed individuals?

I saw nurses standing by a station, but I decided to look for room 512 myself without help. I couldn't bear another stare down like the receptionist gave me when I told her I was Betty Russo's daughter.

Slowly, I walked passed room 508, 510, then 512 was upon me, with the name Russo written sloppily in cursive on paper taped outside the door. I couldn't catch my breath. A panic attack was imminent. I started to count backward from one-hundred, ninety-nine, ninety-eight... God, I didn't want to drop dead here in this awful place!

"Hey, Barbie!"

A tap across my shoulder was felt. I turned around and saw a thin woman, taller than me, with a crooked smile plastered on her face. Her hair was very short and straggly, mostly gray with some darker colors blended in. An attempt was made to wear red lipstick, but she missed some spots.

"Don't be rude, Barbie Doll. I said hello."

"Oh, hello." An endeavor to be polite was made.

"You lost or something? Looking for Ken and your dream house?" She snickered. "You're not gonna find them here!"

I merely smiled, still staring at the name "Russo" outside this miserable hallway, afraid to step inside. Afraid of what I might find in there.

"You can't be Barbie with that black hair. Didn't she have a brunette sister or something?"

"What? Who?"

"You're Barbie's sister! With a really neat wardrobe." She fondled my fur and let out a whistle.

I turned my back on the crazy woman with the Barbie doll fetish and treaded inside room 512.

The bed was empty. A pile of books sat atop a corner shelf. I recognized some of these books, a few Agatha Christie mysteries and Harper Lee's *To Kill a Mockingbird*. They used to be stacked on the hope chest in her bedroom. The same books.

I couldn't help myself. I looked around the small space that became my mother's home. The bed was made neatly with a decorative, forest green spread. There was a small closet with some clothing hanging on wire hangers. A few drawers built inside the wall of her room held personal items like undergarments, socks, pajamas, and a small picture frame.

The photo was old and torn at the edges, but I remembered it. I wore a short, ruffled, yellow dress with sparkling white saddle shoes. My black hair was in pigtails. Maybe I was five or six. Connie was about eleven. She donned a blue-printed dress, and her dark brown hair was in one long braid tied at the end with an elastic band. I chuckled a bit, recalling how it hurt to pull those thin elastic bands from the ends of my hair.

"Whatcha doing in here, Barbie? You shouldn't be in here."

Good Lord, the "Barbie" woman returned. "It's all right. I'm waiting for someone."

"Oh yeah. Who?" She folded her arms as if demanding an immediate answer from me.

As I looked closer into her eyes and observed her stature with those folded arms, there was a familiarity about her.

"I mean it, Barbie. Beat it! You don't belong in here."

"What is your name?" I asked, creeping cautiously toward her.

The woman stood still and kept her arms crossed. A serious look washed across her face.

"You call me Barbie. What should I call you?"

No response.

"Should I call you… Betty?"

Her face softened. Slowly, her arms unfolded and went limp by her side. "Who the hell are you?"

Taking a deep breath and attempting to swallow hard with a dry mouth, I answered her. "It's me, Mother. Angie."

Baby steps were taken, inching her way closer to me. She lifted her hands and squeezed my arms, staring me in the eyes, studying every detail of my face. A half-smile appeared. "We've got some catching up to do, kid. Follow me!"

Reluctantly, I followed her down the hallway. She moved quickly. Thinking about her age, she was only fifty-one, considerably younger than many of the other people I saw on this floor. The end of the hallway was less busy. She fumbled with a door knob to a room that appeared to be locked. She twisted the knob hard toward the left. Then with a bobby pin from her hair, she popped the lock, literally breaking inside the room. I wasn't sure if I should be horrified or impressed.

"Mother, should we be in here? What are you doing?"

"Shh, quick, get inside." She pulled me by my fur into the room then closed the door swiftly behind me. She walked up close to me and gave me a big smile before a tear shed from her eye. "Is it really you, Angie?"

"Yes, it's me. Do you know who I am?" Because she seemed a bit daft, I really wasn't certain she knew who I was, or if I had the right woman. No, it was her. She aged, and I'm sure the effects of the drugs and this awful ward she called home didn't help to keep a youthful look.

"Of course I know who you are now. Look at you! You're beautiful!" Her fingers opened up my fur for a close inspection of me. Then she grabbed my cheeks and gazed deeply into my eyes. "I've waited so long, hoping you would visit me."

"I didn't know where you were or what happened to you."

"Does your father know you're here? He won't like this at all. You need to be careful, Angie."

"Daddy? No. Uh, he died, Mother."

Her body plunked onto the chair in the corner, sitting on her leg. She rocked her body back and forth, a habit that made me nervous. "He's dead. Really dead? Like dead, never coming back, dead?"

"Yes."

"How did he die?"

"Daddy was shot by a burglar who broke into our house. We think Daddy tried to stop the man, and he was killed in the process."

"Hallelujah! My prayers have been answered!"

Surely, she detected the contempt smeared across my face.

"Don't look so grim, sweetheart. He's in a much better place than that giant house. That house that kept us all imprisoned!"

"With everything you did, how dare you be so cruel about Daddy's death."

"You were your daddy's pride and joy. Daddy dearest was not a perfect man, deserving of all those stars you had in your eyes whenever you looked up at him. Did you come here to tell me he died?"

I felt the need to clear my throat. "He died in 1967 actually."

"1967? Wait. What is today? The date, today's date, what is it? I don't have a calendar in my penthouse," she mused.

"February 7, 1979."

"Twelve years ago? He's been dead twelve years and no one told me? Why did you wait so long to come? I waited for you. Waited for you to be old enough to understand what happened all those years ago."

"I know what happened, Mother. I was there. I witnessed things."

She shook her head. "You don't know. You don't know anything! You should be glad that man you call Daddy is dead!" She slammed her fist down hard on the table.

"I felt terrible and was all alone after he was murdered. I was alone because of you, Mother! You chose heroin over us. Connie got hooked on your dope! I went through hell losing all of you!"

"No. No. You don't know what you're talking about. You don't know what hell is. Look at you, walking into this place like some kind of fancy movie star in your fur coat, diamonds, and leather boots."

"You don't know anything about me or my life, Mother, and that choice was yours."

"I had no choice, Angie. Your father controlled everything in our family. The minute he thought he lost control over any of us, he went insane. I wanted to get a job instead of being in a prison cell all day and night. He went mad! I wanted to leave. I wanted a divorce. Women didn't have the right to divorce their husbands back then. At least not to men like your father."

More deep breaths crept up through my throat. These things she's saying aren't true. My father was loving and kind. Maybe he was controlling. He never wanted me to leave the house, especially after Connie started using drugs. He was protecting me. I sat beside my mother and let her speak, as much as I despised her words.

"He saw the suitcases. When I started to pack our things, your father stopped me. I should have just grabbed you girls and ran, leaving it all behind. He threw me in the bedroom and locked the door. My leaving would have shamed him. No more control over me or you or Connie. He wouldn't allow that to happen. He lived for controlling me, all of us. I fought with him, physically. He threw my body down on the floor one night and shot me up with that… junk. I was under lock and key for days, maybe weeks. I don't remember anymore. He shot me up regularly until I couldn't leave. I needed him, and I needed that dope like my life depended on it."

"You're a damn liar!"

Tears filled her sockets before bursting down her cheeks. "I don't remember much after that. I just know I needed his visits to pump my arm, finger, leg, or toes with that poison. I was so far gone and out of it most of the time, and some days I wished I'd die already!"

"What about Connie?"

Mother wiped her eyes with her sleeve and paused before she could speak. "I honestly don't know. I slept most of the day with the amount of drugs being pumped into my veins. Your precious Daddy came to visit me one day in my room. My body was filled with so much heroin, I overdosed. A failed attempt on his part to *kill* me. I vaguely remember waking up in a hospital. Then I was brought to this place sometime afterward, my new home. Your father came to visit me once, only once. I remember the date. He came to see me on June 28, 1965. I was here for at least a couple of years before he dropped by. The only reason he showed up was to tell me my sweet, innocent daughter died on June 16, 1965 from a heroin overdose. He told me if I never tried to leave him, the heroin would have never been in our home for her to sample. He blamed me for her death. Her funeral came and went before I even knew she died. He left me here to die as punishment."

She cried to the point where I actually pitied her, instead of hating her.

"I tried to kill myself that night. I broke the mirror in the bathroom and sliced my wrists." Her arms flung at my face; and she lifted her sleeve to show me the jagged scars. When she saw the agony in my expression, she concealed her wrists and sat back. "I'm sorry," she whispered, then lowered her sleeves.

I stood to my feet, prepared to leave. This was about all I could take. How could I possibly absorb what she was saying? My father was not the monster she described. He couldn't be.

She grabbed hold of my arm in a gentle manner this time. "Don't leave, Angie. I realize you loved your father. But you need a dose of reality. Please, I want to know about you, the woman you've become."

Her hands shook. I remembered that jittery feeling when I stopped using coke. A heavy sigh left my lips. "What do you want to know exactly?"

"Your father died in 1967. What happened to you?"

"I moved in with Uncle Vince."

Her disapproval was evident in her facial expression, yet she remained silent.

"Katie and I are close. Having her in my life almost fills the void of losing Connie. She has three beautiful boys now." I felt my face beam brightly when I mentioned them.

"Do you have children, Angie?"

"No." I hid the sadness from her. In no way did I want to start weeping about not being able to have a baby of my own. "But I have a career. I'm a licensed realtor."

She smiled big and bright. "Wow, my daughter has a career! That's wonderful." She nodded then lowered her head, staring absently at my left hand.

"I see a lot of jewelry on you, but no wedding ring."

"I have a boyfriend, Tommy, but we're not married yet."

"Good. You're better off. Was this Tommy handpicked by your uncle? That's something he and your father would have done, finding you the perfect mate to procreate," she said that statement in rhyme.

She was right about that. Uncle Vince found a husband for Katie, but he first had Louis in mind for me. I hated that she was right, and I didn't respond to her comment. Did this mean she was right about all the horrific things she said about my father?

"Who told you a burglar shot Frank?"

"The police I think. It was so long ago. Maybe Uncle Vince."

"You never questioned his death?"

"Why would I? I was barely fifteen years old. Katie and I were having a sleepover that night at Uncle Vince's house. I overheard people say I was lucky I wasn't at home with Daddy when it happened."

She shook her head. "You do realize the kind of business your father was in, and your uncle is surely still in, right?"

"Uncle Vince's club is really successful. He opened clubs in Reno too."

"The club, right." Her tone was suspicious. "How's Dolly doing? Or is she in a nut ward like me? Dead?"

"Aunt Dolly is just fine. She visits Katie and the boys regularly. Why?"

"Ask her about your father, uncle, and their business."

I shook my head at her. I wasn't about to start investigating the two men who took care of me my whole life at her word.

"At least ask her about her car accident years ago."

"Car accident?"

"Yes, it must have been in 1961. It was before I decided to leave your father when Dolly left Vince for the same reason, to stop being controlled. Dolly packed up and left the house with Katie. She actually did the unthinkable and got a job. She left Katie at her mother's house. On her way to her new job, her brakes didn't work. The brake line was cut. Well, actually, the cops found no evidence that someone cut her brakes. Could have been normal wear and tear, they thought.

"A cut brake line, well that was something your father and uncle knew how to do all too well. The last time I spoke with Dolly all those years ago, she was scared to death. Vince didn't care if she left him, but she couldn't take Katie with her. To save her life, she left Katie with Vince and left town alone, with nothing but the clothes on her back. Now, I envy her."

Chills ran up my spine. Uncle Vince would never do that. He couldn't kill the mother of his daughter. My father couldn't have tried to kill my mother. My head was spinning, and my stomach felt nauseous.

Mother was thinking hard with her fingers, scratching her chin. "You're what? Twenty-six? Twenty-seven years old now?"

I nodded.

"You aren't married but you've got a boyfriend. Tommy, right? Do you plan on getting married?"

"Yes, someday."

"You've been controlled your entire life, my sweet child. You don't even realize it." She stared into my eyes, more serious than ever. "If there is anything I want you to remember me telling you, it's this. Make sure you can take care of yourself. Don't ever count on a man to support you. Don't let anyone control you. Your life, your terms, my darling daughter."

The door opened abruptly and a hefty woman entered, wearing green scrubs as if she just performed surgery. "Mrs. Russo, what are you doing in here?" The woman's dark eyes shifted toward me. "Who are you?"

"I was visiting Betty," I responded a bit nervously.

"This is not a visitor's room," she scolded. "Mrs. Russo, lunch was served twenty minutes ago. Everyone's been looking for you! You need to leave this room and eat your lunch before it gets cold. You know you're not supposed to be in here."

"Is it macaroni and cheese, Liza? You know I like the macaroni and cheese."

"Well, it's a grilled chicken and cheese sandwich with vegetables today. I'm sure you'll like it just fine, Mrs. Russo." Liza smiled, patting Mother's back with kindness.

Mother moved past me as if I wasn't there. I followed them out of the room, and watched her sit at the table next to the woman with the baby doll and dig into her meal. She caressed the pink dress worn by the doll and said, "Good afternoon, Lola," to it, then smiled at Baby Lola's mother.

Was she as crazy as everyone else in this place, or did she learn to adapt to all of the bizarre behavior around her?

171

Chapter 50

WHEN I STEPPED off the elevator, mindlessly wandering back to the lobby, I didn't stop to look for Tommy. My head was too focused, attempting to contemplate the theories Mother told me. He saw me approaching and jumped up, causing me to lose my train of thought.

Talking with Tommy about my visit with her helped. This place was maddening! The residents were mentally ill. Still, I'm not certain if my mother is mentally ill, irrational, or eccentric. I told him her crazy story, accusing my father of shooting her up just to keep her under his thumb. Saying he attempted to kill her with an overdose seemed ridiculously far-fetched. Not the man I knew. The man who played dolls with me, taught me how to ride a bike, helped me with my science homework, and kissed boo-boos when I was hurt was not evil.

Tommy said nothing. He merely listened.

"You knew my father, Tommy. He couldn't be capable of these things, could he?"

He didn't respond immediately. "I never met your father, babe. I heard of him."

"What did you hear?"

"I don't know. I don't remember really. I heard he was a tough guy. Not someone to mess with."

"Wait, what does that mean exactly?"

"I can't say. I think you should focus on your mother right now. Whether or not the story is true, she believes it's true."

"Oh, she also doesn't think a burglar killed my father."

"Who does she think killed him?"

"She didn't say a name. She thinks it's related to his business or Uncle Vince's business. What would my uncle's nightclub have to do with my father's death?" I paused, waiting for a reaction, but didn't get one. "Tommy? What could that mean? Can there be any truth to her theory?"

Quietly, he mumbled, "Nah, I doubt it."

Chapter 51

May 4, 1979

SINCE VISITING MY mother, I was in contact with Doctor Hart, her main physician. As Betty's daughter, I had a right to know about my mother's condition and treatment plan. He reviewed her history with me. Heroin addiction is not something people can get past as with other types of drugs. Basically, to remove the cravings of the drug, she had to be treated with a liquid dose of methadone. Unfortunately, methadone is as habit forming as heroin. Regrettably, this was the only option to rid her body of heroin and keep her free of it.

My mother contemplated suicide and made several attempts on her life. Visions of those scars on her wrists came to mind. Other medicine was used to help with her depressed state. The bottom line was my mother belonged living in such a facility to manage her condition and prevent her from harming herself or others.

I was curious who was paying for her care. Did she have medical or hospital insurance? Doctor Hart advised me to contact the facility directly to inquire, and I did.

Mrs. Wilcox suggested we meet in person, however, I explained I lived in Las Vegas. Maybe I needed to explain the long distance from my mother to rationalize why I never called or visited her until now. I owed the woman no explanation, but saying those words felt proper.

The facility's administrator told me Mother had health insurance. Expenses incurred at the home, and any medical charges not covered by insurance, were sent to the estate of Frank Russo, and paid off in full each month.

My father was not paying those bills from wherever his spirit went. Uncle Vince was the executor of his will. He must have known where my mother had been all this time. He knew of her condition and state of mind. Hell, he had to be the one paying her bills.

I called Mother every week to talk to her and make sure she was all right. We never spoke for long and that was fine with me. Her attention span wasn't very lengthy.

I purchased some new clothes for her, nothing fancy. Some new pants, shirts, and pajamas with a note telling her that I was thinking of her. New books were in order and a watercolor paint set. I cleared those items with Mrs. Wilcox. I remembered how much Mother loved to paint. The books I saw in her room were from fifteen years ago. Surely, she needed something different to read. Mrs. Wilcox advised me that a pair of reading glasses would help her. Of course, reading glasses were shipped to her soon after.

Three months had passed since I saw Mother without a word to my uncle. I couldn't forget the sheer lunacy she shared with me about my father. The awful things Mother said about Aunt Dolly's alleged accident and that my uncle was responsible. If I spoke about my visit to her facility, bringing her suspicions up about that accident wouldn't be wise. I wasn't afraid of my uncle, but he did not want me to find my mother for a reason. Was that reason for my own good, or his?

It's Friday, and Tommy had business at the hotel. I had some paperwork to complete for Jerry and dropped it off at the office this morning. Everyone seemed busy today, so I didn't stay to talk with my male colleagues. They didn't speak to me too much anyway. I had the impression they didn't like their work given to a woman.

Instead of returning home to a quiet house, and tackling a pile of laundry to wash, I decided to visit Uncle Vince. His home was not far from my office.

I pulled up in the vacant driveway outside the mansion. His Mercedes may be in the garage, I considered. As I stepped out of the car, laughter and screams of delight were heard from the backyard. Maybe the boys were visiting. I scurried around the potted plants toward the side of the house to the backyard and surprised my uncle and little David. Michael and Louie were surely in school.

"Angie! This is a nice surprise." He turned to the baby sitting in his high chair. "Look whose here, Davie, Aunt Angie! Yay!" He clapped his hands, causing David to giggle and jump.

I couldn't resist this little one, my godson. "Come here you. Look at those little feet and toes you have." I picked him up and tickled his piggies as he tried to squirm from my arms. I kissed his plump, rosy cheeks. Placing him down on the patio cement floor, I held his hands for balance. The strength in this baby's legs and arms was surprising. He was taking steps now, with help, at only eight months old. My eyes glanced at Uncle Vince. "He must want to chase after his big brothers. Look at him ready to run already!"

"Katie wasn't feeling too well this morning, so I told her I'd watch this little man for her while the others are in school."

"I hope she's okay. What's wrong?"

"Just a headache. She said she needed to lay down and rest a little without worrying about David. Three boys keep her busy all day. She doesn't get a lot of opportunities to rest."

Surely he saw the worried look on my face.

"So what brings you by?"

"I wanted to share some news with you. News I probably should have told you about already."

"News? Is Tommy divorced?"

Uh, I should not have presented this situation in such a way. Everything always circled back to Tommy's marriage. "No, news about my mother. I asked Tommy to find her for me, and he did. I went to see her a few months ago." I waited for a surprised look on his face, but didn't see one. His expression was blank.

"I know you did."

"You know? How? If you knew where she was, why keep it from me?" My voice stayed steady and soft. No need for raised voices around the baby.

"You saw your mother, Angie. I'm sure the visit wasn't pleasant. Unfortunately, all the drugs she took really messed with her mind. She hallucinates and makes up stories. I didn't want you to see her like that."

"You're paying her bills there?"

"You know your father left an inheritance for you. He also left funds to pay for your mother's expenses at the facility until she dies. His house and cars were sold. That money went into the estate to help fund her stay there. I receive bills and make sure they're paid. That's it."

"Well, thank you for taking care of the finances, but have you been there? Have you seen her?"

"I have no reason to visit your mother, Angie."

"That place is awful." I covered David's little ears, so he wouldn't sense the tension in my voice. "I hate that she's there on that horrible floor. I know she needs help, but there must be better places for her to live, Uncle."

"Angie, this was your father's request. He was responsible for your mother's care and that facility had the means to help get her off that dope. It messed up her mind. She'll never be the woman you remember before the drugs."

"Maybe there are better places nowadays where she could live. I'd like to look into that and maybe move her to Nevada, closer to me."

His head whipped in my direction. "No, that's not a good idea, Angie," he stated calmly.

"Why? She's too far away and in that terrible place. Uncle, I am grateful you've been paying for her care, but she's my mother, and I think she should be closer to me. She has nothing there. She needed clothing and activities to keep her busy. She had the same books that were in her bedroom fifteen years ago. I sent a supply of new books and reading glasses for her to be able to read if she wanted."

"That was very nice of you, sweetheart. I'm sure if she realizes that you sent her those supplies, she would appreciate it. But, Angie, she won't. Did she know who you were when she saw you?"

"Not at first. I didn't recognize her either when I first saw her."

"When she knew who you were, what did she say to you?"

"She didn't know Daddy was dead."

"And?"

I struggled to say the words, but I wanted to see his reaction. I monitored his facial expression closely. "She believes Daddy fed her the drugs because she wanted to divorce him. She thinks he wanted to control her."

"You see? Do you see what I mean? That's preposterous! She's blaming her drug use on my brother? You don't believe her, do you?" It's only natural he'd want to protect my father.

I paused to continue, studying his face before answering him. "No, of course not. What happened between my parents? Why would she, all of the sudden, start to use heroin of all things?"

"Why did you start to use cocaine, Angie? People go through difficult times and make poor choices. You're no stranger to that. I'm sure she didn't realize what she was getting into and how addictive that junk would be."

How could I argue with his reasoning? Maybe I'm more like my mother than I realized, a frightening notion.

"You have the means to visit your mother whenever you want. I don't think moving her from an environment she's become used to is the right thing to do. She knows her doctors and the staff there. Her mental state may deteriorate if you moved her long distance, across the country to an unfamiliar place."

I couldn't disagree with his logic.

Little David reached for a small Tupperware cup and spilled the milk on the ground. He began to cry as a minor temper tantrum erupted. Uncle Vince lifted him up to calm him as I squatted down to clean up the spill with a towel and napkins.

"Uncle, you never told me how you knew I went to visit my mother."

"I get updates from the staff each quarter. Your visit was a matter of record at the facility, so I saw it. I didn't ask you about it because I thought it may have been a painful experience for you. Clearly, it was."

My uncle managed the money used to keep my mother at that nursing home, complete with medical care, food, and shelter. He was the decision maker. I planned to continue searching for a better home for her. If I found a place closer to me, I would discuss a transition plan with her doctor and my uncle. Hopefully, he'd listen to me. I know there has to be a nicer facility suited to help her on the West Coast. I was not about to give up. He may have been in charge for all these years, assigned by my father legally. However, I had rights. I was her daughter. Surely, my opinion mattered.

Chapter 52

July 15, 1979

TOMMY AND I flew to New York in July every year. Knowing we would be returning to the city, I wanted to see my mother and introduce Tommy to her. There was a nursing home in Nevada outside of Las Vegas where my mother could move to if her doctor agreed that moving her closer to me would be in her best interest. I scheduled a meeting with Doctor Hart in person.

The city was hot today. I pulled my hair back into a single ponytail and threw on a pair of shorts with a solid purple t-shirt. I wanted to look neat without the diamonds and fur coat to visit my mother at her home this time. Tommy wore burgundy slacks with a cream-colored, knit shirt. He wasn't comfortable wearing shorts to meet my mother. For this visit, we brought a dozen, long-stem, white roses and a box of Russell Stover chocolates for her to enjoy.

I wasn't sure what to expect when I saw her this time. Would she remember me by sight? We continued weekly phone calls. I told her doctor she could call me anytime, but she never did. She seemed to know who I was when she answered the phone. She never referred to me as "Barbie" again. The conversations were short but cordial. If I asked how she was, she always responded that she was good. She told me she liked the paints and books I sent her. Usually, she'd hang up the phone because there was a Bingo game going on that she didn't want to miss.

Maybe I was wrong to try to have her moved. Maybe it was selfish on my part to move her closer to me. However, I felt a sense of obligation to ensure she was taken care of in a high-quality facility.

Tommy and I walked into the building and checked in with the receptionist, a different woman than the last time.

"Ms. Russo, Doctor Hart wanted to talk to you."

"Our meeting is at two. I thought we could visit with my mother first."

"Please wait here, and I'll tell the doctor you arrived."

We waited a good ten minutes before the doctor greeted us. I didn't understand why we couldn't see Mother first. A part of me was anxious for Tommy to meet her.

A short, thin man with glasses, wearing a white lab coat, walked around the corner and called out my name. As I stood, he eyed me up and down. I felt Tommy's hand squeeze mine hard. He complained my shorts were too short when we left the hotel.

"It's nice to meet you in person, Doctor Hart. I'm Angie. This is Tommy Cavallo."

After the standard salutations with handshakes occurred, he asked us to follow him down a long hallway with pale blue walls, displaying various oil paintings and photographs of what seemed like this facility from at least fifty years past, judging by the clothes worn and nurse's uniforms. Soon we strolled through a door and around the corner to an office with glass windows.

"Please, have a seat." He pointed to the two chairs opposite his desk.

"Is everything okay with my mother, Doctor? I planned to meet with you after my visit with her. The receptionist insisted I see you first."

"Yes, I needed to meet with you." He sat down in his large, leather chair behind this enormous desk that made him appear even smaller than he was for a petite man. His hands folded, entwined fingers. "I tried to call you, but I realize it takes time for you to fly out here, and with the time change and all…"

"What is it? Is something wrong?"

"Angie, I'm sorry to tell you this, but unfortunately, your mother passed away during the night."

"What?" Tommy asked, because I couldn't.

"The police were notified and an investigation began."

"The police? What the hell happened?" Tommy asked, rightfully concerned.

"She hanged herself in an office on her floor. I'm terribly sorry for your loss. Your mother was a deeply disturbed woman who had attempted suicide a few times. Unfortunately, this time she was successful."

I absently placed the rose bouquet on his desk. "How did this happen? And why? I called her every week. She seemed to be happy to hear from me. She knew I was coming to see her today. Why would she kill herself before seeing me?" Guilt filled my senses. Maybe if I moved her sooner to a different facility, she would have been monitored more closely.

"The office doors are locked all day and all night. You need a key to access these rooms."

He had no idea how skillful my mother was with a bobby pin, and I didn't inform him of her talent.

"She took a sash from her bathrobe and made a noose that she apparently tossed over a beam in the office. I don't think I need to explain further."

A sash from a bathrobe? The robe I bought her. My hands covered my eyes, but no tears were shed. Shock, sadness, and remorse consumed me, but no tears fell.

Tommy set the box of chocolates on the desk next to Mother's roses, then he gently clenched my hand. He studied me as if he could read my mind, knowing I couldn't speak. "You said the police were called?"

"Yes, standard procedure if an incident occurs. No one saw Betty leave her room. There are a few nurses and some aids who work the night shift. The police questioned them. We documented everything that occurred."

Doctor Hart stood from his chair, picked up a small, cardboard box and placed it in front of me. "We haven't gone through her clothing yet, but these are some personal items of hers you may want. She also left what seems to be a suicide note. The police opened it and kept the original. I requested they make a copy of it for you." He stood over Tommy and me, watching us attempt to absorb this tragic information.

I stared at the note. I hadn't seen Mother's handwriting in many years to recognize it.

"I'm so sorry, baby." Tommy kissed my cheek and watched me as I stared at this folded piece of paper. "Are you going to open it?"

My mouth couldn't move to speak.

"Hey, do you want me to read it to you?"

I nodded before Tommy read the short and sweet words aloud.

The last thing I wanted to do before I left this wretched life was to see Angie. I'm proud she turned out good. It's time I make peace with Connie now.

The sobbing began as soon as she mentioned Connie's name. Tommy pulled me into his arms and gave me his shoulder.

Later on, we met with Mrs. Wilcox to discuss options for a funeral service in New York. She had no friends here to my knowledge. I made arrangements for her body to be cremated, and I would return home with my mother's ashes and figure out later where to spread them.

I requested her clothes that were in good condition go to a local church for people in need. The rest of her belongings included bobby pins, lipstick, hair clips, the photograph of Connie and me, her books and paintings. I kept the photograph and her paintings, then advised Mrs. Wilcox to share the other items with the residents if she thought that would be appropriate, or discard them.

Mother's paintings were quite nice. There was something familiar about them. Then I realized one painting resembled the flower garden she loved to tend to in our yard. Another was a moonlit view of the Golden Gate Bridge in San Francisco. We visited there when I was little to see my grandparents when they were alive. She loved seeing the bridge lit up at night. She was a talented painter, a gift I never had.

These paintings were worthy of frames. I will honor her memory with these pieces and find a place to hang them at home.

Chapter 53

Christmas Eve 1979

ANOTHER CHRISTMAS AND Tommy disappeared for a few days from me as usual. It's been nine years since we met. He's still married to Sadie and still spent Christmas with her family. This bothered me as well as my uncle. They all waited for me to give Tommy an ultimatum, or walk away on my own. I loved him so much, I couldn't bear the thought of living life without him. We were a part of each other, together every day, and we traveled constantly. A few days around Christmas had been a hurdle to endure every year. The love of my family helped.

Knowing that Tommy and I will be headed to Paris next week for our New Year's trifecta healed my heavy heart. The eighties were upon us! The decade seemed to fly by.

Holiday lights were strung along the outside of Uncle Vince's house. Streams of green, red, and blue colors blinked excessively. Overkill in my opinion. Staring at the blinking lights made me dizzy after a while, even if they looked pretty. Candles flickered in the window panes, dazzling the boys when they pulled up in Louis's Ford Country Squire, a practical vehicle for three growing boys.

I had arrived early to help finish wrapping the presents for Michael, Louie, and David. They made the holidays so much fun, tearing at the paper and seeing the contents inside. Clothes never earned as big of a reaction as a basketball hoop, Big Wheel, or bicycle, but Louis and Katie taught them to be respectful and always smile and say thank you.

The excitement was heard through the kids' praises of the light display and the giant Christmas tree spotted through the picture window. My uncle outdid himself this year with the monstrous Spruce.

I had quite a surprise myself, and it wasn't from any gift beneath the tree. What surprised me was Aunt Dolly's entrance. Uncle Vince didn't mention she would be attending Christmas Eve dinner, but he certainly didn't seem surprised when she appeared, holding David in her arms.

Uncle Vince spoiled his grandsons so much. When they charged in and saw the massive array of gifts beneath the tree, they ran toward them to see whose names were written on the tags. Michael was extremely bright and a very good reader. Louie recognized names quite well for his age. The boys were each allowed to open one gift before dinner. The rest had to wait until afterwards. This became a tradition.

A new tradition for me was thinking about Mother in a favorable manner. I hadn't thought fondly of her in so many years. I thought about the time wasted, hating her for an addiction I never understood. An addiction I could relate to. Whether her accusations about my father were accurate or false was irrelevant. She had a disease. Addiction is a disease. Her mental issues exacerbated her health.

"Angie." Aunt Dolly disrupted my thoughts. "I wanted to tell you again how sorry I am about your mother's death."

"Thank you. The plant you sent was lovely, Aunt Dolly. I appreciated it so much."

"Your mom and I had some fun times. She was such a stitch! Always told a joke and made me laugh. What a great card player too. She was an expert at Bridge and Gin Rummy."

Wiggling my pointer finger, I encouraged Aunt Dolly to follow me down the hallway. "My mother asked me about you."

"She did? That makes me so happy. What did she say?"

"I told her I'd seen you, and you were a grandmother. She brought up a terrible accident you were in years ago. Do you know what she was talking about?"

Aunt Dolly stepped backward, stretching her neck for a clear view of the other room where my uncle was reading *T'was the Night before Christmas* to the boys.

I lowered my voice and glanced over my shoulder to confirm no one stood close enough to hear us. "My mother said you thought your brakes were tampered with. She thought it was because my uncle was angry at you for leaving him and taking Katie with you."

Her voice was rattled as she whispered, "You choose now, here, in this house, to bring this up? Jesus, Angie. Did you talk to Katie about this?"

My head shook from side to side. "No."

"It was an accident, end of story. She adores her father. You can't share such a theory with her. It's complete nonsense!" Her eyes were large and her hands were animated. Her demure persona changed drastically. "Your mother was a wonderful woman once, but you can't believe her ramblings in the state she was in. Imagine a woman accusing her husband of attempted murder."

"I'm sorry if I upset you, or made you relive a terrible memory."

Still whispering, Aunt Dolly continued, "Listen to me. We never had this conversation. You will never talk to Katie about this. And most importantly, you will never share your thoughts about that accident with your uncle. You won't share this with anyone because you never thought it, and your mother never told you anything about it. Is that clear?"

In my entire life, I never heard Aunt Dolly scold anyone the way she just scolded me, a grown woman. She attended some special family gatherings to see her daughter and grandsons. My uncle tolerates her presence for the same reason. His demeanor always improved the moment Aunt Dolly left.

Something my aunt said clicked in my brain about a woman accusing her husband of murder. Sadie accused Tommy of a similar accident. Her brakes were tampered with. At least that was her accusation. The police had no evidence to charge Tommy. Thoughts of my mother entered my head, telling me a cut brake line was the Russo men's specialty. Sadie's brake line was broken.

"Angie." Uncle Vince snuck up on me. His voice sent chills up my spine. "Come, the antipasto is being served."

"I'll be right there. Don't wait for me, Uncle."

He approached with a suspicious smile. "Is everything okay? You look like you've seen a ghost or something."

That loving, soft glance he sent me seemed so genuine. Was he capable of such crimes my mother told me about? Would he have harmed Sadie? He was never happy about my relationship with Tommy. Did he want to free Tommy from his marriage in order to make an honest woman out of me?

Aunt Dolly was pretty riled up when I brought up her car accident. I'm uncertain if her heightened anxiety is from frustration with my insinuations, or plain ole fear.

Chapter 54

June 14, 1980

IT WAS SATURDAY, a warm, spring evening in June. Tommy's lawyer, Len Stein, and his wife, Wanda, opened up their spectacular mansion to host a formal dinner party with some important associates of Tommy's.

Wanda Sherman is a beautiful blonde with a larger than life personality. I always admired her for keeping her given name, maintaining her independence. She lived in Germany before moving to the United States when she was a child. For as long as she's lived in this country, her German accent was thick and authentic. She and Len were inseparable. Wanda and I coordinated the extravagant details of this black-tie affair as cohostesses.

The Stein's Victorian mansion was lovely with an antiquated yet elegant look and feel. In the front of the property were numerous statues and fountains, spouting water in a whimsical fashion. If I didn't know them personally, I'd think they were movie moguls.

There were horses in a large barn in the back of the infinite property. The thick green grass appeared to run for miles. The couple had a tremendous love and respect for animals. There were a couple of cats in the house. I didn't see them, but my itchy, watery eyes gave me a clue of their presence.

Wanda is also a huge NASCAR fan. For years, she hounded Len to invest in a car. Finally, he caved after she met Dale Earnhardt, an up-and-comer in the business, with an aspiring career. Wanda insisted Tommy and I join her and Len at the Indianapolis 500 next year.

Approximately twenty couples were expected this evening. Len had valet parking set up outside. For this type of event, Tommy drove the yellow Ferrari. He loved the sporty look and feel of the car, but he drove it so fast, my heart beat practically right out of my chest.

Tommy had his tux cleaned, and I bought a lilac-colored, strapless, evening gown with a detachable wrap to cover my shoulders.

Caterers in black and white uniforms were hired to serve hot hors d'oeuvres on silver platters. A cold buffet with a variety of cheeses, crackers, and sliced meats was placed in the corner of the dining room. There was an open bar set up with top-shelf liquor, beer, and wine. Tommy and I drank club soda with lemon slices.

I met most of these VIP clients before, but not many of their wives. It was nice to meet the women in their lives. Tommy introduced me to everyone as "Angie." He never explained if I was his wife or girlfriend. If people made an assumption that I was his wife, he didn't correct them.

In the library were some lovely sculptures and new artwork on the wall. Tommy brought me in there to see these pieces before the men trailed off behind closed doors to talk business, while the women made small talk or polite conversations about the market, cooking tips, or if desperate enough, the weather.

Barry and Jillian Riley beat us to the library. The couple gazed at the art, seemingly impressed, while Barry nipped at his pipe. One of the wait staff found us and offered crabmeat puffs and marinated steak kabobs.

Tommy began to describe in great detail our recent trip to Lake Como to the Rileys, and encouraged them to stay at our penthouse with the breathtaking view.

Jim suddenly appeared, interrupting our conversation, requesting Tommy leave the room. When Tommy excused himself, I continued describing the lake, boat rides, and the sheer tranquility of the Como region to the Rileys.

"Angie." Tommy's voice rang out to me.

I turned to see him and Jim standing in the doorway, waving at me to join them. Smiling at the Rileys, I raised my index finger, requesting they excuse me for one minute. Then I walked toward Tommy, who appeared to be jumping out of his skin, frantic. "What is it?"

Jim held my wrap and purse in his hand, I noticed.

"I'm sorry, baby, but Jim's going to take you home."

"Home? Why? Has something happened?"

"There's no time to explain. I'll see you in the morning. I promise."

"The morning? Wait, what is going on?" I held my hand out, refusing to leave without an explanation.

Tommy took hold of my arm, snatching me away from my conversation with the Rileys; then he moved me down the hallway and inside a small bathroom.

Jim trailed quietly behind us.

"Tommy, what the hell are you doing? Why are you shoving me in here like this?"

"Sadie's here," he whispered, eyes looking everywhere except at me.

"What?"

"I don't know why she's here or what she's thinking, but Jim has to take you home."

"Why would she be here, Tommy? How does she even know about this party? This party that I helped plan." Flashbacks of organizing John's funeral returned. I had to miss his service because of Sadie's presence.

"I don't know!" His voice was angry and his face turned red as if his blood pressure were rising.

My blood pressure was boiling for certain. "You are really asking me to leave?"

"Angie, what am I supposed to do? Introduce you to her?"

"She doesn't act like a wife preparing for a divorce, Tommy. It's nearly ten years now. Damn you!"

"She's checking up on me. Maybe she wants to catch me here with you and use it against me in court. I don't know. Baby, please, let Jim take you home. I have to go. You know I love you."

Without thinking, my hand raised and slapped him hard across the face. The blow stung my hand, tingling my fingertips. Tommy looked shocked as he lifted his hand to his damaged cheek. Let him explain the reddened face to his wife.

My legs felt like Jell-O, but I managed to sluggishly pace toward the front entrance until Jim stopped me with a delicate tug of my arm. He and Tommy exchanged a look. If I wasn't so damn angry, I'd ask what that suspicious signal was.

"Angie, let's go out the side door through the kitchen," Jim said as he escorted me along.

Sneaking me out the back door. One more humiliation after another.

Chapter 55

June 15, 1980

I FIGURED OUT what that look was between Tommy and Jim. Jim sat outside all night in his car like a cop at a stakeout. I was in no condition to go anywhere anyway. Between my anger, rage, and bursts of foul-mouthed expressions, I stayed home. Will he ever leave Sadie? Could I leave him? I thought about it. God I wanted to leave at that moment, but it was the fury talking. I even started to pack a suitcase during my first fit. What would I do? Move back into my uncle's house? Prove him right about Tommy?

Around three in the morning, I decided I would drive to the office at dawn and look for properties on the market. With my salary, I could easily afford a home. Of course, because Tommy was my exclusive client, I may not continue to earn the same pay if I left him. Not to mention that getting a loan may be a challenge for a single woman. Perhaps I could tap into my inheritance; the money my uncle controlled.

Why did I feel so trapped? I knew Tommy was married when I met him. I've known all along he had a wife. This was not news to me. Every so often, Sadie made her presence known in a big way, clashing with my faith in Tommy and our relationship. My uncle's voice floated through my ears, smacking my brain saying, *you're not his wife, you're his mistress. A mistress doesn't reap the same benefits as the wife. The wife is respected.*

I packed some clothes in my suitcase. I wanted to leave before Tommy arrived. Sunday morning at the agency would be quiet since the office was closed. I'd stay there for a while to think things through before going to Uncle Vince's house. Anything to avoid seeing Tommy and feeling trapped in this house.

Peeking out the window, Jim sat wide awake and erect in his Chevy. I knew he would try to stop me from leaving if I carried this suitcase outside with me. I had to escape this place for a while. The suitcase remained packed and in the hallway. I grabbed my keys and my purse, then marched toward my car. Jim's car door flung open, and he jumped out, as predicted.

"Angie, where are you going?"

"I have some things to do, Jim. I don't need a babysitter."

"Where are you going?"

"You don't need to know and you're not going to follow me. You need to give me some space. Tell Tommy I said that too."

"I can't let you leave."

"Are you going to tie me up, Jim? Kidnap me? I have errands to run. Someone has to manage this house, right? Please, leave me be."

He stepped aside, allowing me to access my car. I watched from my rear-view mirror, expecting him to drive after me, following me to report my final destination to Tommy. If he were following me, he was damn good at being invisible. Maybe I was paranoid. To be sure he didn't follow me, I took several back roads and drove the long way to work instead of taking the shortcuts I normally used.

Around noon, I decided to drive to my uncle's house early for dinner. I should have gone home to freshen up, but Tommy could have been there waiting for me. I wasn't ready to face him. Seeing the boys would cheer me up. David was nearly two years old, and his face lit up whenever he saw me. I cherished my time with them.

Before going inside, I smoothed on my pink lady lipstick and tossed my hair back with a barrette. Admittedly, I was distracted after looking up photographs of houses for sale. Maybe I would have an easier time renting an apartment.

So many thoughts in and out of my head kept me from minding the biscuits in the oven I told Roseanne I'd watch for her while she prepared a salad.

Katie and I brought the food from the kitchen to the dining room table. As everyone sat down to eat, the doorbell rang. The Franciscos had a wedding to attend and were not expected at family dinner today. Katie hadn't sat yet, so she walked to the door. When she returned, Tommy sauntered behind her, sulking. His face was somber as he looked at me, barely acknowledging the others at the table.

Michael sat next to me, but Louis asked him to switch seats so Tommy could take his seat beside me. The young man quickly scurried out of the chair as his dad requested.

When Tommy sat, he turned his face, those gray eyes intently fixed on me. But I stared at my plate, refusing to make eye contact. I felt his hand trail my leg and knee beneath the table. I swiftly pulled my leg away from his grasp.

"Aunt Angie is playing with her food," Louie squealed on me. "We're not allowed to do that."

I smiled at him. "You're right, that is rude of me. I guess I'm not very hungry today, Louie."

"Are you okay, Angie? You've been quiet since you arrived. You look pale." Uncle Vince said with concern.

"I'm fine, Uncle. I didn't sleep well last night. I'm tired, that's all." As I stood up to carry my plate to the kitchen, an effort to prevent the kids from watching me play with my food, I noticed my uncle was unable to take his dark eyes off of me.

"Tommy, what's wrong with my niece?"

"She said she didn't sleep last night," I heard him answer before telling Uncle Vince he'd check on me. That means he would be in this kitchen behind me at any moment.

"Baby, I am so sorry about last night."

"Not here. We're not doing this here. You shouldn't even be here! You need to make an excuse to leave and go home." I desperately attempted to keep a low volume on my anger.

"Come home with me and we'll talk."

"I meant go to your other home."

"No, you aren't going to push me away."

"Last night you pushed me away, throwing me out of that party like I was garbage. It was humiliating." I desperately tried to fight the tears that wanted to flow.

"That's not true. I understand why you feel like that, but that's not true."

"Aunt Angie, I spilled juice on my shirt!" Louie ran into the kitchen, looking for me to help him.

I grabbed the towel on the counter and wet it with some soap and water before dabbing it on the boy's checkered shirt. Tommy stood watching me, arms crossed, waiting patiently to finish a conversation I didn't want to have with him. "I'm afraid the juice may not come out until Mommy washes it at home, Louie. Did she pack you an extra shirt to change into?"

He nodded his head.

"Okay, Louie, tell Mommy we tried to save your shirt but you need a new one."

"Thank you." He planted a wet kiss on my cheek before running out of the kitchen.

As soon as Louie bounced back into the dining room, Tommy took hold of my hand and led me outside to the backyard, far enough away from the house for some privacy. "I know you're angry. I don't blame you. Sadie wasn't supposed to be there. She was checking up on me. With all the time I spend with you and the trips we take, she's been suspicious and wants to prove I've been cheating on her. I called Len this morning and told him I really need him to speed things up and get this divorce finalized."

"I don't believe you. It's been almost ten years, Tommy. Ten years! We should have been married by now. You said we'd adopt a baby."

"We will, sweetheart. I want nothing more than to make you my wife and adopt a child to raise with you. You'll be an incredible mother. I see you with these boys, and I know you have the biggest heart." He approached to wipe a few drops that plunged from my eyes.

How I wanted to believe him. I wanted his muscular arms to wrap around me and make me feel safe and loved again. "I can't keep waiting, Tommy. Last night was a dose of reality." I had to ask him a question I dreaded to know the answer to. "Are you sleeping with her?"

"What? No. Baby, I told you about our living situation."

"Why would she show up at that dinner last night if you're separated? Why would she care if she wasn't in love with you? Why isn't she pushing for a divorce if she suspects you're in love with someone else?"

"I foolishly left the invitation in my room at the house. She found it and showed up, expecting to catch me cheating. I argued with her about it last night when we left the party. If she caught us together, that would only drag this entire mess out longer. She would have caused a scene too. She's like that. I know you hated that I asked you to leave last night, but I couldn't put you through that. What would you have done if she fought with you in front of the guests? Sadie loves conflict. She lives for a good fight."

I hadn't thought about that.

"Please come home with me, so we can talk about this in private."

"I need some space."

"No, don't say that."

"I can stay here at my uncle's if you prefer."

Judging by his expression, he didn't like that suggestion.

"You need to give me time to think. I can't go on like this, Tommy, when there is no end in sight. Either give me space at home, or I'll ask my uncle if I can stay here for a while."

"All right. I'll give you whatever you need. Don't stay here. Go to our home."

"I don't need Jim sitting in the driveway either."

"Okay. Just come home, please. I'll call you in the morning."

Chapter 56

June 18, 1980

TOMMY CALLED ME once or twice daily to say hello and see how I was. With every phone call, he asked if he could see me. As hurt as I was, I missed seeing him and holding him. I agreed to talk to him tonight. It had been three days since family dinner. As angry as I was, I longed for him.

His car engine revved in the driveway when he pulled in. My stomach was in knots, confused if this feeling was excitement or nausea.

The door opened wide. His arms were full, carrying an arrangement with at least two dozen, long-stemmed, pink roses, my favorite. Most people liked red, but he knew I loved pink with baby's breath blended in. I sensed disappointment from him when I didn't smile or thank him. I couldn't reach out for them when he attempted to hand me the bouquet.

"Will you ever forgive me? What do I have to do, Angie?" He placed the flowers down on the coffee table.

"I want you to be mine. Completely."

"I am yours, baby."

"I'm tired of sharing you!"

"It won't be much longer. I talked to Len to push the divorce through. I will do whatever it takes for you to forgive me. I won't lose you, Angie."

His fingers reached inside his jacket pocket and pulled out a small black box with silver ribbon, before bending down on one knee. "Angie, I love you more than I ever thought I could love another woman. I know we can't technically get married until my divorce is final, but I am committed to you. As soon as I am free of Sadie, we will be married in Paris or wherever you want. I will do nothing but make you happy from now on. You are forever in my heart." The large diamond was custom made in the shape of a heart with an inscription that read, "Forever."

The sparkling diamond was surely larger than two carats.

"I had this ring made six months ago when we were in Paris for New Year's. I hoped to give it to you before now, but the divorce still wasn't final. I know that's important to you. What's important is that you know how much I love you; and I'm devoted to you. You will be my wife someday soon if you say yes."

I stood there, looking down on him, still and silent, with eyes pleading for my answer.

"Angie? Please accept this ring as a symbol of my love and commitment to our relationship."

I heard the word "yes" leave my lips, although I don't recall thinking about the answer.

Tommy stood to his feet, still holding the ring. He placed his forehead against mine and embraced me tightly in his arms. He took the ring from the box and softly picked up my left hand and slid the ring on my finger. It was the most beautiful ring I'd ever seen, and it looked amazing on my finger.

"We've been together a long time, sweetheart. You are my life. My home is with you. My heart is with you. We've come so far. Please don't give up on me now."

My fingers lifted and ran through his thick hair. His lips met mine. The passion and love between us was undeniable.

Chapter 57

August 31, 1980

I HADN'T WORN the ring around the family, but it killed me to take this precious gem off, and setting it in my jewelry box at home every Sunday. Uncle Vince wouldn't understand my accepting an engagement ring while Tommy was still married. He assured me his divorce was imminent.

Pop had a bit of a health scare and was rushed by ambulance to the hospital. Tommy sat by his bedside. Even though Pop was ill, Tommy told me Len was working on the divorce, and he hoped it would be final by the end of the year.

Before we left our home to attend family dinner, I slipped off my engagement ring. However, Tommy placed the diamond back on my finger, stating it was where it belonged. He wanted to tell my family about his upcoming divorce and prove his loyalty to me.

Today was David's second birthday. I picked out a tricycle in blue and black with a little bell on the handle for added sound effects. He wouldn't be able to ride as fast as his big brothers on their bikes, but he could try.

We walked into the house, Tommy carrying the trike with a giant, red bow affixed to the seat.

David tumbled toward me when he saw us enter, arms stretched up for me to pick him up. I nibbled on his cheeks and wished him a happy birthday. As soon as he saw Tommy with the tricycle, he couldn't leave my grasp fast enough to run toward it for a try. I took out our camera and snapped some shots of him riding through the living room. Maybe I'm an overprotective godmother, but I hovered over the lad as he peddled down the hallway.

Using my left hand, I showed him how to ring the bell. That's when Katie spotted the large, twinkling diamond on my finger and screeched loudly. Loud enough to call attention, making everyone curious to see what the fuss was about. This ring was hard to miss.

"Wow, Angie, this is gorgeous! Does this mean?" Her eyes glowed with delight.

"Yes," Tommy answered Katie. "We are engaged."

I noticed Tommy's eyes locked with Uncle Vince's.

Katie and Louis gave us their congratulations, followed by the Maronis and Franciscos. The DeLeones hadn't arrived yet. Michael and Louie didn't quite understand what this meant, but they each gave me a hug and shook Tommy's hand. I was afraid to make eye contact with my uncle.

"Angie, Tommy, can I speak with you in here please?" My uncle pointed toward the study. His tone was mellow and dry.

Everyone else became very quiet, even the boys, as we followed Uncle Vince to talk in private, behind closed doors.

"What is this ring on my niece's finger?"

"Uncle..."

"I'm asking him!" he snarled, glaring at Tommy.

"I am committed to Angie. I love her very much. This isn't news."

"What's not news is the fact that you're still married, unless that's changed recently?"

"I expect the divorce to go through by the end of the year, Vince. It's going to happen."

"But right now, you're married." He turned toward me. "Don't you have any self-respect? How could you be planning a wedding to a married man you've been having an affair with for ten years? He's still not divorced!"

"Don't speak to her like that, Vince. Come on. I know you never approved of our relationship."

"Affair." My uncle corrected Tommy.

"You have to know that after ten years, I love her. My divorce has taken a long time, but Angie is my life. She's my future. I will marry her. I know it's important for her to have your blessing."

"Uncle, please. This is my decision. I love Tommy, and I accepted his ring. I've always wanted to be his wife. We plan to adopt a baby too."

His look was dismal. "Angie, don't get ahead of yourself. Let him get divorced first. Then you can accept a marriage proposal and talk about a wedding and children. This isn't the time."

"Would you approve when his divorce is final?"

No response.

"Uncle Vince, he makes me happy."

He stood up, approached me, and left a kiss on my right cheek. "All I want is your happiness. If he makes you happy, you will have my blessing *after* he is divorced and not a moment before, Angie."

Chapter 58

November 10, 1980

POP'S HEALTH HAD declined further. Between spending time at the hospital, the hotel, and planning the impending divorce, Tommy's stress level increased. When he found time during the day to see me, he wasn't really here. He was aloof. The divorce was slated for December 11. Unless the courts had to reschedule the hearing, he would be free to move into our home permanently and marry me by year end.

I'd been patient long enough. Ten years was a long time to wait, but it would be worth it! Wedding plans wafted into my mind. Tommy suggested we be married in Paris, but I wanted my family present with Uncle Vince walking me down the aisle. A simple ceremony, followed by an elegant dinner in a private room at Tommy's hotel here on the Vegas Strip, was my first choice.

Wedding gown styles changed drastically since Katie's wedding. Gowns are bigger, fuller, but beautiful like Cinderella's classic dress with puffier sleeves. Perhaps white is not the color for me, or maybe that's my conscience whispering in my ear. Ivory, off-white, or a cream-colored gown may be more appropriate given the circumstances of our relationship for the past ten years.

Tommy canceled seeing me again today. This was out of character for him. With the amount of stress he's been under, I was concerned about him slipping back into bad habits. A phone call or a knock on a door was all it would take to score coke. His state of mind concerned me. I can't go to the hospital with him. His father had not been lucid, but if any other visitor or the staff saw Tommy with me, they would question who I was. Unfortunately, I would never have the opportunity to meet Pop.

Thoughts of Tommy using drugs again toyed with my mind. I sat in this big, empty house alone for the last couple of days. The boys were sick with a stomach bug, so I couldn't visit Katie to occupy my time. Since Tommy was my exclusive customer, I didn't have much work to do today. He had other priorities.

I slipped on a sleek red dress and heels. Maybe I could waste some time catching up on literature at the office later, but I had another thought. Something was wrong, off about Tommy. I did something I never thought I'd have to do or feel the need to do. I checked up on him. He said he was at the office at the Montgomery and leaving soon to go to the hospital, then handle some business issues.

My Oldsmobile sat outside the hotel with a good view of his BMW in his usual parking space. After thirty minutes of waiting, Tommy glided out of the building, hopped into his vehicle, and zoomed off, with me not too far behind. How silly I felt when he pulled into the parking lot of the hospital, surely to see Pop. I ducked when his head turned toward my direction. My god, what would I tell him I was doing here in the parking lot of the hospital if he saw me? This was ridiculous! Here I sat, in my car, waiting like an idiot. All he was doing was seeing his father, who may not last on this earth much longer. What was wrong with me?

Twenty minutes passed before Tommy rushed out of the hospital entrance, jumped back into his car and sped off again rather quickly. His visit with his father was short. I started the Oldsmobile and raced to catch up to him on the street. I didn't want to follow too closely. We left the Las Vegas area, and he drove onto a ramp that led to the freeway.

His BMW exited off US 93 in Henderson. I'm not sure how I kept up with him without following too closely. I thought for sure I would lose him in traffic. He made several turns after driving off the main route.

He stopped at a corner store. After a few minutes, he strode out of the store with a paper bag then continued moving along. I hoped he couldn't see my car behind him.

He turned down Mountain Road, a dead end street. I drove very slowly, praying he wouldn't spot me. When I saw his car park in front of a very large house atop a hill, I parked and stayed put until he was no longer in sight. I couldn't sit here out in the open and have him drive by me when he left. I drove closer to the beautiful home and continued driving a few yards down. Then I parked behind another car in the street on the opposite side. Unless he looked very carefully, I doubt he'd recognize me or the Oldsmobile. There were no other cars in the driveway, but there was a four-car garage for vehicles to be parked.

He was in the house for nearly an hour before I watched his vehicle drive away. Because I never saw him leave until his car sped off, I wasn't able to catch up with him. I stared at the house for a moment. Who lived here? Why was he here for an hour? My curiosity got the better of me.

Luckily, my realtor cards were in the backseat along with a clipboard and some documents about the agency. A good twenty minutes passed before I had the nerve to step out of the car and knock on the door. What would Tommy think if he knew I had checked out his story? What if he came back here and found me lurking around this property?

The driveway was paved and a thick cement wall stood tall around the edges for privacy. There were several steps in multiple sections to climb before reaching the English Tudor-style home. The architecture was marvelous. The landscape was impeccable.

A tight knot formed in my belly as I rapped on the door. I turned to leave after a few seconds until the door opened and a petite blonde woman, barely five feet tall, showed herself through the top half of the screened door.

I'm not sure why it didn't occur to me sooner. Was this his home with Sadie? Am I face to face with his wife after all these years? I couldn't speak the first time she said hello.

"May I help you, miss?" she said a little louder.

"Good afternoon. I'm a realtor, walking around the neighborhood. I wanted to leave my information with you and see if you had a need for maybe a new home, or if you were thinking about selling. You never know when someone may be having a life-changing event." I rambled on, bringing up that last part, hoping she might speak about needing another place to live soon, like December 11. "As a female in this business, some men don't think I can cut it." I attempted to solicit a chuckle.

She displayed a half-smile. "Good for you, paving the way for women who want a professional career." A fuller smile appeared, but I couldn't tell if her response was genuine.

"Would you have a need for a realtor? You have a lovely house. I'm sure you'd get a fabulous price for it if you were to sell it."

"I doubt my husband wants to move, but you can come inside and tell me what you think."

As she opened the door, my eyes drifted down, unable to avoid her swollen stomach. "You're with child?" My face must have exposed my shock.

"Yes, I'm about five months along." She rubbed the small bundle with both hands.

This couldn't be Sadie. It just couldn't be. "My name is Angie, by the way. And you are?"

"Sadie. Sadie Cavallo. You just missed my husband. I've been really sick lately, so he's been checking in on me every day. He's usually very busy."

I tried so hard to prevent the agony within me from releasing. Was this one of those "out of body" experiences? Sadie clearly had no idea who I was or what Tommy does. Clearly, I had no idea what Tommy does when he's not with me either.

"What made you want a career, Angie? I mean, you're a pretty woman. I'm sure you could scoop up a husband for yourself." She glanced at my finger. "Wow, that's quite a rock. You must have a good man in your life."

Good man, she thought. No. I struggled to speak, but somehow I managed. "I suppose I wanted to do more with my life. Not that there's anything wrong with women who choose to be housewives.

206

At least we have a choice to work in a professional career if we want. Unfortunately, men still don't consider us equally competent in the workforce, and I doubt my salary is as high as my male colleagues."

She nodded then waddled her petite body through the foyer, encouraging me to follow her to show off the magnificent house she lived in with my lover. That was the last thing I wanted to do. I wanted to run out the door and think this was just a horrible nightmare. I wanted Tommy to come home and see me here with his pregnant wife. Sadie was giving him a child, something I could never give him.

As she showed me the main living room, it was difficult to miss the large portrait of Tommy and Sadie together, placed above the fireplace. The photo was recent too. He wore the dress shirt I bought him for his birthday in March.

"That's my husband, Tommy," she said with pride.

"Yes, very nice." A lump was stuck in my throat. "Is this your first child?"

"Yes, and it's about time. We've been married for a long time, and I finally convinced him to have a baby." She looked around her enormous house. "Maybe if we have more kids, we'll need a bigger place."

I glanced at my watch. "I really need to get going. Sorry to take up your time, but please take my card. And be sure to tell your husband I stopped by to meet you."

Chapter 59

WERE THE LAST ten years with Tommy a lie? Obviously! What a fool I'd been! My uncle was right. He wasn't getting divorced next month or ever. What the hell was he going to tell me when December 11 rolled around? Another delay? Another excuse? Hell, I allowed him to make excuses for me for the last ten years. He probably never had Len working on a divorce at all. Damn him!

I parked the Oldsmobile in the driveway when I arrived home and marched inside, my feet burning the pavement the entire way. This place had been home to me for the last ten years. So many memories, wonderful dreams. All lies.

Gingerly, I treaded around the inside then the outside of my home, our home, or so I thought. This was some kind of sick joke. I dropped into the recliner in the den and sobbed until the sun went down.

The phone rang. Katie's dealing with her sick boys. Tommy canceled our plans, but it doesn't mean he wouldn't try to call me. I ignored the continuous chimes. If I don't answer soon, he may find the time to show up and check on me.

Then I remembered leaving my card with Sadie. If he knew I went to his house, he will surely try to find me. He'll make up some ridiculous story to tell me.

I needed to pack. I had to leave. I didn't want to face him, but a part of me wanted to slap him hard across the mouth, scream at him, and tell him how badly he hurt me.

The phone's constant ringing gave me a headache, rivaling my heartache, the entire time I packed. Where would I go? A hotel?

Uncle Vince's house? I'm not sure I could listen to him say, "I told you so."

My bags were almost all packed, but I couldn't leave without my office files, Mother's urn, and the paintings she drew that I had framed and placed on the wall in our bedroom. Once I walked out that front door, I wasn't coming back. This I knew.

Chapter 60

AS I ENTERED the garage to find some boxes to stuff my office files in, a flash of headlights beamed through the garage windows, catching my attention. Shoot! I wanted to be gone before he came here looking for me. I ran inside to slip the chain on the front door, then brought the boxes to the office and started pulling folders out of the drawers, dumping them quickly inside in any random order.

Then the banging and hysteria began.

"Angie! Angie, let me in!" He tried kicking in the door. "You came to my house? What the hell were you thinking?"

The tears flowed from my eyes, but I managed to yell through the front door. "I knew something was wrong! I needed some answers. The *truth* for once. Something you've never been able to give me! Go home. I don't want you here! We're finished!"

He continued to beat on the door until I heard his heavy steps walking away. I didn't hear his car engine roar. He hadn't left.

Footsteps outside became louder, followed by an ear-piercing crash. The window that framed the front door was smashed with a large rock from the garden. Shards of glass shattered over the entranceway. He unlocked the chain through the broken glass and stepped inside.

I smelled whiskey the moment he staggered toward me. I wondered when he started drinking again, or if my seeing his real life with Sadie sent him over the edge.

My feet carried me to the bedroom to grab my suitcases and strip the paintings from the wall, but he chased me and slammed the bedroom door behind him. Those gray eyes of his peered at the mess in the room. Hangers lying across the carpet. Some of his clothes lay tossed about the room from when I rummaged through the dressers earlier. He picked up my filled suitcase, opened it up, and dumped out all of my clothes onto the closet floor. He pulled the other suitcase from the corner of the room to do the same.

"Stop it! You can't keep me here! Not anymore. I'm done."

"I'm not letting you go!" He reeked of desperation and Jameson.

I tried to run, but he grabbed my arm and pulled me close to him. "You don't understand what's going on, Angie."

"I can't do this with you anymore. Sadie is pregnant! You told me you weren't sleeping with her! You lied. Damn you!" I pounded on his chest with my free hand. "I can't give you a child. Now you've got one on the way, with her."

His muscular arms held my shoulders and moved me to the bed, forcing me to sit. "I never cared that you can't have a baby, Angie. All I want is you! I don't know if that baby she's carrying is even mine."

"That's ridiculous! Just stop talking! Stop lying! We're never getting married. Never adopting a baby." All of my hopes and dreams were imploding.

"I swear this child may not be mine, but I need to wait until it's born to have a blood test. All these years we've been together, Sadie's had lovers too. I couldn't tell you she was pregnant. I knew that would hurt you."

"Hurt me?" My tears formed a steady stream. "The fact that the baby *could be* yours is just as bad. I asked you outright if you were having sex with her, and you said you weren't! You were supposedly sleeping in another bedroom. I can't go on like this. It's over."

"No, baby, no. It's not over! Don't say that. We are this close." He pinched his pointer finger and thumb together. "This close to having everything! After all these years when we are so close, you can't walk away from me."

"My father meant the world to me. In spite of everything my mother told me, I adored him. You're going to be a father now. You need to be a father to that baby. I'm not going to be the reason that baby doesn't have a father! God, I hate you for this!" The waterworks resumed.

"Don't cry. I love you. I don't love Sadie. I don't want her. I had to *pretend* sometimes, that's all. I couldn't have her take everything in the divorce that's mine. Once I prove this baby isn't mine, I can leave freely."

"Just stop talking. It doesn't matter." I wiggled my body, trying to escape his arms.

"I swear I will make everything right again. We will be okay. I know we can get past this."

He caressed my cheek and tried to dry my tears, but I slapped his hands away hard. His arms grabbed me and pulled me in for a hug. I tried to move from his grasp, but he was far too powerful and much too drunk.

"You are a part of me, and I'm a part of you. Our love is too strong, baby." His lips kissed my neck and shoulder. "I'm so sorry I hurt you. You have to forgive me."

He devoured my mouth. The liquor on his breath made me dizzy. His strong arms secured me to the mattress as he continued to kiss me.

"Your drunk, Tommy."

"I can't let you go. You're my life. I can't live without you. Don't you remember how good we are together?" He took in a deep breath, catching the scent of my hair. "God, you smell so good. You always smell so good."

I tried to speak, but his lips consumed mine. His body moved atop me, and I felt a hand hike up my dress and pull off my panties.

"I love you so much, baby," he kept repeating those words over and over, like a broken record.

I knew I hadn't the strength to fight him, especially while he was drunk. I allowed him to take me. It was easier this way. He would leave soon. No matter how tired, drunk, or high he might have been over the years, he never spent the entire night here in this bedroom. My body felt numb as he pushed his way inside me. I stared at Mother's painting of the Golden Gate Bridge and heard her voice speaking to me. "Make sure you can take care of yourself. Don't ever count on a man to support you. Don't let anyone control you. Your life, your terms."

Had Tommy been controlling me all these years? I never saw it through the intense love we shared, until now.

When he was finished, he held me with such deep, tender affection. "I love you so much. We're going to be okay. You know that, right?"

I nodded, merely to appease him.

He gently tapped my chin then turned my face to meet his penitent, gray eyes. "Tell me you love me, sweetheart."

With a shaky voice, I replied, "Of course I love you, Tommy." Somehow I managed a smile.

"That's my girl." He embraced me tightly. He may have passed out. At least an hour flew by before I felt him move, or that's how long it seemed. He kissed my cheek then my lips. "I'll be back in the morning. I'll take tomorrow off so we can talk. I will tell you the whole story. Everything will be different, I promise." He stared into my eyes with so much love, passion, and tenderness. The same man who obliterated my heart.

This would be the last time he ever touched me. The last time I'd see the man I loved with everything I had. All these years he called me his girl, but I was just his mistress.

Chapter 61

THE CRUNCHING OF the glass pieces from the broken window was what I remember hearing after Tommy left the bed. He fussed with the mess a bit, but he was probably too drunk to clean it up tonight. He shouldn't have been driving in his condition, but I wasn't about to stop him.

My body laid frozen in the bed. When I heard the front door close, my hands and legs trembled. I'm not certain how long it took for me to be able to lift myself up.

The white digits on the clock displayed eleven twenty-seven. Although it was late, I needed help. I couldn't move too quickly, despite my efforts. I had to leave tonight. Somehow, I managed to walk to the kitchen to make a call. A call I dreaded to make. A call he warned me I'd make someday. A call he hoped I'd make. Talking through the tears was not easy.

Uncle Vince always drove a Mercedes, a smooth-sounding car. I didn't hear him park in the driveway. If it weren't for the broken glass he had to step through to enter, I wouldn't have known he arrived. He called my name loudly, but I couldn't respond. I sat upright at the edge of the bed, staring at the clothes from my suitcase spilled all over the floor.

"Angie?"

From the corner of my eye, I noticed the worried expression worn by my uncle as he gazed around the destruction of the bedroom. I was certain he could see the disheveled mess I was, devastated to learn Tommy lied to me for years and impregnated his wife.

"What did he do to you?" He slowly drew near and sat gently beside me. I felt his hand touch my arm with soft, delicate ease before he stood, angry. "Oh my god. Where is he? I'll kill him!"

My head turned. The look on his face scared me. My trembling worsened. "Please don't, Uncle. I just need to leave." My words spoke at a mere whisper.

"Your arms. They're red, bruised. Your dress is torn. Did he rape you? Jesus Christ!"

"Rape? No. I'm okay. He didn't hurt me… physically. I… I want to leave now."

"Let me help you." He propped me up and off the bed, grabbed the blanket from the chair and wrapped it around my shoulders. The warmth of the cozy blanket didn't stop my chills.

"Wait, my mother's urn and her paintings."

"I'll have my men come by here to get your things, sweetheart. Don't worry about it."

"No, I want my mother, her paintings, and the files from my office tonight. I don't care about the clothes." I vaguely recall slipping my engagement ring off my finger and handing it to my uncle.

Chapter 62

November 11, 1980

WHEN MORNING CAME, the pain in my heart deepened. My head throbbed and my eyes ached, red and swollen from a billion tears shed. The bruises on my arms were more pronounced, turning a shade of midnight blue. I found a sweater to pull over me, hiding the marks. I could still feel his hands squeezing me tightly. He was drunk. Yes, that's an excuse. Tommy hadn't consumed a drop of alcohol since April 30, 1973, when we were in Nice, or so I thought. Apparently, he kept many secrets from me.

Sleep was all I wanted to do. A dreamless sleep to avoid the vivid thoughts of all the lies he fed me for so many years.

Sadie was a pretty woman. Very different from me. She stood maybe five feet tall with short blonde waves and blue eyes. Her build was slight for a pregnant woman, small hips and breasts.

How could he live two lives? That's ultimately what he was doing. His job didn't stress him out. His father's illness didn't stress him out. Having two different homes with different women with expectations of him had to be the major stress factor. If only I could sleep straight for the next six months without waking, the pain may lessen.

A soft knock was heard. I didn't want to talk to my uncle or relive last night. The night that ended it all for Tommy and me. The door opened, although I never welcomed anyone inside.

"Angie, are you okay?"

The sweet, soft-spoken voice of my cousin was a welcomed sound. I didn't have to answer her. She sat next to me, handed me a cup of tea, and didn't say a word until I was ready to speak.

"Thank you for coming to see me. How are the boys feeling?"

"They're better today. Louis is on top of it. I'm needed here. Do you want to talk about it?"

I took a sip of tea and collected my dour thoughts. "I left him for good, Katie."

"Did he hurt you? My father said he raped you. God, Angie, why? What happened?"

"He didn't rape me, Katie. I simply pretended everything was okay between us, knowing he would leave much faster than if I fought with him."

"You know you can tell me anything. Obviously, he was physical with you." She lifted the sleeve of my sweater that hid the bruises my uncle must have told her about.

"I met Sadie yesterday."

"His wife? What? How?"

"I knew he was keeping something from me. He'd been distant but would talk about his upcoming divorce." I stood to my feet, felt a bit wobbly then sat back down. "I followed him yesterday. He led me to a big, beautiful home in Henderson. When he left that house, I knocked on the door."

"His house? You actually went to his home? With her?"

I nodded. "Not only did I see her, I spoke with her and noticed she was… pregnant."

Katie said nothing. Her hand covered her mouth in surprise. Not as surprised as I was.

"I didn't tell her who I was, well, not to Tommy anyway. I made up a bullshit story about real estate and asked about her home." I paused to catch my breath. "He's not leaving her, Katie. He probably never planned to. They're having a child. He can't leave the baby. I told him it was over and we argued. He held onto me tightly because he didn't want me to leave. He wanted to prove his love to me. He started drinking again. Yes, he was out of control, but he didn't rape me, Katie."

I sucked in a few deep breaths and squeezed my fingers, an attempt to free my hands from the incessant shaking. "Sadie is giving him something I never could, a child. He was still sleeping with her, and now she's pregnant. I feel like such a fool!

"Last night I merely pacified him. But I'm not okay with this situation. I need to stay away from Tommy. He has a family now. I won't interfere with that. I'm waiting for him to show up here looking for me, causing a scene, or convincing me we can still be together."

"My father won't allow that."

"I'm worried about that. Last night he threatened to kill him."

"He was very upset. Called me first thing this morning to tell me about it. He's worried about you, and so am I."

Tears began to flow. "The bruises are nothing compared to my broken heart." My head found its way to her shoulder.

"Your heart will heal, Angie. I promise it will."

Chapter 63

January 5, 1981

GETTING THROUGH THE holidays was tough. I was used to Christmas without Tommy, but New Year's was our holiday. Our special time together. I turned twenty-eight years old, and for the first time in ten years, he wasn't there to celebrate with me or surprise me with something special. I never cared about the gifts. It was him I wanted. I just wanted him to myself in our Paris loft. The pain was as piercing as a dagger through the heart.

Did he make amends with Sadie? Did he touch her the way he touched me? Did he love her even when he told me he didn't? He hadn't called or dropped by, demanding to see me, which surprised me. A part of me wants to see him, but I know it's not possible. I won't keep him from his child. I thought recovering from a cocaine addiction was hard. The withdrawal symptoms I had for Tommy were more severe.

This afternoon, Katie called me sounding anxious. She wouldn't speak to me unless my uncle wasn't in the room. To prevent him from eavesdropping, I called Katie back from the phone in the study behind a locked door.

"What is it, Katie?"

She spoke fast and furiously. "Tommy was here, at my house."

I couldn't answer right away.

"Angie? Angie, did you hear me?"

"What did he want?"

"You, of course. He wanted to make sure you were okay. I told him he needed to leave, and you didn't want to see him."

"Did he leave?"

"Not right away. He gave me those puppy dog eyes, filled with sorrow." Her voice was rattled.

"I'm sorry to put you in the middle of this, Katie. Was Louis home?"

"No, Louis was at the office. I asked Tommy about the rape."

"Katie, stop saying that! He was drunk and out of control. Why would you say that to him?"

"He said he never meant to hurt you, but he's not going to give up trying to make it up to you and win you back. I asked him if he was divorced yet. That was when he left."

"He's not going to let me go, is he?"

"He came right out and said that, Angie. It's only a matter of time before he shows up at your job or follows you somewhere and…"

"Stop, Katie. He won't hurt me physically. But it doesn't mean I should see him. It won't be good for me. At least not right now. I won't take him from his family. It's too late for us to make it work. I've been thinking about relocating."

"Leave Las Vegas?"

"Yes. I'm in the realty business, right? I've been looking at different locations, not terribly far from here, but outside Nevada. It would be best if I left town. At least for a while."

Chapter 64

February 26, 1981

I COULDN'T ALLOW Tommy to harass my family; and it wouldn't be good for me to see him. I needed to be far away from Tommy and his world. I'm a grown woman with skills and money to make a fresh start. This type of life change would be key to healing from a broken heart.

Jerry was very understanding when I gave my notice.

Apparently, Katie was right. Tommy contacted the office several times, leaving messages for me. I didn't read them.

Jerry hired a receptionist named Gail. She was a young, attractive girl, as innocent as I was at her age. Gail told me I was an inspiration to her. She planned to take courses in real estate and work toward her license. What a wonderful feeling to know that my career aspirations inspired another young lady. Gail had no idea how much strength her words gave me at a time when I needed to hear them.

Since my career successfully launched, Jerry hired three other licensed, female realtors at his office.

In order for me to find a comparable job, Jerry wrote a letter of recommendation. He went as far as to tell me that with my talent, knowledge, and business degree, I could potentially have my own agency someday. A huge part of me didn't want to leave this job. I admired Jerry so much. He took a chance on me, an inexperienced female, newly licensed in an office dominated by men. He took me under his wing to show me the ropes then gave me hope to run my own company. He's quite a businessman and friend.

I needed to select a location not too far from my family and a warm climate. If I wanted a job in the real estate market, I needed to find an agency in a state in which I can easily obtain a license if I didn't already have one.

While I was looking at a variety of options, Uncle Vince made the suggestion to have my last name changed. That suggestion came as a surprise. He didn't want me to leave, but I couldn't continue living in his home. I'm twenty-eight and can manage on my own. He was concerned for my well-being, and he believed Tommy would find me no matter where I went.

Changing my last name would make it more difficult for him to locate me. My uncle had connections to have my name changed quickly and quietly. No guarantee Tommy wouldn't find me, but Uncle Vince felt better. Still, I didn't think Tommy would hurt me physically. I just didn't want to give into his excuses and declarations of love. My heart still ached for him. I knew I couldn't trust him after all of the lies he fed me for many years, but he had this ability to melt my heart and brush away any disappointment felt within. Seeing him was not possible right now.

Driving out of state for interviews required a car. Uncle Vince helped me purchase a 1980 Toyota Corolla. It was a small, black, sporty-looking vehicle with a hatchback. I'm used to driving American cars, but I liked this Toyota. It had a lot of get up and go! As long as it was reliable to get me where I needed to be, I was happy.

I had a couple of interviews in Arizona and Los Angeles that didn't pan out. A small agency in San Diego agreed to meet with me. The drive was under six hours if I wasn't stuck in LA traffic. I was offered the job on the spot.

A woman named Tammy was the only female currently working as an agent. She seemed nice and welcoming. Maybe she liked the idea of another female in the office, less testosterone.

San Diego would become home.

Within a few weeks, I found an adorable cottage not far from the beach with a small piece of land, which was perfect for me. I never had a green thumb and don't care for yardwork. San Diego was a lovely place with upscale homes, businesses, and many activities. I especially liked the fact that my family was a day's drive or a quick flight away if I wanted to visit them.

Katie and I spoke regularly, and the boys would grab the phone from her to say hello. They would tell me about school or sports. Mostly sports. Sometimes tears were released after speaking with them, missing them all. However, I encouraged Katie to visit me any-time. I had three bedrooms, enough space if she, Louis, and the kids visited. They would love the beach and the numerous activities in the area. The San Diego Zoo and Sea World were a stone's throw away. Disney Land wasn't terribly far from my new home. How I wished she would bring the boys to visit me and experience all the sights San Diego was famous for. She wanted to come as soon as Louis would be able to take some time off.

My new last name is Petrillo. According to Uncle Vince, it was his grandmother's maiden name. Technically, I am a Petrillo a few generations removed. A new name, a new life!

Life after Tommy

Chapter 65

1981: New Job, New Friends

I SOLD MY first house after a few weeks to a couple who were about my age, Mitch and Gwendolyn Bonner. They had been married for three years and lived in a small house in the area. They decided it was time to start a family and upgrade.

Gwen had a very domineering personality. The fact that she was so strong and stood at least five feet, ten inches tall without heels, intimidated some women and men. Her hair was long and curly, blonde with a touch of red easily spotted in the sunlight. Something about her presence drew me in. She was popular in town and involved with numerous organizations and charities. When she heard I was new to California, Gwen insisted she and Mitch show me around and introduce me to their friends. They were a part of an interesting circle with mixed backgrounds, careers, and political views. Gwen was someone to admire. She managed a pediatrician's office in town, skilled in accounting principles.

Mitch was more docile to Gwen's dominating personality. They paired well together. He had to be six feet tall with an inch added, thanks to his mullet hairstyle with a mass of neat, brown curls at the top. If Gwen wore heels, she seemed to tower over him, but her strong character had a lot to do with that as well. His eyes were a piercing blue, bright and brilliant, with a strong chin and chiseled features. A very handsome man, he was. Certainly they would have gorgeous children someday, and I envied them.

California appeared to be a more liberal state with a higher chance of equal rights for women, minorities, and the gay and lesbian population. I finally found people who shared my political views. Society's beliefs were changing some.

For so long, my only girlfriend was my cousin. My only other friend was Tommy's brother, John, who I thought about a lot. I thought about both Cavallo brothers often. Life without Tommy was a challenge, but the change of scenery, a new job, and new friends helped me battle that addiction.

Most people in Gwen's circle were married couples. I'm not sure why she felt the need to find me a man. Was I really ready for that? It was too soon to tell. However, when a single man would show up at a charity event, church function, or a dinner party, it was clear my new friend, Gwen, wanted me to have a mate. She'd throw me a wink anytime she introduced me to someone new. I went on a few dates, but no one interested me too much. Not enough to have a second or third date.

It took time for me to explain my relationship with Tommy to Gwen. Naturally, I left out the parts about being Tommy's mistress and the way our love affair came to an explosive end. The Bonners were rather straight-laced, so discussing 1973 and my craving for cocaine was out of the question. I was allowed to have some secrets no matter how good of friends we became.

Before they planned to have a child, the couple discussed taking a long vacation somewhere remarkable. They were entranced by my stories of the Caribbean and Europe. They had no idea I traveled extensively.

Paris, of course, was always my favorite place with the most meaning. I shed a tear, thinking about how much Tommy and I loved each other, and our amazing time in our loft with the view of the Eiffel Tower. Suddenly, I realized I was speaking out loud in front of them. Gwen finally understood I may not have been over my last love, and she was right. She took a break from the endless parade of men for me to meet.

Chapter 66

March 7, 1982

OUT OF THE blue on a rainy day in March, Katie called to announce her visit with the three boys. Louis was unable to join them, but she missed me, and God knows I missed her and those three little guys. They were growing up so fast. I planned the whole weekend, starting with a trip to the zoo and the beach, weather permitting. If the beach wasn't an option, we'd take a drive to Sea World. I don't have much vacation time to bring them to Disney Land, but maybe the following year, assuming they would return for another visit, and have more time to schedule a trip.

Her visit came at the perfect time. Tommy's birthday was a few days away so memories were clinging. I often wondered about his baby. Was it a boy or girl? Did he and Sadie stay together? Did he still think about me? Had he tried to find me?

Pop's obituary was in the paper before Christmas of 1980. I'm sure his death was hard on Tommy. He lost all of his family now. I knew exactly what that felt like.

When Katie and the kids arrived at my cottage, I anxiously raced outside with anticipation to greet them. The trunk of her car was filled with suitcases and large trash bags stuffed to the brim, I noticed. A lot of hugs and kisses were exchanged. The boys teased me so much for being emotional. I didn't ask Katie why all the loot was with her.

The tour began outside the house. There was a swimming pool the kids could use as long as they were supervised, I warned them all. The beach could be seen from the backyard in between the palm trees, and I promised if they behaved, we could go.

The kids were already comfortable in my home, helping themselves to canned soda in the refrigerator. I loved that! Katie tried to explain how rude they were, but I reminded them they are family, and in my house they can help themselves to food and drinks if their mother approved.

I prepared the bedrooms and bathrooms with fresh linens. One guest bedroom had a king-size bed, which would be the room for Katie and Louis if he were able to visit. The third bedroom had two twin beds. I hoped Louie and David could share one or I could pull out the sofabed in the den, but I didn't think it was very comfortable. Katie thought David should sleep in her bed with her and to let the older boys have their own room. Surprisingly, there were no arguments about the sleeping arrangements. David thought the king-size bed was enormous. However, I decided to add another bed in their room or buy bunk beds for the next time they visited.

Michael wanted to play Atari. He set the game system up to the television in the living room with his brothers following behind, already pleading for a turn. I fixed the coffee pot with some grounds, grabbed two mugs from the cabinet, and sat on the kitchen bench beside my sweet cousin.

"What's wrong? I could tell the moment I saw you outside something was off."

She smiled on the right side of her mouth, a telltale that she had something on her mind. "Louis and I have been having some… problems." She turned her head to make sure the boys were occupied in the other room before continuing. "I think there's another woman."

"What? Louis? Katie, I don't think so."

"Angie, a wife knows these things."

"What things?"

"It's the little things. He doesn't call me every day from the office to talk to me or the kids. When he's home, he's distant, like he's not there. I try to have conversations about his day, and he doesn't want to talk to me. He just stopped talking."

"What about…" I paused before asking such a personal question. The boys were yelling about *Pong* in the other room. "Your love life?" I whispered.

"Huh, what's that? He hasn't touched me in months. When I bring it up, he makes excuses about being tired or stressed at work. I think there's a woman at the office. I'm not sure who, but it's an instinct."

I squeezed her hand, unsure what to say. Did Sadie feel this way? Were her instincts screaming that Tommy was cheating on her? He lied to me, telling me he slept in a separate room. As awful and hurt as Katie is now because of another woman, I was that other woman in between Tommy and Sadie's marriage.

Chapter 67

March 13, 1982

KATIE AND THE kids spent the week with me. Although I had a job to do, coming home to sheer madness and kids fighting was a remedy for feeling homesick. That sounds strange, I know.

Louis called several times to talk to the boys and me. Katie refused to speak to him. I was the "middle man," so to speak. I never accused Louis of anything, but I subtly let him know he had a beautiful family, and he should try to put it back together and get his priorities straight.

A part of me thought I had no right to intervene after my affair. But this was Katie's life, and her heart was breaking. She may not have been in love with Louis when they married, but she grew to love him. They built a life together.

The boys would need to get back to school. Katie couldn't keep them out of school much longer. As much as she was welcomed here, she had some decisions to make. Was she going to leave Louis? Take the boys far away from him or remain in the Las Vegas area? I offered to help her find a home should she decide to leave him. That's my job, after all. Although I hoped they would reconcile.

It was Saturday, and the kids were eager for a day at the beach. I picked up sand pails, shovels, and a beach ball to take with us. The boys raced outside in front of me when we noticed a red Cadillac had parked in front of my house.

The boys started yelling, "Daddy's here!" They were elated to see their father after a week.

Louis surprised us all, driving five or six hours to meet up with his family.

I glanced at Katie, unable to tell if she was happy, nervous, or both.

After high-fiving with his sons, he cautiously crept toward Katie. It seemed like such a private, intimate moment. I felt my cheeks blush, watching their somber eyes meet. I scurried the kids along for the walk to the beach and confirmed with Katie it was okay to take the boys without her. She agreed, although David wanted both his mommy and daddy to go to the beach with us.

We spent about two hours soaking up the sun. I wanted to be sure to give Katie and Louis some time alone and hopefully work things out. Maybe Katie was wrong about him having an affair. I hoped she was wrong.

The boys and I scooped up sand and added water in an attempt to make a castle. Naturally, they all ganged up on me about my inability to build a cool castle. These boys loved to tease me. They tortured me with their taunting.

David agreed to lay down in the smooth sand as his brothers buried his feet and legs. The beach was a little crowded to throw the ball around, so they jumped into the water, splashing relentlessly. Keeping my eyes on three active boys made me very nervous.

I decided it was time for ice cream. Even though it was before dinner and their parents may not have approved, I was overwhelmed watching them all by myself along the serene stretch of ocean that seemed to extend for miles. The calm waters turned to larger waves that crashed frantically against the rocks. A distraction from the suddenly turbulent sea was needed to ease my troubled mind.

The soft-serve ice cream shop was a short walk from the beach. David didn't want to hold my hand because he's three and a half and too big for hand-holding, according to him. I pretended to wobble and nearly fall down. I told him I'm getting too old for all of this walking, and asked for his help. He gladly took my hand, slightly annoyed, but said he wouldn't let me fall.

As we stood in line, waiting our turn for ice cream, the boys argued over which flavor was the best. They love to dispute about everything!

The sugary smell of the candy, ice cream, and toppings wound these kids up before we were served. I'm not sure how Katie does this all day long, separating them from fighting and kicking. As I attempted to gain control of the arguing, I spun around and felt an ice-cold, wet, sticky mass smear across my breasts.

"Oh, I'm terribly sorry," a man with a British accent said after colliding with my breasts, ice cream cone first.

The boys' fighting ceased.

White globs of very cold vanilla ice cream once dipped in a layer of cherry-coated, candy goodness, spread across my chest. I lifted my head and met eyes with a familiar face.

"Angie? Angie Petrillo."

Doug Speers, one of the many floats in the Bonner parade Gwen set me up with a year ago. I wasn't entirely interested in anyone at that time, and Doug started to date another woman, or so I was told.

He reached for extra napkins from the counter and handed them to me to wipe up the mess, considering most of it landed near the cleavage of my bikini top.

"I am really sorry. I should've watched where I was going," he said.

"Well, I stood in your way, distracted by my cousins."

"Hey guys! I'm going to buy you whatever ice cream you want today." He glanced at me. "It's the least I can do to make up for you wearing mine."

We all laughed at my expense. Doug ordered the ice cream, and we sat at a table together outside. The bees were drawn to me, sensing the sweet sugar that melted against my skin in the warm sun. I wanted to use the restroom to wash this up better but didn't want to leave the boys alone with Doug since I didn't know him very well.

Doug and I went out to dinner once, but that was it. I thought he was a very nice man, smart, ambitious, and very good-looking. I liked the British accent too. Tommy was still in my heart and mind then. I never gave Doug a second thought after our date.

He was really good with Michael, Louie, and David for a single man with no children. He explained he had many nieces and nephews. He's the youngest of seven kids. We talked more today than I remembered on our first date. He had a firm, stocky build and a thick neck. His brown hair was short, clean cut, and parted on the side. Very professional-looking, even in a bathing suit and t-shirt. He loved to talk, and I enjoyed his stories.

Something about him made me think of him differently from when I first met him. Maybe he wasn't different at all. Maybe I was different.

I glanced at my watch. We had been gone for nearly four hours. Katie would wonder what happened to us.

"Thank you for the ice cream, Doug. Boys, what do you say to Doug?"

"Thank you, Doug," they said in stereo.

"It was my pleasure." He moved in closer. "I had a nice time catching up with you, Angie. Do you think we could get together again?"

I sent him a smile. "Yes, I'd like that." Using a crumbled napkin on the table and borrowing a pen from the cashier, I jotted down my phone number and handed it to him before taking the boys home.

When we arrived at my house, suitcases were packed and sitting outside in the driveway. A good sign that Katie decided to go home with her husband. Nice move on Louis's part, coming here and reclaiming his family.

As the boys and I raced inside, I grinned, knowing they worked things out, judging by the smiles they wore. As happy as I was for them, this meant they were leaving. Saying goodbye was tough.

Chapter 68

The Summer of 1982

DOUG AND I spent countless hours together. Getting to know him was fun, unlike the first time we met and had dinner due to Gwen's scheming. I explained to him about my long-term relationship that ended very badly, and at that time, dating was not something I was ready for. He hadn't had luck in the dating department either. He is next in line at his company for a vice-president position. His professional goals and motivation were quite impressive.

Once we spent time getting to know each other, my attraction to Doug grew fast. The major plus to the situation was the fact that he was single. Naturally, confirming that fact was simple with a friend like Gwen. She knew everyone in the church circuit, town committees, the library, and she managed a doctor's office.

I was falling for Doug. It had been so long since I wanted a man to kiss me, touch me, or make love to me. Close to two years passed since I had been with Tommy, the only man who ever knew my body and how to play it. There was no comparing Doug to Tommy in any aspect of a relationship. Completely different men in so many ways.

Somehow being with Doug for the first time didn't make me nervous. We developed a good friendship. His touch was gentle and sweet. His kisses took my breath away, leaving me gasping for air. A thirst for passion. A hunger to be fulfilled. Desire prevailed, wanting to explore every inch of his body from his delectable lips to the tips of his toes. Without haste, he discovered every pleasure point, sending me soaring to unimaginable heights. Our bodies played as one rhythmic symphony in perfect harmony.

And he spent the entire night in my bed at my house. The whole night.

My love life was successful and so was business. Gwen and Mitch helped, sharing my business cards with friends and colleagues. I was busy and making a very nice salary. Doug was succeeding further in his career, cinching his short-term goal of becoming a vice-president soon.

Chapter 69

September 1982

TAMMY AND I bonded nicely at the office, and once in a while, we would meet for lunch or catch a movie if we were both available. As much as our friendship grew, she was a bit competitive at the office, not necessarily to gain a client, but rivaling for the attention of our male colleagues at the agency.

The business expanded, and more men and women were hired. Tammy and I were two attractive women. The only single women in the office besides the young girl, the boss's daughter, who answered the phone. She knew I had a boyfriend, yet she went out of her way to let me know which mark was hers to find herself a husband. I had no intention of vying for any of the men at the office.

She went as far as sleeping with Charlie, who was married. Without sharing my history with her, I advised her against that. Not only does she have to work with him, he may not leave his wife for her. I tried to warn her, but she assumed I wanted him for myself and upped the ante. Needless to say, we remained friendly colleagues, but I never spent time with her outside of office hours again. Once Charlie sampled her wares, he ignored her as if she didn't exist.

Her reputation swelled, the men didn't take her very seriously, and the women could barely tolerate her shameless, flirtatious antics. She became a fun girl to hang out with in lieu of an intelligent, capable team member. I believed she resented me further because I earned their respect.

By the end of the year, she left the company. No one was sure if she quit or if she was fired.

Chapter 70

October 25, 1982

GWEN AND MITCH welcomed a beautiful baby girl into the world. They named her Lindsey. I must say I had fun shopping for items of pink, dresses, bonnets, and ribbons. It was a very different experience, shopping for a girl after having three boys to buy clothes and toys for.

Gwen's brother, Steven, and his wife, Dorothy, attended the christening. Steve was Gwen's older brother and godfather to Lindsey. Surprisingly enough, he looked absolutely nothing like Gwen. They were complete opposites. Steve was maybe a half-inch taller than Gwen's five feet, ten inches. His hair was blacker than mine and he had steely, sharp green eyes.

I mentioned the difference in their looks to Gwen, and she smirked before explaining to me that they had different fathers. Steve's father disappeared on their mother when she told him she was pregnant. She was a single mom for a short time until she met Gwen's father, Walter Morgan. He married their mother, Delia, and adopted Steve. They don't speak about it though. Steve never knew his biological father. He only knew of one father, the one they shared.

Instantly, I thought about young Michael. Would he ever know Louis was not his biological father? Did it matter? Louis adores Michael and treats him no differently than Louie or David.

Adoption was something I always considered. I would love a child if he or she wasn't from my own flesh and blood. Naturally, I don't have a choice in that respect.

Although my relationship with Doug was very new, I started researching the adoption process, making phone calls to local agencies in California. I created a list of questions to ask. I was overwhelmed with the intense details and the long waiting list of eager couples wanting to adopt an infant.

Chapter 71

September 1983

GWEN'S BROTHER AND Dorothy, who I learned to call Dot, moved from Santa Barbara to San Diego. The move allowed Steve to be closer to family as well as a job opportunity as a stock broker. His educational background is in finance. I knew nothing of what a stock broker consisted of, except he must be good with numbers and skilled with schmoozing people since they had to trust him to invest their money. In some cases, their entire life savings were at risk.

Dot was a nurse who managed to transfer to Sharp Memorial. Her family lived in Long Beach, so the distance wasn't too far. They had an infant daughter, Alicia, and planned to build their family with other children in the near future.

Doug and I spent a lot of time with Gwen and Mitch and Steve and Dot. The six of us had plans every Friday night to meet for dinner and cocktails. No cocktails for me, though I never explained why. Doug eventually asked. It was time to be honest with him about some of my past.

Needless to say, he was surprised that I tried drugs at all, never mind used them extensively for a brief period of my life. I had some concerns he thought less of me. I didn't want to overshare much more, but when he asked me what made me start to use drugs, I took the honest approach again.

The look on his face said a lot. I told him the whole story about my hospital visit, which led to a devastating diagnosis that prevented me from having children. As much as I tried to fight the tears when

I shared my story, I couldn't hold back. When could I ever hold back a cry, whether it were a good cry or a bad cry?

"Oh," was his only response.

He sat back on the sofa and remained silent, staring at the television. The eleven o'clock news was reporting more information about a new virus, AIDS, infecting thousands of people already in the United States, mostly the gay population.

He didn't say much else to me the entire night. Doug hadn't been married yet. He had no children, but loved his nieces and nephews.

I didn't push for a conversation about my infertility issues right away. Maybe he needed time to absorb this information. A detail about me that made me feel defective.

By the time Sunday night rolled around, I had to bring it up. He wasn't distant toward me the rest of the weekend, but he didn't appear to be his goofy, fun self either.

"Can we talk about the other night?" I asked while he was staring inside the refrigerator, searching for a snack.

"What about the other night?"

"I gave you some pretty powerful information about me. You've been so quiet about it. I'm sure it was a blow for you to hear that my getting pregnant may be next to impossible."

"You know, there may be medical advances now to treat the problem, don't you think?"

"Maybe." I didn't want to entirely crush him. Of course I had more tests done since my diagnosis. My doctor advised me I'd need a hysterectomy at some point. I was too young for that procedure right now, and my situation wasn't dire enough to warrant a surgery that would finalize my inability to conceive.

"Why don't we look for a specialist to talk to?"

"Doug, stop." I didn't mean for my hands to slam on the counter. "Even if there is a glimmer of hope, it's very possible I can't get pregnant. What does that mean for us? Our future? How important is this to you?"

He blew out a deep breath. "I don't know. But I love you, Angie. If there is any possibility that we could be married someday and start a family, we should look into it."

Chapter 72

November 2, 1984

I'D BEEN THINKING about my mother recently. When Doug isn't around, I talk to the urn, her current burial plot, or stare at her paintings on my bedroom wall. I talk to Daddy and Connie too. I sensed their presence often, not to sound too creepy. Somehow I feel at peace. Whether or not they can hear me, I'll never know for sure. However, I like the idea of believing their spirits are with me in this world.

Anytime I felt lonely, I'd call my uncle or Katie.

Uncle Vince really liked Doug. I suppose any single man would gain his approval after I left Tommy. Katie, Louis and the boys visited frequently and had the pleasure of getting to know Doug very well. They were glad I found a decent man who made me happy. However, I wasn't entirely sure where our relationship stood. We're not married and never discussed marriage until I brought up infertility.

I had the pleasure over the last year to meet Doug's parents in England and some of his siblings, nieces, and nephews. We flew overseas to York, a region in England I never visited.

York is a lovely town deeply absorbed in the medieval spirit. The area is surrounded by a thick stone wall acting as a fortress that once protected the charming city from its enemies. York is rich with history, enchanting stories, and numerous activities that kept us busy every day throughout our visit.

Doug's sisters and parents joined us for a walk through the Shambles, a popular tourist attraction with enchanting shops to browse through. Its antiquated, cobblestone paths twist and bend exposing its medieval flair.

On a separate day, Doug's father, his brother, Bill, and his family of six, joined us for a boat ride along the lovely River Ouse with extraordinary scenery to drink in.

York Minster was an important monument to visit on this trip. This gothic cathedral stood proudly despite a horrible rooftop fire set ablaze by a fierce bolt of lightning this past summer. Fortunately, only a portion of the church suffered, including some slight impacts to the famous organ, instigating heartache amongst parishioners.

Doug inherits his handsome features from his father, except that luminous smile he wears so well. That delightful trait is surely from his mum. I wasn't surprised to witness first-hand that the Speers family is very close-knit. Doug and I barely spent a moment alone together on this trip. I could see how much he missed them all, and why having children of his own may be important to him someday.

His family are lovely people, anxious to see Doug settle down, hoping he'd return to his homeland. I must say, that bothered me a little. I couldn't imagine leaving the United States and starting a new life in another country. It's challenging enough for me to live six hours from my family. To be in a different country and time zone wouldn't be ideal for me.

Chapter 73

August 1, 1985

A NEW BABY was born into my San Diego family. Gwen and Mitch had a son, Christopher. The family was growing because Steve and Dot were expecting another baby in January. Being around all of these little ones was fulfilling for me. I adored them. However, Doug felt left out.

Sometimes he didn't want to visit with them and look at baby pictures or hear baby stories. He wouldn't discuss it with me, but it bothered him, spending time with our friends who were devoted parents, a pivotal part of life we wouldn't experience if we stayed together.

I suggested we consider adoption if we ever married. We both had the finances to adopt a baby. So many children are in need of a good home with loving parents.

He shrugged at the thought.

A phone call to social services was in order. So many young children were in need of temporary foster homes or permanent homes with loving parents. Without discussing this with Doug first, I met with Mr. Vickers, a representative of the state organization in Los Angeles. Hundreds of children were in the foster care system. Listening to some of their stories broke my heart. Some children were born with a drug addiction or a disability. Others were abandoned or taken from abusive homes. There was so much to consider.

After my meeting with Mr. Vickers, I sat Doug down and shared the pamphlets and details I learned. At first, I couldn't tell if he was surprised or angry with me.

"Why would you do something like this without consulting me?"

"I wanted to look into this option and understand it before we talked about it."

"Angie, I know you want to be a mother someday, but some of these children really need help. More help than two working parents could give them. Would you give up your career?"

"Doug, if we were able to have children of our own, that question would come up too. It has nothing to do with fostering a child versus having one of our own."

He smiled at me, but I could tell this wasn't the solution he wanted. I started to doubt if the love and feelings we had for each other for the last three years would be enough.

Chapter 74

September 10, 1985

DOUG WAS OFFERED the vice-president of operations position at his company. This was a major stepping stone. A job that could lead to his dream of becoming president or CEO someday. When he shared the news with me, his eyes were heavy, no smile to be seen.

"What is it? I thought you'd be thrilled. You've wanted this for so long."

"Yeah, I have waited a long time for this, love."

"Talk to me," I urged, approaching closer, sliding my fingers between the buttons of his blue dress shirt.

"Bloody hell! The job is in York." His eyes gazed upon mine, waiting for my reaction.

"England? You're leaving?" I was too surprised to cry or feel anger.

"I didn't give them an answer yet. I have the weekend to think about it, but I have to let them know on Monday."

I felt my insides twist and turn. "Oh. Wow. I know you want this job, Doug."

"You can come with me, you know."

My eyes caught his. The offer was sincere, but I just stared at him, dumfounded.

"You don't have to make a decision at this moment. I mean, England needs good real estate agents too." He showed a hint of a smile then pulled me into his chest. He held me so tight, I could barely breathe.

He guided me to the bedroom, lifted me up, and placed my body atop the black and white quilt on the bed. I watched as he removed his clothing then lay beside me, kissing my lips while his fingers unbuttoned my blouse. He loved me so slowly and tenderly that night, our bodies glued together, completely connected and entwined, not wanting to let go.

Chapter 75

October 17, 1985

DOUG AND I had one month left together, and we were insep-arable. The small amount of time remaining seemed to make the upcoming break up harder. He refused to call it a break up, but ultimately that's what it was. I hated to lose Doug, but understood he needed to do this. This was his dream. I turned down his offer to join him in England. My mother's voice screamed through my muddled mind, chanting *take care of yourself* and *live your life on your own terms*. Moving to England on a permanent basis was not in my future.

Saying *so long* to Doug was grim. Taking him to the airport would have been heart-wrenching. He refused to say the word *good-bye*. Thought we'd keep in touch and maybe get together soon. I couldn't commit to that. Seeing a man I loved once or twice a year would not make for a realistic relationship. The agony of saying goodbye again would be painfully redundant. I'd feel like a mistress again, seeing him only on his terms and when our careers allowed us to be together. Of course, if the gig in York didn't work out for him, I hoped he'd come back to San Diego and to me.

There was an emptiness within my heart. My love for Doug was very different from the wild, passionate love I had for Tommy. The pain was there, but somehow less severe. I didn't feel broken, just sad. Very sad.

My dear friends let me sob to them. Katie was my first phone call. Gwen lent me her shoulder. She and Dot tried to keep me busy on the weekends to keep my mind on other things. Thank God for good friends and my family.

Chapter 76

November 27, 1985

THE NIGHT BEFORE Thanksgiving, I laid in my big, empty bed, staring at my mother's painting of the Golden Gate Bridge. I decided it was time to put Mother to rest.

That weekend after Thanksgiving, I hopped on a plane, taking a brief flight to San Francisco, where Mother was born and lived out her childhood. I carried a backpack with Mother's ashes in a sealed bag. I couldn't very well carry an urn on the airplane. Imagine the looks I'd receive!

I booked a room at a quaint inn and rented a mid-size car to drive around this amazing city, bursting with culture and dramatic history. It had been many years since I visited. Grandma and Grandpa Barbuto both died young from heart attacks. They smoked like chimneys before significant, clinical evidence linked smoking to conditions like heart disease, stroke, and cancer.

The Buick I rented sat parked in a lot not far from the Golden Gate Bridge. Listening to Journey's *Escape* cassette, "Don't Stop Believin'" played as I waited for nightfall when the bridge would light up with the moon in the background, just like Mother's painting. I carried Mother's ashes with me over the bridge, nearly to the half way point. It was such a long walk. I'd forgotten how long this bridge was. I said a prayer and wished her peace before releasing her ashes to the dark, deep water below.

One more Hail Mary was said before my eyes wandered to the eerie structure of Alcatraz in the distance. The evening was foggy and cool, casting a shadowy haze over the island, adding mystery to its chilling character. A cool sensation suddenly dashed through me, snapping me back to my purpose of bringing the feeling of serenity to my mother and our relationship.

Tommy came to mind. He pushed me to see Mother. If he hadn't brought it up and found her for me, I would have never made peace with her. For that, I'm grateful.

Chapter 77

March 23, 1986

I REQUESTED VACATION time and drove to Las Vegas. Easter Sunday was the following weekend.

Uncle Vince had been diagnosed with lung cancer recently. The disease was caught early enough so his prognosis was good if he listened to his doctor and followed instructions. My uncle was used to giving orders, not following them. His treatment began, and a nurse would visit daily to check on him. He told me on the phone he was just fine, but I needed to see him in person. I wanted to ensure he had all of the necessary conveniences and comforts to survive chemotherapy; and tell him how much I loved him.

Of course, Katie was ready to pitch in and help as needed. She was always there for her father. She started hairdressing school, a profession she always wanted to launch, but hadn't accomplished. Becoming a mother at a young age changed her life path, but she appeared to be reinventing herself. I was happy she chose to do something that pleased her instead of everyone else. Katie always put her kids, husband, and parents before her own personal needs.

Anytime I returned to Vegas to visit the family, I thought about Tommy. If I drove down the Strip, I wondered if I'd see him. What was he doing? How was the baby, who'd be about five years old now? I avoided our usual haunts. In my current condition, still hurting from losing Doug, being face to face with Tommy again could be dangerous. Had I forgiven him for all of his lies? No. But I knew he loved me. If he were honest with me back then about not divorcing Sadie, I would have left him sooner. He had to know that. Again, I continued to make excuses for him. He's probably moved on with his life now anyway.

Chapter 78

Good Friday, March 28, 1986

KATIE RAN TO the grocery store to buy the items needed for Easter pies. We planned to make pizzagaina, a rice pie, and a chocolate cream pie for the boys. Louis had to go to the office to prepare for a big meeting on Monday. I agreed to stay with Michael, Louie, and David while my uncle rested. Lately, fatigue would set in quickly for him.

The boys were playing a *Mario Brothers* game, and I was checking the pantry to ensure we had everything we needed for a traditional Easter Sunday dinner with ham and all the trimmings. Maybe I'd make lasagna too.

The doorbell rang. The boys were too involved with their video game to hear the chime, so I walked to the entrance and opened the door to see three men in suits flashing identification my way.

"Good morning, ma'am. We're looking for Angela Russo, aka Angela Petrillo."

I hesitated to answer, unsure what this was about. "That's me."

The tall man standing in front of the others spoke. "We're agents Griffiths, Hudson, and Murdoch with the FBI. We'd like to ask you some questions. Please come with us."

Michael overheard these men talking and approached the door, standing beside me. He was taller than me now at almost fifteen years old. His arms folded, prepared to protect me.

"What is this about?" I asked.

The agents glanced at Michael and didn't respond.

"Michael, would you please keep an eye on your brothers while I speak to these men?"

He rolled his eyes, unhappy that I sent him away, but he listened to me.

"We need to talk to you about a former client of yours, Thomas Cavallo."

Hearing Tommy's name sparked a fire within me. "Tommy? Well, he's not a client of mine at this time."

"We have some questions about your friendship with him."

"I don't understand."

"Please, ma'am, we need you to come with us now," an agent firmly demanded in a polite manner.

"Would you give me a moment, please?" I didn't want to upset my uncle while he was resting. I scurried into the living room.

Michael and Louie were eavesdropping. David was still playing the video game, completely oblivious to my frazzled state.

I looked at the two older boys. "Michael, let your mother know what happened when she returns, and please call your dad at the office immediately. Surely, he could uncover what this is about and why they need to question me."

"I remember Tommy. What did he do?" Louie asked.

"I'm not sure, sweetie, but it looks like I'm going to find out."

Chapter 79

THE FBI AGENTS drove me across town to an old building that looked like an abandoned warehouse. I was nervous. These men showed me their identification, but I wouldn't know if their documents were real or fake. There was a lot of activity inside the building. Relieved to see other people in uniform, offices, file cabinets, telephones, and a couple of computers, my trembling subsided a bit.

Agent Hudson offered me a glass of water or a Pepsi as he escorted me into a room and held out a folding metal chair for me. I refused the beverage, and he left the room, closing the door behind him. Almost twenty minutes passed before the three men returned. Agent Griffiths seemed to be in charge, and started drilling me with questions in an unbelievably pleasant manner.

"Ms. Russo, or do you prefer Petrillo?"

"Petrillo is my name."

"For the record, you were known as Angela Russo when you were involved with Thomas Cavallo, correct?"

"Yes."

"May I call you Angela?"

"Angie is fine."

"Okay, Angie. What do you know about Mr. Cavallo's business operations?"

"His business? He owns hotels in various states and in other countries. Some hotels have casinos."

"You were his real estate agent from approximately 1977 through 1980, right?"

I had to think about the dates before answering. "That sounds right."

"You were a part of the business transactions?"

"When he purchased a new property or hotel, I was part of those transactions as one of the agents involved in the sale."

"What do you know about the money used for those purchases?"

"I don't understand the question."

"Where did the money come from?" Griffiths asked, annoyed by my perplexity.

I couldn't help but laugh nervously at the question. Was I not understanding him? "His bank account."

"You never talked to him about where the money in his bank account came from? Which bank account? He had numerous accounts in the US and overseas."

"Why would I question his finances? He had a thriving business. That's how he made money. What is this all about?"

"You traveled extensively with him before you were his agent." Griffiths snapped his fingers at Murdoch, who handed him a large, manila envelope. He opened the envelope, pulled out photographs and started to slap the pictures down in front of me, one by one. "You were a lot more than his agent, Angie."

The photographs couldn't be disputed. Pictures of Tommy and me in each other's arms in New York, Hawaii, London, Paris, at airports, clubs, and other very intimate photos in compromising positions at our home. I wondered how long they were spying on Tommy, on us.

"Obviously, you know we were a couple. Yes, we traveled together, but I wasn't involved with his business, outside of his realty needs. Why were you watching him? What do you think he's done?"

"He has some investors in his business. Those are the people we're really after, but the trail always takes us to Tommy. We hoped to have your cooperation. Money laundering is a serious charge with a prison sentence attached to it."

"Money laundering?" What on earth were they talking about? Yes, I knew Tommy had multiple bank accounts, but I never accessed them or inquired about them. "I'm trying to cooperate with you, but I really don't know about his business partners or his bank accounts."

"You lived with him. There are phone records showing calls made from the home you lived in with him to these persons of interest. Are you seriously denying knowing anything about this?"

"Tommy used a separate phone line in his office at our home. He sat behind closed doors, and I did not sit outside the door eavesdropping." My blood was starting to churn, but I tried to remain calm.

"And where were you on all the business trips you took with him?"

"Yes, I traveled with him. But if he ever attended a business meeting, I didn't go with him."

"Bull!" Murdoch responded with tremendous arrogance.

"If you didn't accompany him to these meetings, how did you spend your time?" Agent Griffiths asked.

"I was probably at the beauty parlor, sightseeing, or shopping." Tommy always kept me busy while he was in business meetings. He always arranged for me to do something like have my hair done or go shopping and use his credit card. Keeping me at a safe distance from any business discussions. Perhaps that was intentional.

"We're hoping you can get him to talk about it to you? You know, revisit the past with him."

"I haven't seen or heard from Tommy in more than five years. I can't help you. I'm sorry." I pushed out the uncomfortable metal chair and stood to my feet to leave.

"Hold on. You do realize we went back a lot of years, looking at Cavallo's business dealings and associates?"

I shrugged my shoulders, unsure what that statement meant.

"A name very familiar to you was on the list of people with an association to Tommy's business. Someone we have enough ammunition against to charge." He waited for a reaction, of which he never got from me. "Vincenzo Russo. He did some business with the Cavallo family when Tommy's father ran the show. Now your uncle isn't our main person of interest, but if we don't get the information we need, he could be the sacrificial lamb."

"My uncle? He's a very sick man right now."

"All the more reason you wouldn't want him to get his treatments from prison. I'm also not sure a jury is gonna believe this 'I swear I don't know anything' act either."

"How am I supposed to do this? Tommy never talked about his business with me. Only real estate. He hasn't tried to contact me in five years. Why do you think I can help you?"

"Tommy's been trying to find you. He hired a private investigator. He doesn't know about your name change. He's so desperate to find you, he may tell you anything you ask. You just need to wear a wire so we get him on tape."

I shouldn't have been surprised to hear Tommy attempted to find me. Perhaps I was thrown a bit by this information, considering it's been more than five years since I've seen him.

"We can make sure he finds you. Throw his PI a bone without knowing it's coming from the FBI. He will make contact."

"Are you going to arrest him?"

"That depends on what he's done, what he knows, and if he'll cooperate with us. We are after the bigger fish here, but Tommy may be in some trouble, using his business as a front for organized crime."

"Organized crime?" My god, what had Tommy gotten himself mixed up in? "I can't set him up."

"Would you rather visit your uncle in jail? I'm not sure how good those prison doctors are, treating people with cancer. And we can work to make a case against you too, Angie."

"Me? I really don't know anything." My heart sank to the pit of my stomach. I can't go to jail! How could I allow them to sentence my uncle when he's so sick? I don't care what evidence they had against Uncle Vince or what he may have done. If I had the power to keep him out of jail, I would. Tommy was on my mind too. What was his involvement? Could I go through with setting him up? No matter what happened between us, I had no intention of punishing him like this, with a big, fat prison sentence.

They told me he had been trying to find me for all these years. My name change and relocating to San Diego must have made it difficult for him. That was the plan. I needed him to stay away from me, so my heart could heal, and he could be a father to his child, without any interference from me. I didn't take a flight out of town under the name Russo. My car was purchased under Angela Petrillo, and I drove out of town, only to return a handful of times, by car, to visit my family.

The FBI had a plan they shared with me. They would send a team to my home in San Diego. Once they leaked my location to Tommy's PI, they anticipated him finding me at my home. My house would be set up with cameras and the phone would be tapped. If I left my home, I needed to tape a wire between my breasts in case Tommy met me outside the house. I couldn't tell anyone about this. If Gwen called me to gossip about her crazy neighbors, the FBI would hear.

I agreed to tell my family that the FBI merely questioned me to see if I knew anything about Tommy's business. I couldn't discuss the plan, my tapped phones, or my uncle's immunity in exchange for my cooperation.

I asked they put this in writing to exonerate my uncle and me from any charges if I cooperated, whether Tommy chose to tell me anything or not. I couldn't make Tommy tell me anything about his business. He never told me about his business, outside of his realty needs, before. Why would he suddenly tell me now after all these years? For the record, if it's the bigger fish they wanted, bigger than Tommy, I attempted to bargain for Tommy's immunity. But I failed terribly. Tommy was involved in some way. How much was undetermined. They refused to negotiate for his freedom.

Finally, I was free to go. Hudson was to escort me back to Uncle Vince's house. He had me wait for a few minutes at the end of a long hallway.

I couldn't help but hear a woman's voice who sounded angry. My head turned toward the outraged tune; and I recognized the pretty blonde sitting in a room with the door ajar. The woman was Sadie. The FBI brought in Tommy's wife too.

Chapter 80

The Summer of 1986

AFTER EASTER, I returned to my life in San Diego. What kind of life would I have now? Was Tommy going to knock on my door? Seeing him again didn't frighten me. I just can't go back to the way things were. Him being married to Sadie and me as his mistress. I need more than he could give. And now there's a child. He always had this way about him. A way to make me believe him. Believe in us and our love. It would never be enough.

Entrapping him for a crime that warranted jail time was a horrific thought. So many years passed, yet he continued to search for me. I never asked how the FBI leaked my information to his PI. Several weeks after Easter, he had my new last name. Once he had that detail, they didn't suspect it would take long for him to find me in San Diego, if this PI was worth his salt. Tommy knew I loved working in real estate. He could find me through my job.

I was a nervous wreck. If my telephone rang, I jumped out of my skin. If I heard a noise outside, I wondered if he'd be standing in front of my door. For months, I painstakingly waited for an update.

On Sunday, August 24, the feds forewarned me that Tommy's pilot registered a flight plan to San Diego. He would be on his way at any time, and they were watching him.

I drove to the office every weekday, not to change my routine. My office phone was tapped too. I'm not sure who had to authorize that, or if my boss knew about this ongoing drama.

Friday nights were the same, hanging out with Gwen, Mitch, Steve, and Dot, but I never stayed out late. My gardens were in need of some weeding, but I dreaded going outside at all, thinking he may be watching me. Not to mention, wearing a wire to the office and out with friends was extremely uncomfortable. Even if the feds couldn't see me with Tommy, they would have the ability to hear our conversation with this irritating wire that gave me a prickly rash.

I didn't want him to find me. I didn't want to set him up.

Chapter 81

September 5, 1986

I WAS SHOWING a house to a middle-aged couple outside the San Diego town line. A black sedan was parked across the street. There was a man wearing a 49ers cap in the driver's seat. Maybe it's someone interested in the house. Maybe it's an FBI agent staying close to me. Maybe I was paranoid. I tried to avoid looking in his direction.

The last time I saw Tommy, his brown hair was thick and fell below his ears. The driver sitting in this Mercury sedan had very short hair, clean cut, but his build was somewhat familiar to me.

My heart raced feverishly. My thoughts were all over the place, distracting me from the questions my clients asked. The house was really out of their price range, but I continued to do my job and showed them the backyard. After a lot of hemming and hawing, the young, preppy couple requested time to think about it, and soon drove off in their Ford Escort.

I locked up the house, dashed to my car, loaded my paperwork in the back seat then sped off as the Eagles "Life In The Fast Lane" blared through the speakers. After a few seconds, I noticed that black Mercury turned out into the street and followed me. At least it seemed like he was following me.

From my rear-view mirror, I recognized those strong, powerful muscles that once held me with deep affection. Was it really Tommy? I slowed down to turn, hoping he would catch up to me, so I could take a closer look. He didn't follow too closely. Do I drive to the office? Home? I hated trapping him. I loved him once. Loved him so much it hurt. I don't know what he did or what he knew that the FBI wanted, but I couldn't be the one to send him to jail. I couldn't have him follow me to a place where cameras could see us, evidence against him.

If the FBI had sufficient proof, he'd already be behind bars. If they had evidence against Uncle Vince, he'd be arrested too. They were using me to bury Tommy and blackmailing me with my uncle's freedom. I owed them nothing!

The library was coming up on the left. Gwen, Dot, and I attended several book club gatherings here. No cameras the FBI would have installed. However, they may know if I removed the wire from my chest, hear the tape peel off, or stop hearing my body movements.

Would my lack of cooperation send Uncle Vince to prison? Do they realize Tommy was driving behind me? They must have known what kind of car he rented. But they didn't know I saw him. They had no clue I knew Tommy was following me, and it had to stay that way.

I had an idea, but I was really uncertain if it would work. All of our lives depended on this half-baked plan of mine.

I pulled into the library and parked behind the building to access the back entrance. I purposely moved slowly to the door to see if Tommy's car would pull in. I didn't see him or the car, but I heard a car park around the corner. To avoid suspicion, I eagerly strode inside and noticed the door to the meeting room for our book club was open and empty, blinds partially closed.

To appear as if I were in need of a book, I strolled to the non-fiction section and picked up a couple of hard covers at random. I didn't see any FBI agents, but they could be inside soon, in addition to listening. Could they hear my heartbeat pounding hard through the other end of the wire? I felt it would beat right out of my chest.

The back door swung open.

I saw Tommy peeking inside, treading cautiously. It was him. I'd know his stance anywhere, even after all these years. Without looking obvious, I moved my body in his line of sight. He looked up and stared directly into my eyes. He knew I saw him and gave me that sexy smirk I remembered fondly. His hair was cut very short now, but handsome as ever.

I turned my head in the direction of the empty room to see if he would follow me there. I waited by the door and closed it behind him after he complied with my body language. I reached for the white, thick blinds and closed them completely.

His mouth opened to speak, but I quickly covered his lips. He attempted to say something again, genuinely confused.

My heart fluttered at an ominous rate. I took one step back and used my fingers to sign with him, but he wasn't paying attention.

"Ang..." he tried to say my name, so I grabbed his face with both hands and placed my lips firmly against his to keep him quiet.

Those strong arms wrapped around my waist, holding me snug against his body. He kept kissing me, but I had to pull from his grasp and catch my breath. After all these years, Tommy still lit a fire within me. I urgently raised my index finger to my mouth, begging him to be quiet.

Finally, he obeyed my request for silence, even if he didn't understand why. That kiss was surely unexpected. With good intention, I caught him off-guard.

In sign language, I explained as quickly as I could. I hadn't used this language in years. I hoped he'd understand me. "The FBI is listening to us. Don't say a word."

He shrugged and signed back. "FBI? What?"

"They wanted you to find me. It's a set up. They want me to ask you about your business. Said they want proof of your connection to certain business associates. I told them I don't know anything."

His eyes narrowed and brows curved in as he signed back. "You don't know anything about my business partners."

"They may show up here at any minute and see us together. They threatened me and my uncle with jail time if I don't cooperate with them. I don't want you to go to jail either."

"They're listening right now? How?"

His look was suspicious. He didn't believe me. I had to prove it to him, so I unbuttoned my blouse and exposed the wire taped between my breasts.

His expression changed. His hand balled into a fist and smacked the wall hard.

I tried not to react. Didn't want the feds to hear me say anything. I cleared my throat from time to time. Coughed once or twice to appear I wasn't engaged in a conversation with Tommy or anyone.

"I'm sorry you got involved in all of this." He shook his head then stared deeply into my eyes as if he were trying to assess my thoughts. "I had to see you. It's been so long. I tried to see you sooner, but I couldn't find you. I'm so sorry about everything that happened. It's all my fault. You know I never wanted to hurt you. My marriage, Sadie's pregnancy, it wasn't what you were thinking that day you found out. I never had a chance to explain everything to you." He brushed his hand gently against my cheek.

I knew the FBI could be here any second. "It doesn't matter anymore. We can't be seen together. Go home. Clean up whatever mess you made with your business, so they won't arrest you. I can't let my uncle go to jail. I can't go to jail for you."

"I won't let that happen."

My arm entwined with his as he took hold of my hand. I missed his touch despite all that had happened between us. "Wait! Sadie. Did she tell you the feds questioned her?"

"Sadie?"

"When I was brought in, Sadie was there too. I saw her. They had her in a separate room." I paused, thinking. "If she didn't tell you about it, she may be working with them."

Tommy shook his head in disbelief.

"I wouldn't lie to you. They had photos of us together. Compromising pictures. They could've shown them to her. Made her angry so she'd turn on you. I have no reason to lie. I left you so you could be a husband to her and father to your baby, but I don't think you can trust her."

Tommy drew near. His lips a breath apart from mine until he released me to sign. "I trust you more than anyone. Not knowing where you were all this time destroyed me. I'm lost without you. What happened that last night we were together..." His eyes left mine, hands covering his lids, appearing shattered and torn. "Your uncle told people I raped you. Angie, I..."

"I never said that. I never thought that. You were drunk and my heart was... pretty beat up. That one night doesn't define what we had. We had our chance, but it had to end."

"I started drinking again, yes. Scared to lose you." His hand lifted my chin, turning my face to look him in the eye. "You're so beautiful. I don't want to let you go again." Tears fell from his gray eyes. The only other time I ever saw Tommy cry was when John died.

"You have to let me go. The FBI could see us together. Please, Tommy, walk away. I have a new life here. I'm happy."

He lowered his head, discouraged. "I never loved anyone the way I love you." His hands clasped my face, fingers lost in the black strands. He placed his forehead against mine. Admittedly, I was anxious for another taste of his sweet lips, but he pulled away, forming the "I love you" symbol in sign language.

And with that, he was gone. I needed a couple of moments to compose myself and properly button my blouse. Why does he tug at my heart so much? Even after all of the lies and heartache, I still wanted to protect him.

I grabbed those random library books and quickly approached the librarian to check them out. While waiting at the desk, out of the corner of my eye I noticed two familiar-looking men; FBI agents in plain clothes, glaring at me, signaling to ask if I saw Tommy.

Wearing an expression of pure innocence, I simply shrugged my shoulders. I collected my books and library card, then sauntered passed the agents who aimlessly strolled around the library, searching for any sign of Tommy Cavallo.

They had no record of our conversation. No record I tipped him off. As far as they knew, I honored my part of the bargain. Tommy marched out of the library entrance and never returned, at least not that I know of.

For several weeks, I continued to wear the wire until the feds gave up. I don't doubt my phones remain tapped.

Chapter 82

February 13, 1987

FRIDAY THE THIRTEENTH in February was chilly for San Diego weather. The wind whipped and howled. The rhythm of the breeze sent shivers up my spine on this frigid, damp day.

Friday nights with the gang weren't quite the same without Doug by my side. Life moved on. Doug called me a few times since he left. It was always good to hear from him, but hard to end the call. I was glad to learn he was doing exceptionally well in his position, although I had no doubt. He was meant to be a leader and he had a brilliant mind. It had been at least four months since his last phone call. A man like Doug wouldn't stay single for long. I dated here and there to keep myself busy, but no one special caught my attention.

After seeing Tommy last year, I couldn't help but think about him from time to time, and all of the amazing adventures we shared. Memories were all I had. I left the photographs behind. I never asked him if he had a son or daughter. Did he get out of the mess he was in with the FBI? As long as the FBI didn't expect me to knock on his door and ask about his business, I was golden. I'd probably never see him again, which made me feel a little sad. Anytime I used my phone at home or the office, I still wondered if the FBI was listening.

Gwen and Mitch wanted to try a new Irish pub in the area for dinner tonight. Steve and Dot canceled dinner plans again. This was the third weekend in a row. I called Dot and left a message but hadn't heard back from her.

Steve called Gwen and me and invited us over to their house instead. It would be a pizza night. He suggested Gwen and Mitch bring the kids too. I never minded having the children around. Poor Christopher was the only boy stuck with three girls, but they were first cousins and loved family gatherings. They reminded me of my childhood when Connie, Katie, and I would spend time together. The Irish pub could wait.

I sold Steve and Dot a lovely white colonial house with black shutters, similar to Gwen and Mitch's house, only theirs was yellow with brown trim. Dot was proud of her vegetable garden in the back. They added a swimming pool and swing set, following the birth of their daughter, Samantha.

After we arrived and the babies were fed first, we sat down with pizza and beer. I drank iced tea, and Dot joined me. She looked tired, not her usual bubbly self. Steve was more quiet than normal as well. Gwen was playing with the kids, but I had to ask if they were okay.

Mitch and Gwen continued to give their attention to the little ones until Dot grabbed a tissue from the kitchen counter and began to weep. Steve's eyes filled up. They proceeded to tell us that Dot was diagnosed with breast cancer, stage four. Her doctors gave her maybe six months to live.

Mitch stood still, as if in shock, with his daughter pulling on his pants for attention.

I wrapped my arms around Dot and cried along with her.

Gwen comforted her brother.

No one said a word for several minutes while this horrible news absorbed into our minds. We watched the children laugh and play. How could this young, beautiful mother of two girls be taken away from them? She's far too young for this. My uncle survived his cancer battle. I'm grateful his life was spared, but why my friend?

A fiery mass of anger stirred within my soul. "There must be something they can do, Dot. You're a nurse. There has to be a way to treat this disease," I said.

"I'm too young for a regular mammogram. If I had one, they may have found the lump early enough to treat. Breast cancer doesn't run in my family, so there were no risk factors to warrant a mammogram at my age. I found the lump myself and talked to my doctor right away. They'd been running tests on me ever since, but the conclusion only gives me six months."

I reached for her hand and squeezed firmly. "Six months?"

"What can we do?" Gwen asked, wiping tears from her eyes.

"Help me to live for the short amount of time I have left. I need to be close to home with my girls."

Chapter 83

May 14, 1987

DOT HADN'T SUFFERED at first. She tried chemotherapy, but the treatment made her really sick. She decided to go without it while she was still lucid and capable of playing with her daughters. The thought of her final days terribly ill and unable to live life, even minimally, was strenuous.

I told Dot I kept my own personal journal. I didn't write in it every day. Some days didn't require any replay to mention. Writing important dates and memories on paper allowed me freedom, reflection, and creativity.

She had an idea if I would help her. Dot wanted to write her girls special notes during some important times of their lives. A note to them when they started school, their first date, college planning, wedding day, and motherhood. She was so tired. She wrote most of the notes herself while sitting up in the recliner, so the girls would see her handwriting.

Toward the end, Dot recited her intimate messages to me. Alicia and Samantha would always know their mother loved them, and thought about them for all of the special days in their lives. She would be with them in spirit, like my family was with me.

On the morning of Thursday, May 14, 1987, my dear friend, Dot, did not wake up. She died peacefully in her sleep. The pain medication they gave her made it tolerable for her to live out her final days at home. Nurses visited her daily the last week of her life. Unfortunately, she didn't last the full six months the doctors predicted.

Steve and Dot's family from Long Beach planned a lovely funeral for her. There were at least one hundred guests in attendance to pay their respects to this amazing woman. She was a loving wife, mother, daughter, sister, colleague, and friend.

The flower arrangements were in her favorite color, yellow. Yellow roses and carnations with touches of white and blue displayed in the church, funeral home, and the cemetery. The babies came to the church and cemetery, but Steve didn't want them to see their mommy lying in a casket at the funeral parlor, cold, pale, and not answering them if they tried to speak to her.

I've said goodbye to too many loved ones in my life. Too many funerals. I chose to think about how knowing Dot affected me. All of the times she made me laugh with her crazy patient stories. There was that forensic pathologist at the hospital she tried to fix me up with. He mostly performed autopsies, so he was used to being around dead bodies. Socializing was not his strong suit.

When she was pregnant with Samantha, she let me feel her belly whenever she'd kick her mama. She told me how it felt in a kind way, knowing I couldn't have children of my own. I'd never feel that type of movement or kicking myself. I'd never experience the bonding and love for a child created by me and a husband or lover. Childbirth was a mere fantasy I often relished. I've heard women complain about the hours of pain endured through labor and the visible stretch marks against their skin. If they only knew how badly I wished for such agony to experience, and blemishes across my belly, if the outcome was for me to have a baby of my own flesh.

Dot was understanding, without pitying me. Her time with us was short-lived. A reminder to never take life for granted and live each day as if it were our last.

Chapter 84

December 31, 1987

ANOTHER NEW YEAR'S Eve and another birthday for me. Thirty-five this year, and my friends never let me forget it. Gwen and Mitch hosted a New Year's party at their home for the last few years. Friends from church came as well as a few coworkers of Gwen and Mitch's. This year was bittersweet because we were missing an important member of our club.

When Steve arrived, people were overly accommodating. I felt his suffocation. Endured that reaction myself when I was young and lost my sister and father. Everyone was beyond friendly and had nothing but good intentions, asking how he was doing. Seven months passed and people still felt sorry for him. We all did. Some of us worked hard to not show it.

Since Dot's death, Steve did the best job he could being both a father and mother to his daughters. He had a strong support system. Dot's parents helped a lot. They needed to spend time with the girls, hold onto them tightly, and remember a piece of their daughter was living within them to cherish.

Steve and Gwen's parents were equally supportive and present for their son and granddaughters. They attempted to help everyone get through this terrible tragedy, and heal in their own way and timeframe.

Gwen always offered to watch her nieces if Steve had business to conduct.

I pitched in as well. Although I'm not the greatest cook, the girls loved my homemade macaroni and cheese, and some Italian dishes like my pasta, meatballs, and lasagna. I'd stop by a couple of nights every week with dinner for them. It saved Steve some time worrying about cooking, plus his job, plus managing the house on his own as a single dad.

He missed his wife. His wedding ring was still glued to his finger. There was no rush to take it off. All in his own time.

A rescue mission was in order when I noticed Jan Adams, the church gossip, catch Steve's ear. Jan was a nice woman with thick, bleached blonde curls, thanks to a salon perm. Her fingernails always captured my attention, exceptionally long. I could never figure out how she used a typewriter or dialed a telephone with those claws. I kindly wrapped my arm around Steve's and asked if he'd help me outside to refill the coolers.

"Where's the beer to load up the coolers?" he asked, pointing toward the kitchen as I guided him out on the deck for fresh air.

"The coolers are filled already. I figured after ten minutes with Jan, you needed a break."

He let out a deep laugh. "It was only ten minutes? I thought it was at least an hour. Thanks for the save."

"She's a sweet lady."

"Yeah, in an obnoxious kind of way. Hey, happy birthday, by the way."

"Oh, thank you." I blushed a bit.

"I have something for you," he said with a sweet smile.

"For what?"

"Your birthday. I left it in the car. Come with me." His head tilted, signaling me to follow him.

We walked down the cobblestone path to the oversized driveway filled with cars. "You didn't have to get me anything."

"Sure I did, with all of the help you've given the girls and me. It's just a little something." He opened the back door of his Subaru, and pulled out a flat box, pretty with colorful polka dots and a bright pink bow on top.

I opened the lid of the box and beneath the pink tissue paper was a journal and a pen. Not an average pen. The look and feel of it was elaborate, judging by the wooden box that held it, the weight and luster. I simply stared at it for a moment in silence and surprise.

"Dot told me you kept a journal. Every writer can use a fresh book and pen. Maybe a fresh, new perspective on life too."

"This is very thoughtful, Steve. Thank you." I couldn't help but look at him differently for a brief moment.

The countdown began from inside the house. The guests loudly chanted. Ten… nine… eight.

I packed up the sincere gift in the pretty box. Seven… six… five… four…

Steve sent me a smile, a bright smile, teeth showing. I never noticed his fabulous smile before. Three… two… one… and everyone inside the house screamed, "Happy New Year!"

"Happy New Year, Angie." Then he kissed me, full on the mouth. Not a quick peck on the cheek or a friendly hug. He kissed my lips, passion exploded from deep within. My body gravitated toward him, enjoying every second of the sensation.

I paused to catch my breath then opened my eyes, staring at Steve. Instantly, I jerked my body away. "I'm sorry. I don't know what came over me, Steve."

"I kissed you first."

"I… I can't do this. I'm sorry." My feet couldn't carry me back to the house fast enough. I ran into Gwen's bedroom, grabbed my purse, and raced out the front door without saying goodbye to anyone.

Dot was my friend. I watched her at her best, and I watched her die from a terrible disease. Steve was her husband. She loved him. Yes, he's a widower. He's not a married man. But he still wore his wedding ring. I felt like I betrayed Dot, maybe Steve too. He couldn't be thinking clearly. Surely he was lonely and missed his wife. A year ago, she was alive and vibrant with a delightful personality. She was taken from us much too soon. God, do I give off some type of "mistress" vibe?

Chapter 85

January 1, 1988

THE ANSWERING MACHINE flashed at me after a restless night. The phone rang a few times during the night and early this morning. Talking to anyone was not on my agenda today. Maybe I didn't handle the situation well. I was totally caught off guard by that kiss. That amazing, passionate kiss. Ugh! Thinking about Steve and his kisses seemed so inappropriate. I hoped Dot wasn't rolling over in her grave.

After a long, hot bath with Madonna's "Lucky Star" cranked up, I dried off and wrapped my body up in my fluffy white robe. I pressed the tab on the answering machine to listen to the messages. Mostly hang up calls. Uncle Vince called to wish me a happy birthday. Gwen asked me to call her ASAP. Then Steve's voice was heard, sounding terribly guilty and apologetic. I didn't mean to make him feel like he did something wrong. I didn't really understand what happened last night. Loneliness most likely.

I needed to fix this. He's such a good friend. That kiss shouldn't harm our friendship. I looked forward to my dinners with him and the girls during the week. I wondered when those feelings surfaced. Suddenly, the thought of not seeing him anymore left a pain in my gut.

The doorbell rang. Still wearing my comfy robe, I peered through the beige linen curtains and saw Gwen standing by my front door. With relief, I opened it up for her.

"I thought you could use some coffee and a glazed doughnut."

I quickly snatched the bag from her hand. "The chocolate doughnut's mine!" she demanded.

Grateful for the caffeine, despite the need for sleep, I took a big sip from the cup and nearly tore open the bag in search of that sweet treat. "Thanks, I needed this." I took a bite out of that doughnut like I hadn't eaten all week. "I'm sorry I ran off last night. I didn't even help you straighten up."

"That's okay. Everything got cleaned up." She gave me that once-over look she gives when she's suspicious about something, like when she senses there's a secret to be revealed. "Wanna talk about it?"

My eyes rolled, and my body plopped into a kitchen chair.

"My brother kissed you, and you totally freaked. Why?"

"He told you?"

"Yeah, he told me. Why are you so surprised? The two of you have been spending a lot of time together. I was waiting for one of you to do something about it."

I shook my head at her. "We weren't dating, Gwen. He's my friend. I spent time with him to make sure he and the girls were okay."

"Why?"

"What do you mean, why? We're friends. He needed help."

"Dot's mother cooks for him and the girls all weekend long. His freezer is filled with meals. He hired a maid service to clean the house. He finally got himself a worthwhile babysitter. So yeah, why do you have the need to show up on his doorstep with food, and hang out with him during the week?"

"I... I don't know." I stuttered, thinking about everything she said. Was I doing all of that because I thought I was doing right by him, or because I liked his friendship and company?

"Figure it out! Hell, I noticed the chemistry between the two of you over the last couple of months. If I see it, why don't you?"

"I wasn't making any moves on him."

"I know. That's the problem! Why not?"

"Because of Dot. It doesn't seem right, Gwen. He's her husband."

Gwen stood up, towering a good eight inches over me in those pumps. "Dot is no longer here, in a physical sense anyway. She'd want him to move on and be happy again. And I think she'd be happy he chose a woman she admired and thought of as a good friend. Someone who would have Steve, Alicia, and Samantha's best interests at heart." She eyed me up and down again, staring into my eyes. "Unless you aren't at all interested in my brother? According to him, that kiss was pretty hot."

"He said that?"

"Maybe not in those exact words. I think you should talk to him though. He drove home last night, so he's alone this morning. The girls are at my house with Mitch and the kids." She glanced at her watch. "I really need to get back there. Mitch is waiting for coffee and doughnuts. Think about what I said, Angie. My brother's a great guy and easy on the eyes. If you're not interested, some other woman will scoop him right up. I believe he's ready. The question is, are you?"

Dot was still on my mind. I tried talking to her after Gwen left my house. No sign from above giving me advice. I thought about what Gwen said. Yes, Steve had a lot of help, yet I had the need to cook and drop by a couple of times a week. Were feelings growing subconsciously without my realizing it?

Jan Adams had those claws of hers in Steve last night at the party. She's recently divorced. Gwen was right. Any woman would be thrilled to have a man like Steve in their lives, even me.

How can I be such a complete idiot? That fiery kiss we shared. The fact that I can't get it out of my mind says a lot.

I dropped my robe and ransacked my bureau for a pair of Calvin Klein's. I pulled a royal blue blouse from a hanger in my closet. I was far too anxious to bother searching for accessories. My hair hung loosely against my shoulders. After applying a little mascara and lip gloss, I jumped inside my Toyota and headed to Steve's house.

Chapter 86

AS I PULLED into Steve's driveway, butterflies fluttered their wings throughout my stomach. His garage door was opened with his Subaru parked inside. He was home.

I knocked on the door and waited. Footsteps crept up from the other side of the door. As he slowly opened it, I could sense his look of surprise, seeing me standing there, twisting my trembling fingers. His white teeth showed through his lips when a smile formed. A killer smile I was suddenly noticing.

"Hey, come in." He opened the door for me and led me to the living room. "This is a surprise."

"Should I have called first?"

"Angie, you don't have to call to come here. Listen, I need to apologize—"

"No, I need to apologize. I shouldn't have run off last night."

"Clearly, I was on a different page than you where our friend-ship is concerned."

"Maybe. Maybe not. I didn't think of it. Of you and me being... more than friends." Suddenly, I felt like I was rambling.

"I got that message pretty loud and clear." His eyes left mine, seemingly uncomfortable.

"No, I'm glad you kissed me, Steve. I know that sounds dumb, considering I ran away like a scared, little girl. It made me realize that even though I didn't plan it, doesn't mean it was wrong. It's Dot. I feel like I'm betraying her."

He nodded. "I know. I understand. Wait here a minute." He walked down the hallway to his bedroom and returned with the polka dot box, my birthday gift, which I completely left behind last night.

"I hope you know how much I liked the journal."

"I'm glad." He placed the box next to my Chanel handbag on the sofa. "But I have something else for you." He handed me an envelope. "It's from Dot."

"From Dot? I knew she wrote letters for the girls."

"Yes, you inspired her with that great idea. She left one for me, Gwen, and her family members too. I'm still passing some letters out, like yours."

"Why? Why wait?"

"In the letter she wrote to me, she hinted about me moving on. She knew I'd grieve, but when I was ready, she expected me to move on with my life. She wanted the girls to have a mother. A strong woman who would love them, teach them, and give them direction no matter where life led them." He chuckled softly. "Then she proceeded to remind me about our lovely friend, Angie, who adores our girls and has been a constant, loyal friend to our family. Someone like Angie, she wrote." His chin turned, so our eyes would meet. Mine were flooded. Using his finger, he dabbed the corners of my eyes, catching the liquid before it fell.

"My wife was trying to fix us up before she died. I had time to absorb her implications. I read the note she wrote to me months ago. You didn't read yours yet. I never opened this envelope she left you, but her instructions were for me to give it to you when I thought the time was right. I think this is a good time for you to hear from her. Of course, I can hold onto it if you don't want to read it," he teased, pulling the envelope away from me.

I snatched it from his hand quickly, and stared at her handwriting on the envelope before I found the strength to open it.

Steve squeezed my hand delicately, and I noticed for the first time, he took off his wedding ring. He quietly stepped out of the living room, allowing me some time alone with my friend. Her words were written on lovely lavender stationary with a shaky hand.

Dear Angie,

I may not write as good as you do, but I like the idea of putting my own words on paper to the people who matter to me. You are one of those people. It's been almost five years since we first met, and you quickly became one of my best friends. Maybe I never told you that before, but I'm telling you now. My girls adore you. They love when you visit. I hope you will continue to visit them. Be a part of their lives in some way. They need consistency and the presence of a good female role model. Someone to teach them how to be strong women when they grow up.

My darling, Steve, always comes across so strong. He's not. He may need a shoulder to lean on, but it may take some time for him to realize he needs a good woman in his life. Not someone to replace me. Someone who can help him see that his life could continue. A new partner. I'm not playing matchmaker. I know how much you hate being fixed up—ha ha! That would be up to Steve and the woman he chooses. But if the two of you think about it, I will be smiling from heaven.

I always envied your independence and strength. Just remember, it's okay to lean on another person and depend on him too. Take a chance once in a while. You never know what could be waiting around the corner.

With love,
Dot

I was looking for a sign that made me believe dating Steve was acceptable. Dot's approval was important to me. Now I had it. I wasn't quite sure what would happen between Steve and me, but I thought about taking a chance. I lifted the brand-new journal from the box. I will put these tools to use, and write about this very special New Year and new opportunities.

Chapter 87

February 14, 1989

A LITTLE OVER a year after Steve and I started dating, he flew solo to Las Vegas to ask my uncle for his blessing to propose to me.

Uncle Vince was thrilled I met a good man; a man with some old-fashioned traditions and respect for me and my family. He happily gave Steve his blessing, or so I was told after the fact.

Steve wasn't a fancy, extravagant guy. He didn't fly me out of the country for a grand proposal, or buy me an enormous engagement ring. On Valentine's Day, he barbecued chicken on the grill in his backyard while I made macaroni salad and mixed vegetables as side dishes.

Alicia was five. Samantha was three. He took them to the bathroom to wash up for dinner, and the three of them pranced back into the kitchen and knelt before me simultaneously.

Together the girls held up a small, black, velvet box with a mini red bow affixed to the top. Then Steve expressed how much he loved me, and how much my presence in their lives made them the happiest and luckiest family in the world. Really, I was the lucky one.

"Will you marry me, us?" he asked with a shaky voice.

"Please!" the girls chimed in.

Naturally, I accepted, and hugged and kissed each one of them. How could I refuse such a wonderful offer from a great man and his two beautiful girls I fell in love with?

I used to think about New Year's in Paris with Tommy every year. Now what I remember most about the holiday was the first time Steve kissed me. The surprise of his kiss confused the hell out of me at first, but it also felt natural and right.

With Dot's blessing, we planned our wedding for the summer of 1990, a new decade for our new marriage and life together.

Chapter 88

July 31, 1990

TODAY, I BECAME Mrs. Steven Morgan.

The day was clear, with a blue sky and gleaming sun casting a blistering heat. I must admit, I didn't think about the heat and wearing a heavy bridal gown all day when we chose summer for the main event. Alicia started school, and we didn't want to take her out of class for the honeymoon. Fortunately, we would be indoors most of the day with air conditioning.

Katie, my matron of honor, helped the girls and I get ready. Alicia and Samantha spent the night with us at my cottage while Steve and the men were at his home or *our* home.

I put my cottage on the market. As lovely as it was, I wasn't attached to it. Steve's house was much bigger to support a family of four. We decided once I permanently moved in, and we were settled, we'd visit the pound and adopt a dog to surprise the girls.

ABC news was on the television as Katie fussed with the finishing touches of my hair that she braided and twisted into an intricate bun. She learned some serious skills at hairdressing school. With the boys growing up so fast, Louis did not argue about her working as a beautician. That was something she always wanted to do.

My wedding gown was straight and fitted in pure white. Elaborate, beaded embroidery flowed from the bodice to the floor with a sweetheart neckline. The satin train was detachable. I chose a simple beaded headband that matched the gown and glittered through my jet black hair that Katie primped to perfection.

The girl's favorite color was peach on the day we picked out the bridal dresses. Their favorite color changed every day, but they loved the satin peach-colored flower girl dresses we chose for them. I had the most fun taking them shopping and trying on dresses and shoes. They fought a little bit over the flower bouquets. Alicia wanted to hold a big girl bouquet while Samantha preferred a basket with flowers. I let them pick out whatever they wanted to carry.

Katie was delighted to wear a satin peach-colored dress to match Alicia and Samantha. After having three boys, she had some fun spending time with the girls and me, planning my wedding.

Gwen and Mitch were in the wedding party too. Michael, Louie, and David were ushers, escorting female guests to their seats in the church. They looked so grown up and handsome in their dark gray tuxedos. My dear Uncle Vince walked me down the aisle. He told me how proud he was of me; and he was excited to welcome Steve and the girls into our family.

The church ceremony was beautiful. Aunt Dolly attended. I was so happy to witness her smiling at me as I floated past her in church, sitting next to Louis. Steve invited Dot's parents as well. I wasn't sure how they would feel about him remarrying, but they liked me and knew Dot and I were close. What mattered to them was the happiness of their granddaughters. That was equally important to me.

Steve's parents sat in the front row smiling with delight as I glided toward them. They were thrilled Steve, Alicia and Samantha found happiness with me, securing a new family unit.

After we had announced our engagement, his mother invited me to tea and biscotti with her. She acknowledged my genuine loving nature, beautiful aura, and magnetic energy. She was ecstatic the universe placed me directly in Steve's path. Delia Morgan doesn't speak much about one specific religion, but she believes in a higher power and a grand plan that is in store for everyone. I don't necessarily understand her spiritual beliefs, but she displays a comforting soul that generates positivity.

Fighting the happy tears wasn't easy when I gazed upon Steve standing at the altar, waiting for me with those brilliant white teeth sparkling through his smile. He looked so handsome in his dark gray tux with tails. I never thought I'd be happy again, finding a man to love who was all mine. No threat of him leaving the country for a job. My infertility wasn't an issue since he already had two precious daughters. Steve and I were a genuine couple with two children.

Alicia and Samantha believed this was their wedding day too. They were right. After the wedding, we planned a family vacation to Disney World in Florida.

Our biggest gift was the adoption process. Steve and I talked about this from the moment I accepted his marriage proposal. These beautiful girls already started to call me *Mommy*. I was truly honored and blessed to become their official and legal mother.

Of course, they will never forget their birth mother, my friend, Dot. Every year on Dot's birthday in August, we will visit the cemetery and place a dozen yellow roses on her grave. A picture of Dot with Alicia and Samantha was framed and kept on the mantel above the fireplace. Steve made a photo album for each of them containing their baby pictures with their mother, now their guardian angel.

Dot wanted me to teach our girls important life lessons. I will share with them some of the things my mother taught me when they are old enough to understand. Always be able to take care of yourself; don't rely on a man to support you; don't let anyone control you; and live life on your own terms.

Twenty Years Later

Chapter 89

June 9, 2010

ALICIA AND HER husband, Greg, drove out of town for the weekend for some much needed alone time. I was happy to babysit my grandchildren, Brendan, who was two, and Ava, who was three months. Brendan was dressed up like Batman, and Ava kept her little green eyes focused on her big brother as he whooshed around the room, cape flying.

Steve was golfing with Mitch, and I was enjoying my grandchildren. Since I earned my broker's license and started Morgan Realty, my own business, I had the luxury of setting my schedule and working from home when not meeting clients or showing a house.

Alicia always had her head on straight and knew what she wanted to accomplish in life. She met Greg in college. They were both business majors. Alicia watched me since she was a little girl, selling houses and business spaces. After earning a bachelor's degree, she decided she wanted to become a licensed realtor. Thereafter, she started a beautiful family.

Samantha was a free spirit. She recently earned her master's degree in psychology. With Dot's nursing background, I thought Samantha would take after her in the health care industry. However, after an internship, she lost interest in that field. A lot of money toward a college education, and she didn't know what she wanted to do with her life. Steve was beyond frustrated with her. I had more patience.

She flew to France yesterday with some college friends. I gave her some important tips and expected her to check in with us daily. These life experiences would help her grow. I ought to know.

Samantha is such a good, sweet girl, but a little naïve. I knew she wasn't my flesh and blood, but her innocence at age twenty-four worried me because she reminded me of myself. I told her about my time in Paris. She had the travel bug, and loved hearing my stories about the antiquated places I'd seen throughout Europe. Of course, my stories were kept at a PG rating. She knew I had a boyfriend who traveled, but that was the extent of those details.

Sesame Street monopolized the television. This show distracted the grandbabies enough for me to check emails for a few minutes. Before I had the chance to open my laptop, the phone rang. It was a number from Las Vegas. I recognized the area code on caller ID. A familiar name and voice was heard on the other end. Someone I hadn't seen or spoken to in thirty years, Len Stein, Tommy's attorney. I was beyond shocked to hear his name and his gruff voice. He was a heavy smoker back in the seventies, and his voice suffered from it.

"Len, this is a surprise."

"I thought it would be, Angie. How've ya been?"

"Very well, thank you. What can I do for you? How did you find me?"

"Tommy had your information and provided it to me."

"Really?" Apparently, he still kept tabs on me. I'm not sure why I was surprised. He must have known I got married if he had my information to share with Len.

"I needed to contact you, Angie. It's important if you can spare me a few minutes."

"Of course."

"I'm sorry to say this, but on Friday, June seventh, Tommy passed away."

A lump appeared in my throat, nearly blocking the air from seeping in. How could this be true? I couldn't respond to Len at all. I took a few steps into the living room to make sure Brendan and Ava were okay.

"Angie? Did you hear me?"

"Yes. Yes, Len, I'm just surprised. What happened?"

"Heart attack, they say. I need you to come to Vegas in a couple of weeks."

"Why?"

"Because you're in the will, Angie. You need to be back here in Vegas for the reading."

Speechless again.

"June twenty-first, I need you to come to my office. Do you have a pen and paper to write this down? I can also text you the details."

Still in shock, I managed to confirm my cell number with Len. Within less than a minute, I received his text with the specifics. "Len, what did Tommy leave for me? Do I really need to be there in person?"

"Yes, you need to be here in person, Angie. It was Tommy's request. As for what he left for you, you'll have to wait until June twenty-first."

Chapter 90

WHEN STEVE CAME home, I explained Len's phone call and Tommy's death to him. Before we married, I opened up to Steve about some of my history with Tommy. I even revealed the fact that I was his mistress for many years. It wasn't something I was proud of. I'd grown up since then, and formed a completely different frame of mind after my relationship with Tommy came to an abrupt end.

Steve offered to attend the will reading with me, but that made me very uncomfortable. Tommy always had a surprise up his sleeve. He loved to shock people, especially me. I felt awful that he died at only sixty-seven years old.

No matter what happened between us, my love for him was very real once. I never wished him any harm. Often, I missed him. He taught me how to have fun and how to live life to the fullest. I was a sheltered, inexperienced, young girl when I first met him. I got caught up in the adventures and the wild, passionate love we shared. We had our moment in time. Today, I loved my life with Steve and the girls.

Later that evening, I Googled Tommy. Hadn't thought to check up on him or his life since the Internet was born. I expected to read scandals or arrests. Nothing like that. The FBI may not have had enough evidence against him to prosecute. I'm glad I didn't hammer the nail into that coffin when the FBI wanted me to entrap him years ago.

He was still linked to Sadie, but it seemed he divorced her at some point. He had a son, Daniel John. There were no other children tied to him from the information I gathered. No social media pages.

He still owned hotels and casinos, and was connected to several news articles in the Las Vegas area. The Montgomery hotels won distinguished awards. No mention of a personal life. Had he remarried? Had a steady girlfriend? Who else would be at the reading of his will?

Chapter 91

June 20, 2010

I DROVE INTO Las Vegas Sunday afternoon and met the family at Uncle Vince's home. He looked great for eighty-three years young. He had a caregiver and people who maintained the house for him. He looked forward to Sundays when Louis, Katie, their sons and grandchildren stopped by with all the trimmings for a big meal.

Katie had five grandchildren. Michael and his wife had two sons and a daughter. Louie and his wife had one son and one daughter. David had several girlfriends, no children. We all wondered when he'd settle down, but he's only thirty-two. Maybe he'd enjoy life for a while before marriage. I loved our family occasions.

Steve and I came up for Christmas every year with our entire family. Christmas was extra special for my uncle when we were all together.

Steve and I host an annual summer picnic, a family reunion of sorts, in July. Uncle Vince still made the trip and stayed at our home with us. He liked the beach, but there's nothing like home with the bright lights along the Vegas Strip.

Blood never mattered to Uncle Vince. Maybe because his only living blood relatives were Katie's family and me. The Maronis, DeLeones, and Franciscos still attended Sunday dinners at his home. My uncle always considered his closest friends as family. My daughters were his grand-nieces, despite the lack of Russo blood flowing through their veins. He loved them very much, and they adored Uncle Vince as much as I did.

Uncle Vince, Katie, and Louis knew why I was in town. They heard about Tommy's death. I told them I was mentioned in his will. The reading was in a formal setting at Len's office. Tommy had a lot of money and a legacy to leave behind. I wasn't surprised by the fanfare. That was his wild, fun, and impetuous style. I still can't believe he's gone.

Chapter 92

June 21, 2010

HOW DOES ONE dress for a will reading? I wore a simple black dress with emerald-beaded trim and a matching jacket. I let my hair hang loosely over my shoulders. Steve called my cell an hour before I was ready to leave. He knew me so well, a great big bundle of nerves, I was, twisting my fingers. He spent time with Brendan and Ava yesterday, and it eased my mind, listening to his tales from superheroes to potty training Brendan. I loved this man so much.

Climbing up the marble staircase of the office building where Len Stein worked, I stared in amazement at the artwork on the walls, expensive light fixtures, and exquisite furniture throughout the building. He must have done well over the years. Certainly, Tommy paid him exceptionally well, keeping him out of trouble.

There were a few people standing outside a door up ahead at the end of the hallway. No one I recognized. Wrong room.

Then I located the right suite, sucked in a deep breath, turned the brass latch, and entered. Several people waited near the reception desk.

"Angie?"

My head turned and I recognized Jim. His hair was completely white. He'd aged some, but hadn't we all? "Hello Jim."

He approached me with a warm hug and slight peck on the cheek. We exchanged some pleasantries and shared our shock about

Tommy's death much too soon. Neither of us brought up the "old days." What would be the point?

A few other people in the room looked familiar, but their names escaped me. I may have met them at a dinner or business social at some point throughout my relationship with Tommy.

The door opened, a man strolled in, and I stopped breathing for several seconds. He must be Tommy's son, Daniel John, who I read about when I looked him up online. I'd swear Tommy was still alive when he walked into the office. He was the spitting image of his father. He's close to the same age Tommy was when I first met him at my uncle's club off the Vegas Strip that New Year's Eve in 1970. My god, his height, build, and mannerisms were exactly like Tommy's. I hoped he didn't notice me staring. I couldn't help myself.

Daniel held the hand of a lovely woman with red hair and a layer of freckles against her porcelain skin. His girlfriend or wife perhaps. I glanced at her midsection, where her hand stroked at a small baby bump.

A few paces behind the couple was Sadie. I didn't expect her to be here. I turned my back on everyone, even Jim. Forced myself to draw in some deep breaths to prevent a panic attack. Well, she was his wife for many years. He must have mentioned her in his will and left her something, even if they were divorced.

The receptionist approached each of us individually to confirm our name and personal information. I tried to speak so softly when I said my name, however, I used my married name, Morgan. Soon she escorted everyone in the group into a sizeable conference room down the hall. The table was large with maybe eighteen chairs positioned around it. There were laptops, cameras, video equipment, a large screen television, and other devices I wasn't sure what they were, spread about the room.

Jim took a seat next to me. He sensed my discomfort the moment Sadie and Daniel entered the office. He sent me a wink and nodded, as if he were my bodyguard, protecting me once again.

It was challenging not to stare at the others around this large table, waiting for the event to begin. Some people initiated conversations. Others paid Daniel their respects for his father's death. That would be the proper thing to do, but my legs were glued to my chair and my feet bonded to the floor. I was incapable of moving.

Len ran into the room, fast and furiously. He first approached Sadie and Daniel and whispered something in Daniel's ear. He locked eyes with me and gave me a friendly smile before standing at the head of the table. His feet paced across the tan, Berber carpet as he welcomed everyone. He fiddled with some equipment while he spoke, then dimmed the lights in the room. "You're here in person for a reason. Tommy wanted to speak to you directly. You can hear his wishes for yourselves."

Len flipped the switch of the computer and the television turned on. There on the screen was Tommy's face, a little older since I last saw him in the library twenty-four years ago. A few more wrinkles like the rest of us, but he still had that gorgeous head of hair and firm, muscular body thanks to years of boxing, weightlifting, and swimming. How could someone who kept in shape and looked so healthy die from a heart attack? He filmed this video will by a pool on a calm, sunny day, wearing a burgundy-colored bathing suit, and a deep tan. I'd laugh if I weren't so nervous. Crazy, spontaneous Tommy.

"Hi, everyone! It's me, and for the official record, Thomas Andrew Cavallo. And if you're watching this video, I'm dead. Also, if you're watching this video, that means I wanted you to have something to remember me by.

"A guy walks into a bar and sees his friend sitting next to a twelve-inch pianist. He asks his friend, who's he? His friend pulls out an antique lamp and says I found this, rubbed it, and an old genie popped out, offering me a wish. I asked him why he wished for a twelve-inch pianist. He said the genie was old and hard of hearing. Do you really think I asked for a twelve-inch *pianist*?"

People laughed, not because the joke was funny. They laughed because Tommy was being himself, the life of the party. A poor choice of words at this moment, I admit.

"To my 'mini-me,' Danny boy, you are the best thing I ever created. I love you, son. I cherished every moment with you, your family, and our adventurous vacations. You may look just like me, but you're a far better man." Tommy cleared his throat and collected his thoughts. "I want you to have all my gold jewelry. I have several Swiss watches, Rolexes, cuff links, rings, and chains. My office is filled with autographed memorabilia worth a considerable amount for you to collect. Don't forget about the safe in my home office. The contents of that safe belong to you."

He paused then continued speaking to his son as if he were right there beside him in this suddenly cold room. "You may be disappointed, but I'm not doing to you what my pop did to me. I'm not making you live your life any particular way. I want you to be free to live however you want. That's why my interest in the hotels... will be sold.

"Danny, if you want to use your inheritance to buy a piece of it, Len will make that happen. It's your choice. I'm leaving you one-hundred million dollars. Be smart with it. Your head is on straighter than mine ever was. You may not realize it now, but I'm giving you your freedom. When Pop expected me to run the business, I had no freedom. Someday, maybe you'll understand."

Tommy scratched his head, deep in thought. "Danny, you gave me two of the sweetest granddaughters on the planet! Len set up a trust fund for Emma and Kristina. With another baby on the way, that child will also have a trust fund. I know you'll share stories about me when they grow up. Always remind them how much their Poppy loves them."

I couldn't help but glance at Danny. He stared at Tommy's face on the TV screen as if he were still alive and in the room with us. Then he tapped his wife's hand with pride as he listened intently to his father rave about their children.

Tommy left his prized sport cars to some of the men in the room, including Len and Jim, as well as his business partners, Rob and Jack. I remember meeting Rob Lubitski when he was a manager at the Montgomery, and wondered when he moved up in the ranks to a partner status. He was a good friend to Tommy. Rob had such a hearty laugh, I recalled. No smile or laugh from him today. His sad, brown eyes reflected great surprise when he learned Tommy left him his black Lamborghini.

Tommy's housekeeper, Terri, was given his house in Paradise Palms for her and her husband to choose to live in it or sell it, whatever she wanted. Apparently, he purchased a home not too far from where we lived together. He thanked Terri for her years of service. Terri seemed elated, judging from the smile on her face as he spoke to her.

His boat was left to his friend, Larry, whom I never met or heard of before.

Another man I didn't know, Patrick, was left five million dollars. He sat on the other side of Sadie and appeared thrilled. He even shed a tear. I was curious of Patrick's connection to Sadie and Tommy.

Tommy talked more about the business and explained the process involved to sell it. Any profits of the sale were to be divided up into equal shares to several charities, two I recognized were the National Association of the Deaf, and the School for the Deaf and Blind in Utah, in honor of John.

Danny didn't appear fazed, hearing his father just left millions of dollars to charity. He surely knew his pop was a generous soul.

Tommy dished out some more cash and possessions to others in the room before I heard him call my name.

"Angie, you are one of the very few people I ever trusted with my life. No matter what, you never betrayed me. I messed it all up, I know." He paused, gathering his thoughts. "I'm happy you got the chance to be a mother. Your daughters are very lucky to have you, so is your husband."

He cleared his throat. Perhaps that statement was difficult for him to say. "I'm leaving you… memories. Memories of all the years we spent together. All of the places we visited. We had so many good times. I hope you remember the good times over any of the bad."

Tommy paused momentarily before continuing. "For you, I leave our loft in Paris with the view of the Eiffel Tower. That was the most special place in the world to us. New Year's Eve in Paris. I loved the way your eyes lit up when we stood on our balcony, watching the tower glow with thousands of lights at night. I also leave you the apartment in New York City. Do you remember that hot summer night at Studio 54? We had no clue how wild that place was!"

He laughed at the recollection. "How about the beautiful scenery around Lake Como? We always felt at peace at the lake. I'm leaving you our gorgeous penthouse there too. I'm also giving you the flat in London, the house in Waikiki, and my sanctuary, our home together in Las Vegas." He sighed heavily and played with his drinking glass, shuffling a few cubes of ice. "Anyway, there's also a safe deposit box. Len will give you the key and the details to access it. Angie, always remember…" He used sign language to tell me I was forever in his heart.

As Tommy spoke, I felt the eyes of the entire room upon me. I couldn't look at anyone except Tommy and his handsome features that still had an effect on me after all these years, although less severe than in my youth. A feeling I'll never admit aloud. I listened throughout his speech, and was challenged to hold back my tears. I couldn't believe he held onto all of those properties. Maybe he rented them out to his business associates over the years.

Sadie watched with resentment. I tried not to make eye contact, but I noticed the incensed expression on her face. If Sadie didn't know who I was before, thanks to the FBI investigation and those photos they had, she now knew with absolute certainty that I had been Tommy's mistress for many years.

"Finally to my ex-wife, Sadie Meade-Cavallo, I have money for you in appreciation of all the years we were married. I want you to know just how much that time with you meant to me. Len, go ahead, please."

Len's hands trembled as he reached into his pocket and quickly placed four quarters on the table before Sadie. He made no eye contact with her and swiftly moved away.

She looked down and stared at the loose coins, dumfounded.

Tommy started to laugh on camera, practically on cue.

The entire room was frozen, glaring at her with compassion. I knew they didn't have a good marriage. I was probably partly to blame for that. He never told me the whole story. So many questions about her and their life as husband and wife entered my mind. I'm sure she had her own story to tell about her marriage to Tommy.

Sadie's arm angrily wiped the coins off the table. She stood up, holding onto Danny's shoulder, then casually stepped out of the room.

Danny shook his head back and forth as if he were both surprised and irritated this happened to his mother, especially in front of the other people in the room. He may be protective of her, as a son should be toward his mom.

"And that's everything, folks. I appreciate you indulging me. I'm in a better place now." And with that, his head turned to watch a couple of women in skimpy bikinis lounging by the large, in-ground swimming pool behind him. He placed a pair of Ray-Bans over his gray eyes, then stood up to shut off the recorder. Was the better place he mentioned the action at the swimming pool, or did he mean heaven? Knowing Tommy and his hunger for sex, I'm sure he meant the ladies by the pool.

Chapter 93

JIM WAITED FOR me to stand. He had no idea how difficult it was for me to leave this chair after seeing Tommy and hearing his voice, knowing he's gone.

I wanted to leave, but there was the safe deposit box Tommy spoke about. Len had to provide me with instructions. I said my farewells to Jim, and he began to walk away until Sadie was unexpectedly standing before me, wearing a sinister look. This was the second time I was face to face with her. Only this time, she knew exactly who I was, who I was to Tommy, and how my presence impacted her life.

"Why you? What is so damn special about you?" Her eyes moved up and down my body. Her jaw was stiff, teeth grinding with venom spewing from internal rage. "I remember you. The female realtor who appeared on my doorstep one day, asking about my house. That was so strange. The way you looked at me that day. Checking out your competition, right? Hard to compete with a *pregnant* woman. What did Tommy ever see in you? I mean he never married you after we divorced. You couldn't have been that special. It made me sick, hearing him express his undying love for you, still, after so many years. How pathetic!"

I let her speak. Looked her in the eye, focusing on every syllable she uttered. My heart was ferociously speeding at one-hundred miles per hour. My throat was closing. Taking a breath was difficult. I at least owed her this moment to speak her mind.

"Did you enjoy hearing his praise of you, leaving you all of those houses? Places I didn't even know existed! He gave you a small fortune and left me petty change. That's how our marriage was. We didn't stand a chance with you in the way, getting the best of him while I got garbage! You filthy whore!"

I had no defense. What could I say to her? I never understood her marriage to Tommy.

Jim tried to intervene. He stood in front of me as Sadie lunged her petite body toward me. She was small, but spry and feisty with sharpened claws, pawing at me. Tommy told me she was confrontational, quite a fighter. I recalled the night he had me leave that party at Len and Wanda's home. As hurt as I was, I couldn't have handled this kind of debacle.

Danny and Len dashed out of the room together, surely due to the shrilling sound of Sadie's voice.

Danny rushed to his mother's side. Then he turned to me with that same stern look I saw many times on his father's face when he was pissed off, usually exacerbated by whiskey or drugs. "I think you should leave now, Angie." His face softened; anger dissipated once he had his mother under control.

"Angie, please wait in my office up and to the left," Len said, pointing in the direction.

I couldn't escape fast enough, but I stopped and turned around, facing Sadie and Danny. "I'm sorry."

My apology was sincere, no matter what they believed. I was sorry I was a part of any marital problems Tommy had with her. I'll never know what their marriage was like because he never told me any particulars except that he never loved her. John shared with me that their marriage was arranged on some level. Maybe if I ended the relationship early on or never got involved with Tommy at all, he could have made amends with her. I'll never know.

When Len returned to his office, he apologized. He told me Sadie was tough, a loose cannon. It came as no surprise to him that she confronted me. He gave me the key to the safe deposit box Tommy mentioned, along with the name of the bank and some instructions. He also left me a large file containing the deeds to all of the properties Tommy left me. There was paperwork to sign. If I had any questions, I could contact Len anytime. He had other people to meet with, so I left his office swiftly.

Jim stood near the doorway.

Sadie eyed me with contempt.

Kind-hearted, polite Jim called me over, then escorted me out the door and to my car. Still protecting me as Tommy would have wanted.

Chapter 94

June 22, 2010

HERE I SIT, in this cold room at the bank, mesmerized by these old photographs, reliving my past. A solid reminder of where I came from, and how knowing Tommy changed my life. There were a lot of good times mixed with echoes of bad. My past experiences made me the woman I am today.

When I left Tommy in 1980, it wasn't because I feared him or thought he'd hurt me physically. He had such a hold on my heart. Learning Sadie was pregnant, making him a father, pained me beyond belief. He needed to be a loving and attentive father to Danny, which was evident in the video will, as well as the way Danny looked at the TV screen with love in his eyes and heart.

Tommy had such a way about him that sucked me in. If I didn't leave Las Vegas, I knew he might just persuade me to stay with him. I was right, knowing he kept tabs on me even after so many years flew by. If I stayed in his life, I would have been a distraction. I distracted him enough from his marriage. I'd like to think I moved on for a reason. Tommy, apparently, was a good dad to Danny. And I found a wonderful man with two daughters to love.

I packaged up the photos in the manila envelope to place back inside the safe deposit box, where they would stay. A part of Tommy will always be with me. I didn't need these pictures to remind me. The memories are instilled within my mind and soul. The pictures of my family in my home are all I need.

A familiar-looking black box with a silver ribbon caught my attention. My eyes had been set on these old pictures while my mind reminisced. I hadn't noticed these other items inside the box. I unwrapped the silver bow and opened the small box that held the engagement ring he placed on my finger back in 1980. A symbol of his love and commitment, he told me then. I let out a suspicious laugh, of course. After all, Sadie was most likely pregnant when he proposed.

Another package sat lopsided in the box. A larger manila envelope. As I opened it, a note slipped out. A note from Tommy.

> I remember the first day I met you at Vince's club along the Vegas Strip. I didn't plan to be there that night. But there I was, sitting at the bar and listening to the most beautiful sound I ever heard, you singing that old, crappy Carpenter's song. It was fate. We were destined to meet, if you believe in that sort of thing. I wouldn't have believed it if it didn't happen to me. Real love. That's what we had.
>
> Inside this envelope is a copy of my life story, memoirs the publisher calls it. He agreed to have my story printed after my death. Len will take care of the arrangements. As my legal advisor, Len made sure nothing in it could ever harm you legally. I remember that day in the library, seeing you after several years. Years I spent trying to find you. You were scared to death that your association with me would send you to prison. There's nothing for you to worry about.
>
> If I had a second chance, I would give up everything to be with you, sweetheart. Maybe if you read this, you'll finally know the truth. You'll know everything that was really going on between Sadie and me, Pop, and the business.

The business I inherited came with stipulations. Terms I couldn't share with you or anyone.

You and me made a great team. I'm not proud of the way I handled things in the end. You deserved so much better than a guy like me. I was always afraid you'd leave me for someone else, but you left me because of me. I couldn't be completely honest about my life, but my love for you was pure, honest, and genuine. The real deal. Don't ever doubt that. I will love you forever, Angie.

Tommy

I feared what Tommy wrote in this manuscript. He already had a publisher too. The whole world would know I was his mistress for ten years. My daughters, friends, and business associates could learn some of the most intimate details of my life.

Today, people know me as Angela Morgan, owner of Morgan Realty. Those who'd known me for the last thirty years thought my maiden name was Petrillo. Only Uncle Vince used the last name, Russo.

Perhaps I could convince Len not to go through with this. If Tommy's story goes public, I wouldn't want the drama invading my home and family. However, Tommy made these arrangements before his death, and he wished for this book to be published. Only God and Tommy know why he did this.

All I could do right now was read his memoirs and assess any potential damage to my name and reputation before his book lines the shelves in retail stores.

I left the bank with his manuscript and the ring, leaving the photos and journals secure in the safe deposit box. With good intention, instead of walking to the lot where my Lexus was parked, I strolled around the corner where a woman with her baby sat on a stoop, holding a sign asking for money. A homeless shelter was next door. I handed her fifty dollars then sauntered inside the shelter, requesting to speak to whomever was in charge.

A man introduced himself as Clifford Mendez, the director of the facility. I handed him the black box that carried the diamond ring and requested he hock it for use at the shelter. The value should be no less than a quarter million.

He opened the box and stared at the ring in disbelief.

I quickly left.

Chapter 95

March 18, 2011

STEVE AND I were relaxing on the sofa together. He flipped through the television channels with the remote, searching for something good to watch. There were over two-hundred stations to choose from, yet nothing caught our interest, until one of those real crime drama shows cited the name, Thomas Cavallo. Instinctively, Steve left channel five on when my head bobbed up from his shoulder at the mere mention of that name.

One day was all it took for me to read through the copy of Tommy's memoirs last year when I returned to San Diego after the will reading. I couldn't put it down! He was delicate with some of the details of our time together, like my bought of depression, which led to the drug abuse. Subtle reminders of the similarities between my mother and me.

I can't fathom his interpretation of my father and uncle. Fragile information I still cannot come to terms with. Surely, he exaggerated their ties to the Mafia. Awful accusations Uncle Vince firmly denied when I confronted him. He believed Tommy was seeking revenge against him for helping me change my identity and leaving Nevada under the radar. I allowed my uncle to think I believed him. But I didn't.

Details I never wanted to admit before came alive after reading Tommy's story. The accusations my mother made against my father seemed incredibly far-fetched at that time, yet plausible. Tommy's memoirs confirmed suspicious elements that lingered in my sub-conscious. Particulars about my family's lives and deaths. My poor mother and all she went through.

Tommy led three lives: a husband, a boyfriend, and an entre-preneur. No wonder he was stressed a lot. No wonder he turned to alcohol and drugs for solace. His story answered many of my ques-tions. It also made me ask so many others. Questions I may never get the answers to now that he's gone. There was a lot of darkness that followed him.

I understood why he thought he needed to stay married to Sadie, although it was so difficult for me to read through. Difficult to understand why he kept the truth from me for so many years. Intimate details about Sadie's life were also exposed. Details far more disturbing than my life.

After reading his story in his own words, I sat Steve down and shared everything with him. Our personal lives would be impacted because of its contents about me and my family, revealed from Tommy's perspective. I couldn't blindside him.

Steve understood. He never read the manuscript even though I offered it to him. He trusted me. Steve was never jealous or insecure in our relationship. He never went crazy if a man looked at me or flirted with me.

Tommy had a lot of insecurities.

I was thankful Tommy didn't share my new name or location in his book. I assumed that was his way of protecting me on some level. His book was released by his publisher two months ago.

The TV reporter asked, "Who is Angie Russo, Tommy's long-time lover and mistress? Where is she today?"

I smiled for now, knowing exactly who I was, and where I was.

But they would eventually find me.

Coming soon: *Moonlight Confessions*, the story of Sadie Meade's impetuous life, and her marriage to Tommy Cavallo.

About the Author

Gina Marie Martini is the author of a romantic family saga series, beginning with her debut novel, *The Mistress Chronicles*.

She was born and raised in Connecticut, where she resides with her family. Gina earned a Bachelor's degree in Psychology and a Master's degree in Health Administration. She maintains a full-time career in the health insurance industry with a background in Behavioral Health and Clinical Programs, and a wide array of other specialties.

Follow her on Facebook and at ginamariemartini.com

CPSIA information can be obtained
at www.ICGtesting.com
Printed in the USA
LVHW111326020819
626305LV00001B/43/P